# PRAISE FOR *SOCIAL DEATH*

"Tatiana Boncompagni's *Social Death* is a breathless thriller that takes the reader deep inside the worlds of television news and glitterati New York. Her characters are finely and ruthlessly drawn, and the action never slows for a moment."
—Stuart Woods, *New York Times* bestselling
author of *Unintended Consequences*

"We may not be at beach read season quite yet, but Tatiana Boncompagni's third novel *Social Death* is ripe for inclusion on this year's must-read list."
—*Town & Country* magazine

"A savvy page-turner centered around the murder of a Manhattan socialite. It has plenty of society intrigue and even more suspense."
—Refinery29.com

"Hot Book"
—*Star* magazine

"Best Spring Break Read . . . each page seems to turn itself."
—Bagsnob.com

# SOCIAL
# DEATH

# ALSO BY TATIANA BONCOMPAGNI

*Gilding Lily*

*Hedge Fund Wives*

# Tatiana Boncompagni
# SOCIAL DEATH

THOMAS & MERCER

Text copyright © 2015 Tatiana Boncompagni
All rights reserved.

Published by Thomas & Mercer, Seattle

www.apub.com

Amazon, the Amazon logo, and Thomas & Mercer are trademarks of Amazon.com, Inc., or its affiliates.

ISBN-13: 9781477828533
ISBN-10: 1477828532

Cover design by Mumtaz Mustafa

Library of Congress Control Number: 2014956352

Printed in the United States of America

*For Maximilian*

# Sunday

# one

People cheat and people lie. It's a fact of life I never found particularly newsworthy, except when someone ended up dead. That's usually where I came in, turning betrayal and blood splatter into TV ratings gold. No Emmys yet, but that just kept me hungry—hungry enough to pick up my phone on a Sunday morning in early November when I ought to have been in deep REM.

"We got something on the scanners. Homicide on the Upper East Side." The voice belonged to Larry Shreve, the curmudgeonly head of the FirstNews assignment desk. "You're the only one who answered."

I eyed the clock on my bedside table. "It's not even five thirty, Larry. Everyone's still probably sleeping off last night's cocktails."

"Sorry, Clyde," he mumbled between sips of what was probably high-octane java. "I know you don't do breaking anymore."

I clambered out of bed, stuffing a fresh blouse into Friday's skirt. "Do we know who the victim is?"

"Nope. All we got is an address."

"You sending a team?"

"They'll meet you there."

In the bathroom, I splashed some cold water on my face, pulled my shoulder-length red hair into a ponytail, and assessed the image staring back at me. I had big breasts, good skin, and wide blue-green eyes. I could also stand to lose ten pounds, eat more greens, and get more sleep. Nothing I could change in that instant, so I spackled over the worst of it with makeup and made a feeble vow to start taking better care of myself.

In less than five I was down on my corner, hailing a cab. That's when I realized Shreve was sending me uptown to the Haverford, a sixteen-floor limestone tower on Manhattan's Upper East Side. The building, known as much for its high-powered residents as its pre-war details, was also the home of Olivia Kravis, the socialite daughter of Charles Kravis—FirstNews's founder—and my best friend since childhood.

My cab pulled up to the building just as I was dialing Olivia. We were supposed to meet for a drink Friday night, but I'd gotten held up at work and canceled. Her answering machine picked up right away. "Hey, Olivia, it's Clyde," I said, hopping out of the cab. "I'm outside the Haverford. Don't freak out, but someone's been murdered in your building. Can you find out who it is? The PD isn't talking." I tried her cell next, left the same message, and cursed my friend for being one of those crazy people who liked to jog at the crack of dawn.

I slipped my phone back into the pocket of my trench and took stock of my chances of getting inside the Haverford without Olivia's help. The police had cordoned off the front of the building with blue barricades and yellow crime-scene tape, and police cars were lining the length of the block. A few TV satellite trucks were pulling in behind my cab. One of them was from FirstNews, and I immediately recognized the driver. "Hey, Rich!" I yelled, beckoning him over to the curb. As he parked, the van's door slid open and out popped my team for the day: Aaron, the sound engineer; Dino, the cameraman; and Jen, the field producer. I'd worked with all of them before and knew them to be a seasoned and hardworking bunch. Things were getting off to a good start. "Who we got for talent?" I asked Jen.

She handed me an earpiece. "Alex Amori."

I moaned. "Say it isn't so."

Alex was FirstNews's fastest-rising star. He had been a Washington, DC-based litigator who'd appeared on CNN and GSBC a few dozen times as a commentator before getting hired by our network as a regular. Our bureau chief had lured him to New York with a big salary. In less than six months he'd made the leap from commentator to national correspondent, covering everything from the indictment of a hedge-fund honcho to a congressional sexting scandal. Alex was the industry's version of a triple threat: he could write—and I mean really write—talk the talk, and, as if that weren't enough, he was extremely telegenic. He was also well aware of his talents, and assumed every girl this side of the Atlantic was dying to get into bed with him. Plenty of them probably were.

Not me, though. I'd worked with Alex a couple of times on *Topical Tonight*, the national nightly news talk show where I was a segment producer, and both times he'd used the same tired line on me: "Someone as pretty as you belongs *in front* of the camera." I'd told him that if he was going to hit on me, the least he could do was come up with something more original.

I ducked my head inside the van. It smelled of fast-food breakfast sandwiches, sweat, and electrical equipment. "Alex isn't with you?"

Jen looked up from her clipboard. "On his way. ETA is any minute now."

"Hey, Dino," I called to our cameraman. "Stake out the shot with Jen while I go see what I can find out from the cops."

Most people don't know this, but television news producers don't just sit in editing rooms splicing tape together. More often than not, we're the real newshounds, pounding pavement, chasing leads, interviewing sources, and basically using any means necessary to get the story. I estimated that I had at least five minutes until the satellite link was up and running, maybe more, considering we couldn't go to air without Amori.

Scanning the crowd, I saw the usual assortment of patrol officers, supervisors, and technicians and set my sights on a uniformed guard who was standing off to the side of the main group. Then I asked my remaining crew if anyone happened to have a spare cup of java. Turned out Aaron hadn't yet taken a sip of his. "It's for the team," I told him as he reluctantly handed it over. "I owe you big."

Even with the coffee, I didn't love my odds. The guard was six foot two, about twenty-three years old, and he wore the uninterested expression of someone who'd signed up for the police department for the half-pay pension they got at twenty years.

I handed over the Starbucks, hoping it would loosen his tongue. "Clyde Shaw. Senior producer, FirstNews," I said, flashing him my best smile. "You know who caught the case?"

Officially, we were supposed to get our facts from the PD's information officers—whose job it was to make the department and police chief look good. But in reality, we all had sources on the force who either didn't know the rules or didn't care about them. I was counting on my guy to fall into one of those two categories.

The guard removed the coffee lid and slugged back a mouthful. "You got eyes, Red. Who you see comin' in an' outta the building?" He had a heavy Long Island accent and dark crescents under his eyes.

I peered through the Haverford's front door and caught a glimpse of John Restivo. Restivo was one of the most experienced detectives in Manhattan North Homicide, which meant the NYPD wasn't taking any chances with this investigation. And that meant that the murder victim wasn't just some spoiled hedge-fund wife; he—or she—was a name, and possibly a big one. I knew from Olivia that her building was home to a former governor, two movie producers, an Oscar-winning actress and her country-music-star husband, not to mention a slew of high-powered bankers and lawyers.

"Restivo," I said. "Who'd they pair him up with?" In New York, when a murder happens, one detective gets assigned from the precinct in which the body has been found and another from one of the city homicide departments. We were in the "one-nine," as in the Nineteenth Precinct.

The officer looked at me with stony silence. He wasn't playing ball.

"What about the medical examiner and evidence-collection team? They arrive yet?"

No response. I wasn't getting anywhere and the clock was ticking. "One last question. They tell you who the victim is yet?"

He scratched the stubble on his chin. "Nice try."

"Oh come on. You can tell me. How about this: I say a name, and you can just nod or shake your head?" I'd been in Olivia's building enough times to be familiar with some of the Haverford's better-known residents, and judging by the number of cops on the scene, the vic had a good chance of being one of them.

The officer let out a laugh, amused by my persistence. It wasn't the reaction I was looking for and he knew it. "You get an A for effort, lady. But it ain't gonna happen. Thanks for this, though," he said, lifting his coffee.

I was about to give him a piece of my mind when my phone started buzzing in the pocket of my trench. There was a text from Jen: "Sat up. Live in five," letting me know that the satellite hookup was ready and it was go time.

In thirty seconds I was back at the truck, ready to go. Alex, meanwhile, was nowhere to be seen. "Where is Amori?" I asked Jen.

She looked around helplessly. "He was here a minute ago."

I jogged around the corner, threading my way through the crush of people around the building's entrance. As Alex's producer, it was my responsibility to make sure he was where he was supposed to be at all times, and we were due to go live, feeding into the newscast in less than five minutes. If we couldn't go live and the newscast got screwed up because of it, there would only be one person to blame—me.

Luckily it didn't take long to find him. Alex was hanging out exactly where I thought he would be: the GSBC van.

We had plenty of our own good-looking correspondents, but GSBC had us beat by at least one or two long-legged beauties. They were like the Brazil of network news, and Penny Harlich, the correspondent Alex was busy chatting up, was their Gisele Bündchen. She had long champagne-blond hair, a perfect body, and luminous skin. Resisting the urge to go over there and drag Alex back to his mark by his ears, I whipped out my phone and typed a sternly worded text: "Get your ass to the camera. We are on NOW."

Alex took his eyes off Penny's cleavage long enough to look at his phone.

A moment later, he was by my side. I shook my head as we hustled over to Jen and the rest of the crew. "GSBC? Come on, Alex. You wouldn't flirt with a lawyer from the opposing team, would you?"

He gave me a look. "Well—"

"Don't answer that." We came to a halt at the van. I held out my hand. "Script, please." He proffered up a piece of paper as Aaron clipped a lavalier microphone on Alex's lapel. I scanned what Alex had written. He was a good writer, especially for someone with as little experience in broadcast news as he'd had. I reworked the opening and handed it back to him. "I made a couple changes."

He read through my alterations and flashed me a grin. "Smart *and* beautiful."

Not a lot of girls could resist his puppy-dog eyes and gravelly voice, and had Alex taken notice of me when he first came to FirstNews, I might not have either. But that was before I'd watched him in action at the annual summer picnic. He was more dog than puppy, it turned out.

"Head's up, man." Aaron snaked a wire under Alex's clothes, then plugged it into another wire connected to the phone line in the truck. I already had an IFB—interruptible feedback—device in one of my ears, and my cell phone, which was dialed into the news hour's executive producer, smashed up against the other.

"Wrap it up, now," the director told the anchor over the IFB. "Toss to Alex. Go! Go! Now!"

I scurried behind Dino as he hoisted the camera on his shoulder. "Three, two, one," I counted down with my fingers, pointing at Alex to cue him to start.

Over the next two minutes, Alex recounted everything we knew, which was close to nothing. Dead body. Fancy building. Lots of cops. The anchors then asked Alex a couple of quick questions about whether the police had any leads—if they did, they weren't releasing that information—before the director instructed us to wrap it up. Alex parsed out a few more lines about us continuing to follow the investigation closely. While we were on commercial break, the executive producer let me know they'd be coming back to us in fifteen.

I clapped my hands together. "Let's talk about our next live shot." Everyone groaned except for Alex, who, truth be told, had impressed me with his delivery. Beyond good looks, perfect elocution, and an ability to recite a script verbatim while people screamed in his ear, he'd also nailed the trickiest part of crime reporting—tone. I hated to admit it, but the network was right to recognize his potential.

"You change your mind yet?" Alex walked right up to me, standing close enough that I could smell the soap he'd used in the shower that morning.

I dug my heel into the soil. "About what?"

"Me. Admit it. I'm good."

"Just do me a favor, champ, and make sure you're where you're supposed to be next time we're minutes to air."

He cocked his head to one side. "I'm not a toddler, you know."

"Of course you're not. They'd never give a toddler their own show."

His carefree smile vanished. "You know about the show? How do you know about that?"

I arched my brow. "Do I look like I was born yesterday?"

"I don't think you want me to answer that."

Not that I cared whether Alex thought I was old, but someone needed to show him a picture of Demi Moore. Forty was the new thirty and, by that math, I was twenty-six.

"I have a call to make. Why don't you go bat your eyelashes at Penny Whorelick a few more times and see if she'll tell you who the murder victim is!"

My crew erupted in laughter as I brushed past Alex, my shoulder scraping his. "Nice one, Clyde," Dino hooted.

"Penny told me the victim is a woman," Alex said, stopping me in my tracks.

I turned around. "What else?"

"Her housekeeper found her with the side of her head bashed in and face beaten to a pulp. Gonna take one hell of a cleanup crew."

"Why didn't you tell me that earlier? Why wasn't that in your script?"

He squared his shoulders. "I gave her my word. Besides, she's not going to air with it until she gets confirmation."

I shook my head. "Like hell she isn't." On a breaking story like this, you don't wait for corroboration.

"She said she doesn't trust the source."

"Or maybe it's all just a bunch of bullshit."

He crossed his arms. "At least I got something. What'd you get? That cop tell you anything we can use?" He was gloating.

I stuck out my chin. "What's your point?"

Alex laughed. "That cop's got a day-old beard and bags under his eyes bigger than that wretched thing you tote around." He pointed to the red messenger I had slung across my shoulder. "You prance up to him in your little heels with some fancy coffee and think he's just gonna let it all spill because you're so damn thoughtful."

I shrugged. "Sometimes it works; sometimes it doesn't."

He shook his head, laughing again. "Just admit it was a poor allocation of coffee."

I was about to concede the point when I heard screaming in my ear. It was the executive producer of the Sunday-morning news hour shouting in my ear. "Change of plans, Clyde; we're coming back to you in five."

"Five?" I screeched. "I'm not ready."

"Get ready."

"I'm telling you, I've got nothing." I wasn't going to use Harlich's hot tip until we could independently confirm it. There was a chance Penny had made it all up in hopes of us reporting it on air and looking like a bunch of idiots when it turned out not to be true. My gut told me she wasn't smart enough to pull a move like that, but you never know. The point was that there's a legitimate reason you don't go fishing for tips across enemy lines.

The EP was yelling in my ear again. "Then get me a bystander, for fuck's sake! Let's go with *vox pop.*"

*Vox pop* was short for *vox populi*, or voice of the people. Hanging up, I searched the crowd for someone I could pull into the shot with Alex, but everyone around us was PD or media. Then I remembered Olivia. Alex could interview her over the phone. I dialed her a second time, but once again, my call went straight to voice mail. "Olivia, I'm desperate. Please call as soon as you get this." Reeling around in frustration, someone, or rather some*thing* on the opposite side of the street caught my eye—it was a flash of the distinctive green uniform worn by the doormen and porters at the Haverford.

"Hey, you!" I shouted, threading through a pair of cop cars to reach the opposite side of the street. The night doorman at Olivia's building dropped his cigarette, grinding it beneath a black leather oxford. The top left breast of his uniform jacket was embroidered with the name of the Haverford, and beneath that his name.

Andrew had a compact build, dirty blond hair, pale blue eyes, and a face that suggested a youth spent stirring up trouble in darkened alleys with loose girls. He'd only been working at Olivia's building a few short months, but in that time I'd fantasized about him more times than I cared to admit. What can I say? I found him incredibly sexy, and last time I checked, there was no harm in using one's imagination.

"Want one?" His hand reached out with a pack of Marlboro Golds. I caught a glimpse of a tattoo curling out of his cuff.

I shook my head. "I quit a long time ago." The first of many things I'd quit over the years. Men with tattoos were supposed to be another.

His brow crinkled with concern. "You OK?"

"I could be better." I hitched my thumb in the direction of the media swarm. "How do you feel about going on TV?"

"You work for FirstNews?" His deep voice almost made me forget why I was talking to him. God he was sexy.

I nodded. "Please do this for me?"

He shrugged. "I don't know. Don't you think—?"

I cut him off. "Come on. I'll owe you one," I said, dragging him by one hand and signaling to Jen with the other. Here's one thing I'd learned in fifteen years on the job: when it comes to getting someone to submit to a live, on-camera interview and you've got only seconds to spare, *I don't know* means *yes*.

On the other side of the street, Aaron miked Andrew and made him say a few words so we could test for sound. We only had time enough to push the GSBC crew out of our shot before we were back on air again.

Alex looked straight into the lens, cool as cucumber soup. "I'm standing outside the Haverford, the exclusive building on East Seventy-Second Street where early this morning police responded to a distressing 911 call. According to multiple sources, a homicide occurred in one of the apartments." He gave a quarter turn to face his interview subject. "This is Andrew Kaminski, a doorman who works at the building. Mr. Kaminski, what do you know about what happened here?"

Andrew scratched the back of his neck. The camera got another flash of green scales, the red of a split tongue. "Olivia Kravis was murdered."

# two

My first thought was that he'd made a mistake. I'd talked to Olivia on Friday. We'd made plans to meet for a drink that night, but I'd gotten stuck at the office chasing a missing-person lead and I'd had to cancel at the last minute. Olivia had seemed fine on the phone, but now she was dead. And not just dead, murdered. What was it Penny had told Alex? *Head bashed in? Face beaten to a pulp?* My knees buckled beneath me.

Jen stepped over, grabbing me around the waist. "You OK?"

I opened my mouth to say something, but nothing came out.

"Clyde?" She didn't let me go. I'm sure I would have toppled to the ground if she had. "Take a deep breath for me. You're in shock. Are you breathing?"

I nodded. It was all I could manage. Meanwhile inside my head, all I could think about was who could have done this to her. *Who killed you, Olivia?*

I took the IFB out of my ear and handed it to Jen. "I think I'm going to be sick," I said, ducking behind the van just in time. Wiping the corners of my mouth, I returned to watch Alex finish the broadcast.

"For those of you who don't know who she is, Olivia Kravis is the daughter of FirstNews founder Charles S. Kravis. The victim was active in the world of philanthropy, helping to raise money for several of New York's landmark cultural institutions. Olivia Kravis also ran the Kravis Family Foundation, which funds educational and health initiatives for underprivileged children in the United States and overseas."

I felt the tears prickling behind my eyes and knew I had to get out of there before I lost it. "Jen," I said. "I have to—"

"Go," she mouthed. "I got this."

The Carlyle wasn't far, and I knew at this time of day I had a good shot at having the hotel bar's bathroom suite to myself. I walked there in less than five minutes, pushing through the heavy glass doors that lead to the famed lobby bar. Inside, the lighting was dim and the mood calm—polar opposite from the chaos outside the Haverford—and as I'd hoped, the bathroom was completely empty. I locked myself inside the oversize stall and sank down to the floor. The sobs came fast and guttural and could have lasted all morning if I hadn't forced myself to stop.

I blew my nose and, with blurry eyes, looked at my phone again. I thought about calling Olivia's father or her stepsister, but I didn't know either of them very well. Besides, what would I say? I'm sorry? My condolences? Or what I really felt: I'm going to find the piece of shit who did this and slaughter them in the street. I scrolled through my log of recent calls, looking for Olivia's number, hoping to find the last time we spoke. A quarter to six on Friday night. She'd called, but I hadn't picked up. How soon after that was she murdered? The phone fell from my hands, clattering against the marble tile floor as my mind reached for the earliest memories I had of us together.

I first met Olivia when we were eight. She'd enrolled at the Livingston School for Girls midway through the second grade, right after her father, finally over mourning for Olivia's mother, had married his second wife in a wedding that would later be remembered as a spectacle of wealth, consumption, and poor taste. The papers chronicled everything from the apple-blossom shade of the bride's princess dress (it was a second marriage for both) to the cost of transporting twenty thousand peach-tipped roses via airfreight from Ecuador. Yet the most frequently and gleefully discussed details had nothing to do with the expense or lavishness of the winter nuptials, but instead with the bride's previous occupation as a for-hire mistress (which was merely conjecture), her blue-collar background, and her daughter from a previous marriage.

Olivia and I became fast friends, bonding over the things little girls do: mint-chocolate-chip ice cream, the color purple, the red hair and freckles we both had. Olivia was gawky, all arms and legs and undone shoelaces. I was heavy and bossy. Neither of us was very popular—though for different reasons—and we felt lucky to have each other. A teacher had once called us soul sisters, and I'd always thought of us that way, even after she was sent off to boarding school in Europe.

She came back into my life when I was twenty-six. I'd graduated from J school and had been living back at home with my dad for a few years, basically unemployable—my grades had been lacking, as were my internship experiences and interview skills. I was hustling a gig at Kinko's for a paycheck, which I invariably blew on slushy margaritas and syrupy cocktails. I was also sleeping around with guys who didn't respect me, fighting with my dad, and getting ever more hopeless as the months went by. I was at a dead end, and desperate.

Olivia had just returned to New York after earning a master's degree in public policy and spending a year as a volunteer teacher in Guatemala. She'd started a job at her father's foundation and wanted to meet for dinner or drinks. At first, I ignored her calls. I was embarrassed by my life. I was a loser with no future, a disappointment even to my father, who had once believed I was capable of great things. I was fat and penniless, had no friends, and had nothing close to a boyfriend.

But Olivia wouldn't give up. Livingston's alumni association had supplied her with my home address in addition to my phone number, and one day she just showed up at my door with a bottle of wine in one hand, bouquet of flowers in the other. Her freckles had faded and she'd lightened her hair to a strawberry blond, but my father still recognized her. "Come on in," he'd said. "She's in her room."

Olivia found me on my bed in sweatpants and a baggy tee, my hand in a jumbo bag of Lay's. "I'm taking you out," she'd almost cheered, thinking—quite erroneously—that a night on the town would solve all my problems. I'd see all that was out there, all the life and fun that I could be having, and that would make me want to get my act together. I'd lose weight and get a decent job and move out of my dad's place. One night on the town and *voilà!* I went with Olivia that night because it was easier than explaining. I remembered thinking *Let her see for herself* as I heaved myself off my bed to change into a push-up bra and pleather skirt. By sometime around three the following morning, Olivia had gotten the message.

But once again, she refused to abandon her cause. "Don't worry. I can fix this." She laid me back in my unmade bed, fully clothed and stinking of booze and sweat and the vomit that had gotten in my hair when I'd puked in the street after I got out of the cab we'd taken home.

"This?" I rasped, the room spinning like a top, my short skirt riding up to my stomach, exposing a strip of yellow lace and a hefty slab of thigh.

"You. We'll get you back on track."

I grabbed her arm. "Listen to me. No one's going to hire me. No one's going to love me. Look at me, Olivia. I'm a fuckup. I just want to go to sleep and never wake up. If I could die and know my dad would be OK, I'd do it."

"Don't talk like that." She threw a sheet over my body. Placed a trash can by my bed. Begged me to be quiet so as to not wake my father, who by then had already heard and seen too much of this sort of nonsense and should have kicked me to the curb long before. "Everything will be fine." Olivia smoothed the hair from my head the way my mother had when I was a kid. "A week from now. You'll see. Everything will be different. All it takes is one thing. Just one, to turn your life around."

Two weeks later, she called with good news: I had an interview at FirstNews. There was an opening in the main newsroom, a glorified internship with dismal pay and no benefits. But it was a job in the field I wanted to be in and a great opportunity for someone who had as little experience and as few recommendations as I had.

To make sure I nailed the interview, Olivia helped me clean up my résumé and practice answering potential interview questions. She even took me shopping for a new suit—a three-button black wool jacket with a matching knee-length skirt—and sent over her stepmother's hairdresser to give me one of those Jennifer Aniston shags everyone was wearing.

I got the job, and it changed my life, just like she'd promised. At FirstNews, I found a sense of purpose, structure, and community. I still had miles to go before I really got control over my demons, but I was on my way. I was on the right path. If it hadn't been for Olivia, who knows where I would have ended up. I owed her everything.

I unlocked my bathroom stall and doused my face with freezing water. What if I'd bagged work and met her for that drink on Friday night? Would I have been able to prevent her death? Would I know who had done this to her?

*Face beaten to a pulp. Side of her head bashed in.*

Guilt formed a knot in my stomach. *I will make this right, Olivia. I will find out who did this to you and make them pay. I will be strong for you.*

On the sink was a stack of tiny lavender-scented towels, and I used a number of them to dry my face and repair my eye makeup before exiting the ladies' room. *Get it together,* I told myself. *For Olivia's sake.*

Back at the Haverford, I found the crew inside the van, reviewing the interview tape. As soon as I popped my head through the open doorway, Jen motioned to me not to climb inside. She pulled off her headphones and stepped outside. "Are you OK?"

"Not really."

"Do you want to go home? I can tell them that—"

"No." I cut her off. I couldn't go home. I knew myself enough to know that it wouldn't be good for me to be alone right now. I was better off staying here, on the scene, asking questions, getting closer to the truth, getting closer to finding Olivia's killer. That's what was important.

"Tell me about the interview with the doorman. What did I miss?"

Jen looked at her watch. "They want you back at the bureau."

"Now?" I figured they'd want us to camp out for a while. "Where's Alex?" I asked, suddenly noting his absence.

"Already on his way."

"Don't worry; I have a little time," I told her. "Diskin's coming in from the burbs."

19

Inside the van, she cued up the tape for me and handed me the headphones. The clip wasn't long. After Andrew Kaminski identified Olivia as the murder victim, he said the building's superintendent had contacted him that morning with the news. He didn't know any other details about the crime, such as whether it had been an isolated event, what the murder weapon was, or if the police had named any suspects. Having struck out three times in a row, Alex lobbed a softball. "How are the other residents in the building taking the news?" he asked.

Kaminski scrubbed the stubble on his chin. "They're in shock. You don't expect something like this to happen in a place like this. Or to someone like Olivia Kravis."

The interview ended and Jen stopped the tape. "You'd better get back to the bureau," she said.

"Have a seat, Clyde; I need a sec."

Mitchell Diskin was alone in his office on the twenty-third floor, seated behind an elegant mahogany desk. As a former executive producer, he'd helmed the network as president and chief operating officer for over a decade—eons in television years—and built a reputation as both a brilliant newsman and an able businessman.

His fingers clacked across his keyboard as I settled carefully into one of two brown leather chairs facing his work space. Ten seconds later, he closed his silver sliver of a computer, slid it to the side, and peered at me from across the clutter-free expanse of shiny wood. "How are you holding up?"

In the fifteen years I'd been at FirstNews, Diskin had never once asked me how I was doing. And I'd seen some pretty gruesome stuff: severed heads, mutilated bodies, the kind of carnage that would give most people nightmares for the rest of their lives.

"I know you and Olivia were close," he said, removing his glasses.

"She's the closest thing I had to a sister," I said, my voice breaking midsentence. I had to fight hard not to fall to pieces again.

Something on the grid of muted television monitors mounted on the wall behind me caught Diskin's attention. I twisted my neck over my shoulder to get a glimpse of the news feeds as a double knock at the door frame announced Alex Amori's arrival. He handed Diskin one of the two Starbucks he was carrying. "Nothing for Shaw?" Diskin asked, nodding at me.

Alex lowered into the chair next to mine. "If only she'd tell me how she likes it, I'd be happy to fetch her coffee all day, every day."

Alex's comment would have infuriated me if I hadn't already become inured to the network's boy's club culture. Still, I was glad for the arrival of Georgia Jacobs, the host of *Topical Tonight*, the network's nightly current-events talk show, and one of my closest allies at the network.

"I'm here," she announced in her trademark Alabama drawl, shutting Diskin's door behind her. Her armful of gold bangles clinked together as she strode past me to stand at Diskin's side, her petite frame buttressed against a lacquered console. "Let's cut to the chase," she said. Her direct manner gave her all the charm of a female Dick Cheney and had earned her a reputation in the business for being as implacable as she was irascible, but among her staff she was better known for her fierce loyalty, tough love, and uncompromising ethics. Georgia believed in original reporting, which meant that instead of regurgitating whatever was in the day's papers or getting buzz on the Internet, which is what most networks like ours did, we tried to break our own stories. Didn't always happen, but we gave it a bigger effort than most, and as a result had earned a decent amount of respect from our industry peers. All thanks to her.

Diskin removed a small remote from a desk drawer. He pressed a button on it that made the glass walls of his office go opaque. "As you all know, Olivia Kravis was murdered last night. I've already had a conference call with Monica Kravis—Olivia's stepmother—and the family's attorney. The Kravises are issuing us a statement, which we'll run at the top of the hour."

"That's all they're giving us? A fucking statement? You're fucking kidding me," interrupted Georgia. In addition to all her aforementioned qualities, she also swore like a longshoreman.

Diskin replaced his gold-rimmed spectacles. "Delphine Lamont has agreed to grant us an interview," he said, referring to Olivia's older stepsister, Monica's daughter from her first marriage. She was married with two kids and lived in a brown-brick building with a view over Gramercy Park.

"Which one of us is doing the interview?" Georgia asked.

Diskin sighed. "Can we focus on our immediate coverage? I've called in a few favors with the heads of CNN, CNBC, and GSBC. They've agreed to limit their coverage until we read the family's statement. After that, it's fair game."

"Sort of like when Cronkite died and CBS got to go live with it first," Alex said.

Georgia pursed her lips. "That's awfully decent of them."

"Obviously we have to acknowledge Olivia's relationship with the network, but other than that, we treat this like any other story." Diskin took a sip of his coffee.

"What was Olivia's role here, exactly?" Georgia asked.

"She worked for the Kravis Family Foundation," Diskin answered. "The network is underwriting their big fund-raiser next week."

"Bad timing," Alex commented.

I glared at him.

A wrinkle appeared between Georgia's eyes. "Olivia's not on the board?"

Diskin removed his glasses and squeezed the bridge of his nose. "You're thinking of Delphine. Olivia Kravis had little to do with day-to-day operations, but because the public views her as a representative of the network, any whiff of scandal related to her murder could spell trouble."

"Oh, I get it," Georgia drawled. "This is about the merger."

It was a well-known secret that FirstNews was up for sale. A few years ago, Charles Kravis had suffered the first of a series of debilitating strokes, after which he stepped down as the company's CEO and handed the chairmanship to one Naomi Zell, his chief operating officer and most trusted adviser. By all accounts, Zell was capable of running a multi-platform, multi-billion-dollar media company, but Charles Kravis's poor health, which had continued to decline even after his retirement, had spurred speculation that the family would want to cash out of the business.

Plus, FirstNews wasn't exactly performing up to expectations. The tepid economy and falling ratings had hurt advertising revenue. The board didn't have any reason to reject a reasonable offer from a bigger conglomerate—one that had a better shot at profiting in the current financial climate. But with a merger came redundancies and consolidations—i.e., layoffs and belt-tightening. Nothing any of us were looking forward to. Georgia was right to think that Olivia's death could affect the outcome of any merger negotiations; murder made people reevaluate their lives and priorities. The Kravis family could change their mind about wanting to sell the network. So too might potential buyers reconsider making an offer to purchase the business if they were worried about appearing like vultures after the family sustained such a horrific loss.

Diskin tapped the tip of his Montblanc against the top of his desk. "Above all, we have to stay on message. This is a tragedy and we're going to cover it as such. The other networks may go salacious. God knows we can depend on GSBC to go as lowbrow as they can with it, but we're not taking this story in that direction. Have I made myself clear?"

Georgia was growing impatient. "Yes, I think we all can appreciate the deeply sensitive nature of this case. But what about the facts? Do we know how she died? Do we know anything about the crime scene?"

Alex answered for Diskin. "She was killed in her apartment. No sex play, no drugs."

I wondered how he knew that, but Georgia clucked her tongue before I could ask. "We won't know that for sure until the toxicology reports come in," she said.

"What I mean is that she wasn't found bound and gagged in a latex suit," Alex replied. "We can cross off S and M gone wrong."

Georgia crossed her arms, sending her gold bangles jangling again. "Too early to cross anything off. You got anything else?"

Diskin cleared his throat. "Clyde, this might be hard for you to hear."

# three

I'd spent the last decade of my life submerged in the goriest details of murder. A person can't hold on to a job like mine without building a certain tolerance for violence and tragedy. And then there was my own sob story. You hear about cops with hard exteriors—well, mine was made of steel. But this? This I wasn't sure I could handle. Still, I couldn't have anyone in the room thinking that. They had to believe that I was capable of covering the case if I was going to have any shot of staying on it, and I had to stay on it if I wanted to be able to dedicate myself to catching Olivia's killer. "I appreciate your concern, but I can handle it," I said, sounding more sure than I felt.

Diskin propped his elbows on his desk. "Monica Kravis told me the police are working on the assumption that she was attacked on Friday night, apparently with some sort of crystal object. The killer used it to beat her on her head."

"A bludgeoning," Georgia remarked grimly.

I knew from interviewing countless criminal psychologists that bludgeoning, like strangulation, was a deeply personal method of killing, unlike, say, poisoning or shooting. Those allowed the killer to keep some distance between himself and the victim, but beating someone with an object required the killer to get close. Bludgeoning also indicated rage and was more typical of homicides carried out by men rather than women. Women tended to use poison, cars, and guns to get the job done. I inhaled deeply again, pushing aside the horrific images that were swimming through my thoughts.

"Does anyone know if she had a boyfriend?" Georgia asked.

"She didn't," I said. "Not for a while."

"What's a while?" Alex asked.

"A few years, at least," I said, wondering if Diskin and Georgia actually expected me to betray Olivia's private confidences to enhance our coverage. I wouldn't do it. "What's the game plan for coverage after we break the news?" I asked, hoping to change the topic.

"Updates from the crime scene at four and six," Diskin said.

"I'll obviously want to cover this on *Topical Tonight* at nine," Georgia said, staking her show's claim.

Georgia was a former district prosecutor, a southern spitfire who had risen to fame as a legal commentator back when there was just one cable news network. The show was best known for missing-person cases, especially those involving children or attractive young women, but just about any criminal investigation that had the potential to garner national attention would do, anything from unwanted sexual advances from a politician to a particularly grisly murder. *Topical Tonight* was FirstNews's highest-rated hour, and as such got to call more than its fair share of shots around the network.

Although I had been tapped to handle this morning's breaking news at the Haverford, that wasn't my usual gig. Technically speaking, I was one of *Topical*'s segment producers, a jill-of-all-trades role that had me flying off to cover a shooting spree in Mobile, Alabama, one day and a Boston College hazing prank gone fatally wrong the next. I also kept my eye on the tabs and newspapers for breaking news, scoured regional publications for unsolved cases we could blow up into media feeding frenzies, and pitched in from time to time with guest booking.

"Up to you what you do with your airtime," Diskin said, responding to Georgia. "But everything related to the Kravis case gets vetted through legal and standards and practices. Nothing goes to air without their stamp of approval."

It wasn't unusual for my scripts to go through the legal department. Most of what we put on the air did. But I'd rarely had to deal with standards and practices. Their role, as a department, was to make sure everything that happened at the network was in the best interest of the company. If, for example, something Georgia said on air stirred up trouble with Christian Scientist viewers and as a result caused a company-wide boycott by religious groups, it was up to standards and practices to deal with the fallout. They figured out whether to arrange mediation sessions, issue an apology, or stand by Georgia's right to free speech.

Diskin pointed his pen at Alex. "Also, he's taking the lead for us on the case."

Georgia and I exchanged looks. I could already tell she wasn't going to be happy with this arrangement. Not that she would have wanted to do the on-scene reporting herself—that would be like Katie Couric doing a stand-up in front of the White House—but generally speaking the assignment desk let Georgia dictate which correspondents would cover what cases for her hour. She usually called the shots. But apparently not this time.

"I take this is a done deal." Georgia hooked her thumbs in the belt loops of her jeans. She was wearing her off-air uniform: men's button-down, jeans, and copious amounts of diamonds and gold.

Diskin nodded, looked her straight in the eye. "He was first on the scene."

"And what about me?" I asked. I was there too. By the same logic, this should be my story.

"He's going to need a producer. Alex doesn't have any experience covering murder cases, and we need him to work with someone who does. You've got connections with the PD and I know I can depend on you to employ an extra level of sensitivity in our interactions with the Kravises," he said.

Alex turned to me. I could feel his brown eyes on me.

"It's still Clyde's call," Georgia said, asserting her authority. Technically, she was my immediate boss and Diskin was supposed to clear it with her before assigning me to work with a correspondent.

Working as Alex's segment producer meant I would be glued to him for as long as we were covering the story. I'd have to go with him into the field for live shots and on-site interviews, work my sources for information and leads, set up on-camera interviews with law-enforcement officials and homicide experts, and get my hands on footage of Olivia from public appearances to use as B-roll. There was a lot of work to be done.

"I do have some reservations," Georgia said, clearing her throat. "What about Clyde's relationship to the victim?"

Diskin answered before I could. "Her connection to the family is precisely the reason she's the best person for the job. She'll have access, which, like it or not, is something we have to take into account."

Georgia wasn't convinced. "If this is too hard for you to handle, Clyde, we'll understand. You don't have to do this if you don't want to."

"I'm good, Georgia. Trust me. I want this."

She turned back to Diskin. "You're not at all worried about the conflict of interest?"

"Jesus, Georgia, we're not the *New York Times*." He pawed at the neck of his blue-striped button-down.

Georgia tucked her chin into her neck. "I'll pretend I didn't hear that." She cared about the quality of what we put on the screen, while Diskin was a numbers man—big audiences plus low costs equals mega revenue and happy shareholders. He had a wife, three college-age kids, and a five-acre estate in Pound Ridge. All of them cost money, lots and lots of money.

Diskin regarded me over his glasses. "Professionally, I believe you are capable of remaining objective while working this story, and personally, I feel completely comfortable with this arrangement." He suddenly pointed at his gold watch. "You guys have to get back to the Haverford. We'll want to go live at the scene again after we read the family's statement. Alex and Georgia, you may leave. Shaw, hang back a moment."

As Georgia left the room, she squeezed my shoulder. She and I had been through a lot together—scrapes with network brass, all-nighters in foreign cities, her multiple divorces, and my many failed attempts at relationships. She was more than a boss; she was a mentor and a friend.

The door clicked closed and Diskin turned his watery gaze back to me. "You're sure you can do this?"

"I am. One hundred percent." Olivia was my best friend. I owed her for rescuing me from myself in more ways and on more occasions than I cared to remember. I needed to make it up to her— if not in life, then in death. I was going to figure out who did this to her. And then I was going to bring them to justice.

"In that case, the clock's ticking," Diskin said.

I stood up, straightened my skirt, and made a dash for the door.

# four

*So much for getting a head start.*

The Haverford was even more of a mob scene than it had been when I'd left it just an hour earlier. Diskin may have made a gentleman's agreement with the other networks that allowed us to report first on the details of Olivia's murder, but that didn't mean our competitors were going to stand idly by. The second we wrapped up they'd be live from the Haverford; in essence, we'd get three minutes, five tops, before every other cable news network was jamming their air with the story.

I jumped out of my cab and hurled myself into the crowd to reconnect with my team. This time everyone was where they were supposed to be, thank God, and as we waited for the director's cue to get ready, I put in a call to the PD's chief information officer to confirm some of the facts we were reporting. It was a formality, but this was the kind of case the guys in blue would want to handle by the book. One screwup and there would be hell to pay by anyone remotely involved. The Kravises were big political contributors—despite Charles Kravis's right-wing leanings, he was more of a pragmatist than an ideologue and gave just as generously to liberal lawmakers as he did conservatives—meaning they had plenty of connections to the mayor's office.

"Three, two, one," I counted down again for Alex. He had a sheet in his hand, but he didn't glance at it once as he reported the extent of what we knew: Olivia had been found dead in her apartment that morning at approximately 7:08 by her housekeeper; the police had reported to the scene within minutes of the 911 call and promptly ruled her death a homicide; the cause of death was bludgeoning. The anchors thanked him for his report and we were out.

I breathed a heavy sigh of relief.

The feeling lasted, oh, about ten seconds.

No sooner had Dino—short for Konstantinos—lowered his camera than I got a call from the assignment desk. They wanted another live shot from the crime scene during the four o'clock news hour. And this time they wanted a package, a three- to five-minute-long pretaped segment that included the following elements: B-roll (standard visuals of, say, snow falling if it's a story about a winter storm); voice-overs (the reporter talking over the visuals); taped source interviews; and vox pop.

If you could get past the jargon, it wasn't rocket science. Just a hell of a lot of footwork. And I had only three and a half hours to pull it all together. As I hung up the phone, I could feel the adrenaline surging through my veins. Cocaine had nothing on breaking news.

"Anyone want lunch?" Jen asked. It was ten past noon. Aaron offered to go to a sandwich shop around the corner and started taking orders. "Want anything, Clyde?"

My given name was Cornelia Shaw, but most everyone called me Clyde. Long story short, as a kid I was tall and on the heavy side, to put it nicely. I also liked to wear clogs. Put it all together and the comparisons to a Clydesdale were inevitable. In high school, I managed to lose most of the weight—I'd ditched food for boys and booze—but the nickname, mercifully shortened to Clyde, had stuck. In college, and while I was pursuing my graduate degree in journalism and for some years after that, I was back to Cornelia. And then one day I made the mistake of mentioning my old nickname to Georgia, who'd adopted it straightaway, despite my numerous protestations. "It's androgynous and unique," she'd said, shooing me out of her office with a flick of the wrist. "Now quit acting like a whiny schoolgirl and get back to work."

For the record, I was never a complainer as a kid. I made better-than-average grades at Livingston and participated in a decent number of extracurriculars. Most of them were of the sedentary variety—French club, yearbook, the literary magazine—but one year I worked up the courage to join the swim team. It was the fall of sixth grade, following a summer growth spurt that included, unfortunately, my already-well-developed breasts. On my first day of practice, a thin-lipped eighth-grade blonde named Missy McClintock picked me out in the crowd of newcomers. She positioned herself behind me in the line to start our drills, mocking my breasts with a pull buoy stuffed beneath the chest of her Speedo and making farting noises with her mean little mouth. I'd pretended not to notice as all the other girls laughed.

It got worse, of course. In the pool, Missy kicked and elbowed me every chance she got; out of the pool, she called me names to my face. Fatso, Tubby, and, on a good day, Dolly P. None of the other girls wanted to have anything to do with me. I sat alone on the bus rides to meets and was excluded from potluck dinners and other team-building events. Finally I complained to Olivia, who was furious with me for not telling her about the situation sooner. "What can you do?" I'd said to her. Missy was older than we were, and more popular than both of us put together.

The next day, Olivia showed up during practice. We were all already in the water warming up, so I didn't notice her until she was sitting up in the bleachers with my coach, pointing first to the "Charles S. Kravis" plaque on the wall, then to me, and then to Missy.

That was the end of the bullying. It was also the first time I realized I'd never have another friend like Olivia. She was one in a million, and now she was gone.

"Food, Clyde?" Jen asked again.

I shook my head. Food was the last thing on my mind. "I'll pick something up later." I pulled out my pad and paper and headed back to the building.

It was surprising how much information you could pick up just by being on the scene, watching what happened and talking to witnesses, neighbors, whomever. Good producers were like good investigators in that both believed in leaving no stone unturned. You never knew where you were going to stumble upon a detail that flipped a case upside down or ignited the public interest. Something as small as the color of the victim's shoelaces could do it, and when you're in the middle of a media feeding frenzy you guard those little nuggets like firstborn babies.

I was about ten feet away from the blue police barricade when I spotted Andrew Kaminski, the doorman, coming out of the building. He was heading straight for me.

"You doin' OK?" he asked.

I looked him over. He looked like hell. Ashen face, bloodshot eyes. "Shouldn't I be asking you that?" I said.

He put his hand on my shoulder. "I'm not the one who puked on the street."

Already it seemed like days since I'd lost it behind our van. "Not my finest hour," I admitted. "But I'm OK now. Can we talk?"

Kaminski pulled out a cigarette. I lit it for him. "You don't smoke but you carry a fancy lighter?" He blew a plume of gray smoke out the corner of his mouth.

"It has sentimental value." I dropped the engraved memento in my bag and touched the strand of gum-ball-size pearls I had around my neck. They were both my mother's.

"You want to talk here?" he asked.

Out of the corner of my eye, I saw Penny Harlich approaching us, her long blond hair blowing in the autumn wind. A few fallen leaves swirled at her feet. I grabbed Kaminski by the elbow, leading him away. If Horsedick thought she could steal my number one source out from under me, she had another thing coming. "Can I buy you a cup of coffee?" I asked Kaminski.

He held his hand out so I could see it was shaking. "Too much caffeine already. Cops just loaded me up," he said, hitching his hand back toward the Haverford. No doubt, they'd just spent the last hour grilling him.

I glanced backward. Penny was still on our tail. I quickened my pace. "Juice?"

"I'm headed home."

"I'll give you a lift then."

He shrugged. "I take the train."

"Great, I'll walk you to the subway." Penny had no chance of keeping up with us in that super-tight pencil skirt. I was wearing one too, but I'd had my tailor cut an extra few inches into the back slit. It made it easier to speed walk—or run—if need be.

Once we'd rounded the corner onto Lexington, I dove into my first question. "What did the cops say?"

"They wanted to know the last time I saw Olivia."

"And when was that?"

"Friday night. Around ten."

I stopped in my tracks. "Wait a second—were you the last person to see her alive?"

He took a drag of his cigarette. "Maybe I shouldn't be talking to you."

"Olivia was my best friend. I need to know what you know. I need to know who did this to her." I looked him squarely in the eye until he shifted his gaze to the cracked sidewalk at his toes.

"Are you asking me as her friend or as one of those news people?" he said.

"Her friend."

His shoulders slumped. "I'm sorry, but I'm not supposed to talk to you."

"If you want, we can do this on background," I said.

"What's that?"

I explained to him that *background* meant I could use whatever information he gave me, but I couldn't attribute it to him. We stepped to the side to make way for one of those massive double strollers. "Please, Andrew. You know me. You've seen me with Olivia. You can trust me."

Kaminski shrugged. "You won't use my name?"

I nodded, fishing my pen and a spiral notebook out of my carryall as we started walking again. "So you were just coming off your shift when I saw you?"

"I'd already gone home. I was just about to hit the sack when I got a call from the super telling me I had to come back in."

"Your shift is eleven to seven a.m., right?" Most Upper East Side buildings followed the same schedules: seven to three, three to eleven, eleven to seven.

"The guy before me needed to get off earlier and the super couldn't cover him. I got to the Haverford at nine. Miss Kravis came in about an hour later."

"Ten o'clock? You sure?"

"Yeah, about that."

"Anyone with her?"

"Her friend. The one with the nice—" I could tell he was going to say *rack*, because I caught him looking at mine, but he paused, reconsidered, and chose a smarter approach. "Nice body."

I nodded as my stomach did a series of flips. Things had just gotten about a thousand times more complicated. "Anyone else come up for a visit?"

He shook his head, blew out some more smoke.

*Damn.* "Are you sure?"

He nodded again.

I sighed, forcing myself to focus on what I knew for sure. Bludgeoning wasn't for the weak of heart—or body. Olivia was my height—five foot nine—and whippet thin. But she was stronger than she looked. She jogged the reservoir whenever she could and practiced yoga a couple times a week, and last year she'd traveled to Africa to climb Mount Kilimanjaro. I knew that the woman Kaminski was referring to was Rachel Rockwell, and although we'd never met in person, I had seen pictures of her. She had warm brown eyes, exotic features, and long dark hair. Her small stature made it hard for me to imagine her overpowering Olivia, but neither could I rule her out. Anger was a powerful thing; it turned the meek into the mighty, the humane into the beastly. I'd seen it happen.

"Anything else you remember? Were Olivia and her friend in good spirits, or did they look like they'd been arguing?"

"Well, her friend was wearing a fur coat. Sort of a purple color."

Generally speaking, purple fur is not what one wears to a slaying. If Rachel had killed Olivia, it must have been done in the heat of the moment—in other words, *a crime of passion.* But purple fur? Our viewers were going to devour that detail. I hated that this even occurred to me, but I could already see the line on the ticker tape:

"Suspect in Kravis Murder Case Wore Purple Fur, Says Eyewitness." As a producer, I lived for moments like these. As a friend, I was horrified.

"When did Olivia's guest leave?"

"She didn't." Andrew stopped at the entrance to the Hunter College subway stop. A bunch of kids streamed past us in their backpacks and jeans, talking loudly, jumping around. We let them go past. "I'm on until seven. Then the day guy comes in. If she left through the front door, she didn't do it while I was there."

"C'mon, I'm sure you take breaks. Go to the bathroom? Make a call?"

"That's true."

"And what about the service entrance?" Buildings like the Haverford kept security cameras on all their points of entry and egress, plus the elevators. The latest systems recorded on digital hard drives—not VHS tapes—and could store up to two weeks of video.

He threw his cigarette to the ground, grinding it out with his heel. "I don't know about that stuff. You have to ask the police. Or the super."

It occurred to me that Rachel could have been slain alongside Olivia, but I didn't think we were dealing with a double homicide—the PD would have released that information from the get-go. My guess was that she had managed to sneak out of the building unseen. But was she running from the killer or from the scene of a crime she'd committed?

Andrew gestured toward the flight of stairs leading down to the subway platform. "We're done?"

"For now. How about you go home, get some sleep, take a shower, and then let's talk to set up another interview? This time on camera," I ventured.

He gave me a look.

"Don't judge. We all got a job to do." I stuffed my pad and pen back in my bag. "You ever hear of Georgia Jacobs?"

"Sure I've heard of her." He scratched the back of his neck, giving me another glimpse of green scales decorating his forearm. "But my boss says if I go on camera again, he'll can my ass."

"He can't do that. The union won't allow it."

"Sorry, but that's not how it works. If the people who live in that building want me gone, they'll find another reason. They can write me up for anything."

"As long as you didn't sign a confidentiality agreement, they can't fire you for talking to the media."

He shook his head. "It's not worth it."

*It's not worth it.* Something about his choice of words rubbed me the wrong way. "Olivia's dead, Andrew. She may be just another spoiled rich chick to you, but she had family who loved her and friends who will miss her." I put my hand out to shake his. "Thanks for the interview."

"Wait a second. I didn't mean any disrespect. You know that."

"Sure I do," I said dryly. "My friend's dead and you're worried about your job."

He looked appropriately chastened. "Let me take you to dinner."

I coughed. I hadn't seen that coming. "I don't think so."

"Can I have your number?"

"No."

"Not for a date." He stuffed his hands in his pockets. "In case I find out something about what happened—how am I going to get in touch?"

I was being baited, but there was a chance Andrew would have access to information I could use, and I couldn't afford to dismiss him out of hand. I fished out my business card and handed it to him. "If it's urgent, you can reach me on my cell. I'm hardly ever at my desk."

I was on my way back to the Haverford when I remembered to turn my phone off vibrate. I'd missed five calls, all from Jen.

She picked up on the first ring. "Where are you?" Her voice was panicked.

"Not far. I was talking to the doorman."

"You better get back here."


"Ho-stick scooped us," Jen announced as soon as I reached the van.

While I was talking to the doorman, she'd gotten hold of someone who knew about Olivia's female visitor. Worse than that, this person knew about the purple fur. The first big scoop should have been mine, and Penny Harlich had stolen it right from under me.

Alex didn't share my opinion on the matter. He was in the truck, which now reeked of the greasy sandwiches Aaron must have brought the crew for lunch. He pointed to Harlich on one of the monitors. "She's pretty, so you assume she's not smart, but she is smart, and not only that, she's ambitious. You underestimate her, and that's why she's a threat to us."

"She got lucky," I grumbled.

Alex snorted. "She's gonna hand us our asses if we don't up our game."

"Agreed. But I'm not the only one on this team. Penny's on-air talent *and* she lands scoops. Where are yours?"

"Working on it," he muttered.

"And so am I." I stepped out of the van and made a beeline for the building. Penny Harlich had a source on the PD. There was no other way to explain it. No one else could have possibly known about the visitor except for a police officer. She had a leak; now it was time for me to find mine. I started to dial his number on my phone, but then I saw him. Standing ten feet from the awning—practically right in front of me—was Detective Neal Pandowski, a.k.a. Panda.

Panda and I had met five years earlier. I was covering the rape and murder of a New York University coed and Panda was one of the detectives assigned to the case. The victim, a beautiful Indian girl, had gone missing several days before her body turned up stuffed under a mattress in a vacant room in her dorm. Because the police and university hadn't shut off access to the building as soon as they'd discovered Anjali was missing, some had argued that vital crime-scene evidence had potentially been tampered with or lost. Panda was singled out for making the call not to close the building, but I convinced Georgia to argue that he'd made the right decision, given the facts available at the time. A month later, when Panda cracked the case and the killer admitted to sexually assaulting and strangling the girl, Panda's supposed error in judgment was swiftly forgotten. Still, he remained grateful to me for coming to his defense, and had repaid the favor several times over by acting as my best source on the NYPD.

Since Panda was on the street shooting the breeze with a bunch of patrolmen, and not upstairs studying the crime scene, I could surmise two things: first, that his partner, Tom Ehlers, had been teamed up with the detective from North Homicide; and second, that Panda was miffed about not catching the case himself. At sixty years old, he was nearing retirement and wouldn't have too many more shots at solving a blockbuster case like this one. Selfishly, I was glad Panda hadn't. This meant he'd have access to all the case information *and* plenty of time to share it with me.

I got his attention. He shook his head once. I knew what that meant: *Not now.* Five minutes later, my phone rang. "You eat yet?" he asked when I picked up.

I hadn't. I suggested our usual spot.

"Meet you there in ten," he replied.

Pastrami Queen was a little hole-in-the-wall near Lenox Hill Hospital on the Upper East Side. There was a counter displaying all manner of pickles and coleslaw, knishes, brisket, corned beef, pastrami, and the like. The floors were covered in white tiles and there was a mounted flat-screen television tuned to ESPN. Panda had introduced me to Pastrami Queen's corned beef on rye, extra juicy, and most of the times we met up we did it there, over root beers, half-sours, and massive, artery-assaulting sandwiches. By the time I arrived, he was already there. Two root beers sat unopened on the plastic-covered table in front of him.

I plopped down and popped open one of the drinks, taking a sip straight from the can. Slipping my arms out of my trench, I glanced around the small room. No cops. No media. We could talk. "I need to know everything."

"Holy smokes, Clyde, I thought you'd at least comment on my tie before pumping me for information."

Panda was a good twenty pounds overweight, with a goofy grin and balding pate, and although he could probably afford better, he favored off-the-rack suits to the designer ones some of the detectives on the force wore. He also had a soft spot for kitschy ties, like the one he wore today featuring cigarette-smoking bass.

"Smoked fish," he said.

"Funny," I acknowledged.

"What's wrong? I thought I'd at least get a smile."

"I knew the victim. She was my—" I couldn't finish.

"I know, kid." He patted me on the back of the hand. Panda had lost friends on the force and a child to leukemia. I knew he understood what I was going through. "You sure you're up for this?"

I nodded, shaking off the tears that were threatening to break loose. "They've paired me with a new guy."

"You're not covering the case for Georgia?"

"Not per se. I'm working with one of our new correspondents. We were both the first ones on the scene."

He leaned back in his chair as our sandwiches arrived in a pair of parchment-lined red plastic baskets. "This gotta be a tricky one for FirstNews."

"You can say that again." I didn't touch my sandwich. My appetite was still gone and showed no signs of returning.

Panda bit into his pastrami and rye and chewed in silence for a good minute as I nursed my root beer. Wiping the mustard from the side of his mouth, he pushed my basket an inch closer to me. "You not eating?"

"I'm not hungry."

"That's a first."

I shrugged.

"Eat, Shaw. You need your strength."

Reluctantly, I took a bite, chewed. Took another bite, chewed some more. Auto-eat, I called it.

Panda looked to the back of the restaurant. "Forgot I wanted to wash my hands." He laid a brown paper evidence bag facedown on the table and got out of his seat. "Back in a flash."

I flipped over the envelope. It was marked "Kravis" with a Sharpie. Was he taking it back to the lab for Ehlers? There was a protocol with how evidence was dealt with—the technicians took everything themselves straight to the lab to be dusted for fingerprints, analyzed, and searched for clothing fibers, skin cells, or hairs. Ehlers must have found something after they left and asked Panda to take it in for him. I glanced over by the bathroom door. I had time to peek inside, and if there was ever an assignment worth bending the rules for, this was it. But I couldn't do that to Panda. He trusted me. If I needed to know what was in there, he would tell me.

I took another bite of my sandwich. Panda returned to the table and placed the bag back in his lap with a smile. "Your bosses, they worried about what we found on the scene?"

"What *did* you find?" My leg bounced under the table. "I'm told there was no evidence of drugs or sex play."

He tipped his root beer into his glass. "Toxicology reports won't be back for weeks. But we didn't find any drugs on the scene and the victim didn't have any bruises we'd associate with a sex crime. She wasn't wearing any underwear, though."

I gave him an exasperated look. "That's the fashion. Plenty of girls go commando."

"I may be an old codger, but you can't tell me that's sanitary."

I laughed despite myself. Then I got serious. "What else did you find?"

"You mean this?" He lifted the bag back out of his lap, opened it up, and picked out a bunch of mustard packets.

"Are you kidding me?" I slumped against the chair and tipped my head back to look at the ceiling.

"I'm sorry, kid. But this case isn't like the others. Olivia was your friend and she's the daughter of your network's founder. If I'm gonna trust you on this one, I gotta know I can."

I peeled my body off the back of my chair. "She wasn't just a friend, Neal. She was my *best* friend. And this isn't about protecting the network or doing my job. This is about figuring out what happened to her."

"OK," he said simply. He understood.

"Any sign of a break-in? Burglary? Olivia had a safe—did you find that?"

"No sign of break-in. No sign of burglary. The safe in the master bedroom doesn't look like it's been broken into. Forensics will have to check the fingerprints."

"And she was bludgeoned, correct?"

"She was hit on the head repeatedly with a crystal vase."

"Did you recover it?"

"Shattered," he said. "Blows were mostly on the back of the head, but the killer got in some bad ones to the face too. Looks like cause of death is trauma to the brain, but we'll see what comes back in the autopsy. There was a lot of blood. She mighta bled out."

The little hairs on my neck stood up. A slow death was the worst kind. It gave you time to think about all the mistakes you'd made, all the regrets you had. But Olivia and I were different. Her mistakes were few and far between. Maybe those last minutes had been peaceful for her; maybe—hopefully—she'd died with some knowledge of all the good she'd brought to the world.

"You OK?" Panda asked.

I held my breath, let the moment pass. "Yes."

He eyed my sandwich again. I took another halfhearted bite, put it down again. "Any sign of struggle?" I asked.

"Bruises around the arms."

That meant Olivia hadn't been caught off guard, at least not completely. She'd tried to defend herself. But given that there were no signs of a break-in, my guess was she knew her attacker. That could have included Rachel. I went over the new facts in my head: crystal vase murder weapon, signs of struggle, not a home-invasion burglary. "What kind of building security was in place?" I asked.

"The usual. Cameras in the lobby and elevator, service entrance, and service elevator. But everything was shut off."

"You're fucking kidding me."

"The system is located in the super's office. He says he found it switched off when he checked on it Saturday morning. He figured there was a malfunction or something. Apparently that happened frequently."

"You're telling me you've got no video of who came in and out of that building on Friday night? Do you even know the name of Olivia's visitor on the night of her murder?"

He stopped chewing for a second. I waited as he finished his bite and figured out how he was going to respond. "You know you can't use any of what I'm about to tell you."

"Panda, it's me you're talking to."

"I got a soft spot for you, Shaw, but I can't afford to get screwed over on this one. This ain't slap-on-the-wrist territory."

# five

"For you and me both," I countered, leaning forward on my elbows. "So tell me. What do the cops know about Olivia's visitor?"

"You ever try the knishes here?" he asked, attempting to change the subject. "The spinach ones are pretty tasty."

"Panda, the woman. I take it she's a person of interest?"

He nodded, wiped some of the grease off his chin with a napkin. "Her name's Rachel Rockwell. Name ring any bells?" Panda put his sandwich down.

"Should it?" It wasn't a lie, but the truth was that I knew who Rachel Rockwell was and why she'd been in Olivia's apartment Friday night. I knew, but I couldn't tell anyone. Especially now.

He shrugged. "They're getting a divorce. He filed. Husband's a lawyer at one of those swanky firms. They live in Greenwich, Connecticut. Drive nice cars. Kids attend private schools."

Ten to one, the police were at that very moment trying to ascertain if Olivia and Rachel's husband were sleeping together. Then Rachel would have a motive for bludgeoning Olivia to death with a crystal vase. Detectives loved nothing more than tying everything together into a nice, neat love triangle. I knew better. This was no triangle.

"How'd you ID Rachel Rockwell?" I asked.

"Her fingerprint was on a wineglass. It matched one in the system."

I raised an eyebrow. *A criminal past?*

"She was arrested for a DUI last spring."

"Booze or drugs?"

"The first one."

We'd be able to look that up, get her mug shot. Plus, drunks tend to make spectacles of themselves in public places and Greenwich was an insular community. I'd be willing to lay down another bet that she had a reputation for stirring up trouble. "What other evidence do you have?" I asked. "So far all I'm hearing is circumstantial."

His face darkened. "There may be more."

"What is it?"

"The medical examiner found something under Olivia's fingernails."

"Tissue matter?"

"You know you can't report this."

"You think it's Rachel's?"

"We don't know, and won't for a while. You know how long these tests take. Her husband's lawyer is refusing our request for a sample, so getting the judge to grant the subpoena will add on some time."

"He's lawyered up already?"

That made me suspicious. Either Rachel's husband knew enough about how these things worked to stay ahead of the game, or he had something to hide.

"And of course they had to get a big shot," Panda added, referring to the Rockwells' lawyer.

"Who?"

"Uffizo."

*Oh crap.* Frank Uffizo was a big-dog defense attorney who couldn't resist the spotlight. He'd been on our show more times than any of us could remember and had a decent relationship with Georgia. But the guy was slick. If I called him directly, he'd go behind my back and create a bidding war between us and every other network in the business. He didn't want money—he had plenty of that, and besides, we'd never pay for an interview like this. What he wanted was control. Uffizo liked to hash out the questions beforehand. It wasn't fair, or ethical, but sometimes we had no choice but to play by his rules—and follow his script. You can imagine how Georgia felt about that.

"What does the PD know about Rachel Rockwell so far, besides how much her husband had in the bank?" I asked.

Panda bit into his half-sour. "She's a mother of two. Good-looking. Long dark hair and big eyes. Part Native American."

"Where's she from originally?"

"Birth certificate says South Dakota. Pine Ridge Reservation."

"That's a long way from Connecticut," I commented. All of this was new information to me. I'd be able to use it to work around what I knew and report this instead. I went into producer mode again, thinking about how we could most efficiently locate a gaggle of Rachel's neighbors and friends to talk about her on air. She had to be well-known in her community. She wore purple fur and stilettos, drank too much, and came from the wrong side of the tracks by about three thousand miles. I made a mental note to get someone out to Greenwich to start canvassing her neighborhood for sources ASAP.

"She won scholarships doing beauty pageants. Almost made it all the way to the Miss America pageant. From there, law school," Panda summarized.

"So she's smart." For some reason, that worried me.

"Except after she graduated, she opted out, as you ladies like to call it these days. Married Rockwell right out of law school. Spent the rest of her days running the car pool and playing tennis at the country club. Model citizen except for the DUI."

"Think she'll turn herself in?"

"She better."

"You know I'm going to have to put her picture on air."

This stuff had a formula. First piece is the photo. Maybe her mug shot or a shot of her competing in a beauty contest. Best case I find a shot of her in a bathing suit for our male viewership. Then, for the women, we put a neighbor on air talking about what a great mom she was, how pretty and energetic and what a great baker/ tennis player/homemaker she was. Then we get her parents, "Ma and Pa," straight from South Dakota. And then, if we have luck on our side and can get around Uffizo, we get the husband. It wasn't rocket science. That's why everything came down to finding an inside track. Time is what it's all about. Getting ahead. Booking the guest before anyone else knows to even call them. Because if you get the guest, you get the ratings. I didn't care about any of that, but I did want to find Rachel. She was either responsible for my friend's death or she knew who was.

Panda hunched his shoulders. "Give us another few hours. Let us bring her in first."

I didn't like it. I leaned forward across the table. "And if she disappears? What then?"

"Four hours, Shaw. She's got kids. She's not a flight risk."

I begrudgingly agreed. The truth was it would be tough to get all this new info worked into the package we already had in the works for the three o'clock broadcast. Time was tight enough as it was. I looked at my watch. "It's one now. That means we go live at five."

He balled up his napkin. "Better you than someone else."

49

"Any other evidence?" I asked. If the cops weren't sure that the tissue under Olivia's nails was Rachel's, they wouldn't be able to rule out other suspects—unless they had additional reasons to think she'd done it.

"Neighbors heard yelling after the women returned home."

I digested what he said for a moment. "They heard yelling? Fighting or calls for help?"

"An argument, between two women, they said. Very loud, very serious." Panda drained the last of his soda.

Witnesses played an important role in a criminal prosecution. If the detectives could nail Rachel with DNA evidence *and* witness testimony, she was toast. Case closed, media circus averted. But I knew something the police didn't, and I wasn't so sure things were going to turn out that way.

I took the last bite of my pastrami. I'd eaten the whole thing and barely tasted it. I could feel it in my stomach, though, sitting there like a greasy tennis ball. Better full than famished—I didn't know when I'd get to eat again, between the scheduled live shots and preparing for Alex's recap of the day's events for *Topical Tonight*.

Panda nodded at my empty basket. "Good. At least now I know you won't be fainting from hunger." He took a last sip of his root beer before standing up with some difficulty.

I helped him up.

"My knees are gone," he said, shaking his head. "They say they're the first thing to go."

"For women it's the eyes."

He gave me a quizzical look.

I pointed to the crinkled skin at the outside corners of my eyes.

"You got nothing to worry about. Which reminds me, you dating anyone I should know about?" Panda regularly ran background checks on my suitors. I always protested and accused him of invading my privacy, but secretly I liked the idea that he was looking out for me.

"I haven't had a date in months."

"What happened to the economist?"

He was referring to Pinstripe Joe. We'd been dating for a couple of months when he left his razor and special shaving cream in my bathroom. I packed everything up in a small bag and dropped it off at his apartment when I knew he wouldn't be there, with a note saying, *You must have forgotten this.* Before him, I'd dated a bankruptcy lawyer, before that a museum finance director. All of them were setups by Olivia; all of them were nice guys. The museum guy said he'd tired of my boundary issues and the banker said he'd found someone more "emotionally available" to take my place. The economist blamed our breakup on my job, or my so-called unwillingness to put anything else before it. It had been six weeks since my last outing with Joe. I was lonely sometimes, but most of the time I was too busy with work to worry about my lack of a personal life. "We broke up. It was for the best."

Panda opened the door and stepped down to the sidewalk. "This the truth?"

"Afraid so. It wouldn't have worked."

"Plenty o' fish."

"Easy for you to say. You've got the wife and kids."

"If only you'd take the silver spoon out of your ass, I'd introduce you to one of our boys in blue."

# six

It was true about the silver spoon, but it wasn't something I advertised. In my experience, as soon as someone knew you were born into money, they jumped to the conclusion that you've had everything handed to you, that you've never had to work a day in your life, and that people have given you opportunities because of who you are and who you know—not because you deserve it. The word *sacrifice* is not in your vocabulary, nor is *hardship* or *struggle*. You are entitled, spoiled, immoral, and lazy. I liked to think that none of these things applied to me.

Nor should they; I'm a Shaw in name only.

My mother's family, farmers looking for a better way of life, came to the United States from England in the early 1800s. They settled in Boston, made their money first in trade, then in oil and gas and railroads, and along the way had a lot of children. My forebears were a fertile bunch, and so over time, from generation to generation, the riches were spread thin between the various family branches. Some of my relatives did a good job, investing wisely and managing to add to their inheritances with their own fortunes. As you might have guessed, my immediate ancestors did not. They lived fast and died young; a real go-big-or-go-home crowd. My mother—her given name was Charlotte, but everyone called her Tipsy—was the last in a long line of unapologetic dilettantes.

Shaw was her surname, passed on to me. According to my father, Tipsy wanted me to inherit the one remaining piece of my birthright she thought was still worth something. In her New York, the right last name could open doors and clear paths and, given the option, she wanted her daughter to be in possession of one. Little did she know I would, years later, find it more of a liability than anything else.

My father, James, grew up in a blue-collar neighborhood in suburban Philadelphia. His father was a mechanic and his mother a receptionist at an insurance agency. He defied the local odds and won a scholarship to Columbia, which was where he met my mother. Although I wasn't privy to all the details of their courtship, I did know that it was brief and romantic, and that my grandparents, all four, hadn't been thrilled about the match. My father's parents would have preferred their son marry a good Catholic, while my mother's parents wanted their daughter to marry one of their own—someone moneyed and pedigreed, for whom social status was a given, never an aspiration. The Shaws were not strivers.

Love prevailed, however, and my parents—James Callaghan and Tipsy Shaw—married in a quiet civil service at city hall. I'm told I arrived nine months later. It may have been less. What I do remember of my early childhood is that we lived in a beautiful apartment in a brown-brick building on Park Avenue and enjoyed a lifestyle made possible by the generosity of my maternal grandparents and my father's Wall Street career. Life was an endless parade of niceties—chauffeured cars, fresh-cut flowers, pressed linens that smelled of lavender and sunshine. I wore clothes my mother bought for me in Europe—leather sandals purchased in Rome, cashmere from London, smocked dresses and lace-trimmed socks from France—and my bedroom was a little girl's dream, with walls painted ballet-slipper pink, a canopied bed draped in rose taffeta, and my very own crystal chandelier. I had a nanny, a sunny Swedish girl who kept her coat pockets filled with black licorice and red candy fish. Another woman was employed to do the cooking, cleaning, and ironing.

But then one day, everything changed. My father lost his job working for a big buyout firm under circumstances never explained to me. Without his salary, we couldn't afford the mortgage, to say nothing of the cars and vacations, clothing allowances and charity outlays. My mother appealed to her parents for additional help, but they refused to assist us with anything other than my school tuition, drawing back, even, on their former munificence. I imagine it was their way of saying *I told you so* to my mother.

I was six when we moved into a much smaller condominium overlooking a small concrete courtyard filled with old bicycles and unloved vegetation. Neither prewar nor modern, the building was blessed with the advantages of neither. The ceiling in my bedroom was too low to accommodate the canopy on my bed, so that was disposed of or sold off, along with the chandelier, Mom's party dresses and furs, and the BMW Dad had kept in a garage for weekend jaunts to Locust Valley, where my grandparents kept a Tudor-style mansion, pool, and clay tennis court hidden behind eight-foot hedges.

My nanny and the housekeeper were let go, and my clothing no longer came adorned with seed pearls and lace, or wrapped in crinkly tissue paper that smelled of talcum powder and faraway places. The only aspect of my life to remain unchanged was my enrollment in the Livingston School for Girls, one of the city's more exclusive schools, one of those places where the kids are dropped off in chauffeur-driven Town Cars or SUVs and can trace their lineage back to either the *Mayflower*, the Forbes 500, or both.

"I know it's been a tough summer," she'd told me the following September, squeezing my hand as we made the ten-block walk to school, to my first day of kindergarten. "But don't worry about your tuition. We can still afford to keep you at Livingston."

She'd allowed herself to go downhill since we'd moved to the new place, favoring jeans and old sweatshirts and forgoing makeup and sometimes a hairbrush. But that day my mother had worn a fresh-pressed white blouse, flannel kilt, and dark brown boots. Her dark hair was combed into a neat chignon, exposing the pair of gold shells clipped at her earlobes. Her hand felt rough, though, no longer the texture of rose petals.

I wrenched my hand away from hers, furious. Was it too much for her to use a hand cream? It was the first day of school. I wanted everything to be back to normal. I resented her hangnails, our heavy mood, my ratty old backpack. As soon as we arrived at the school gates, I charged up the stairs without her.

But I was all bluff. At the top of the stairs I turned around, repentant. "See you later!" I called to her across the spiked tips of the wrought-iron gate.

She waved, her small white teeth bared in a brave smile, before turning to walk back down the block.

# seven

I dialed Georgia's cell as soon as Panda left my side. She took the call despite being in the middle of a session with her trainer. "I need an assistant producer to help me pull together the B-roll for my next package," I explained.

"Hang on a sec." I could hear the sound of weights clinking in the background as Georgia hunted for a private place to speak. "Now, girl, how in the hell did we lose that first one to GSBC?"

She was talking about Penny's scoop. "I had it, Georgia. She beat us to air."

"All right," she said. "So we move on. You remember what I always say on cases like this?"

"It's a marathon, not a dash."

"And right now we're in fucking last place, Clyde. Find me something to dig my teeth into. You say you can do this, then do it."

I'd been on the receiving end of Georgia's tough love enough times to know not to take her words personally. All she wanted was for me to do my best work and perform to my highest potential, and sometimes I needed a kick in the pants to do that. Not that day, though. I was already miles ahead.

"An inside PD source says the cops have identified the woman who was in Olivia's apartment Friday night. Her name is Rachel Rockwell. Lives in Greenwich. The PD is calling her a person of interest. She's wanted for questioning but hasn't turned herself in yet. I promised my source to keep her name and picture off the air until five o'clock. They want to bring her in first."

"They establish probable cause?"

I turned off Lexington Avenue onto a quieter side street. "They're getting warrants to search her house, computers, and car."

"How sure are you that this won't leak sooner? Greenwich police. Her family and friends. There's any number of ways this could get out."

Georgia had a point, but I'd given my word to Panda. "I can't go back on a promise."

She sighed. "OK, so we hold till five. In the meantime, do the research on Rockwell. Do we know what her connection to the victim is?"

"The source didn't reveal anything." It wasn't a lie. But it wasn't the truth either. "The husband already hired Frank Uffizo."

"Love triangle?" Georgia posited.

"I'm sure that's where the cops are going with it."

"You need to figure that out before we make any big statements," she said.

"Of course." Most networks, us included, wouldn't bother with the due diligence. On a hot story, with everyone scrambling for a piece of the action, you could go live with speculation and get away with it by framing the breaking news as a question rather than a statement (e.g., *Was Rachel Rockwell, a pretty Connecticut mother of two and former beauty queen, the last to see Olivia Kravis alive on Friday night . . . ? Was a scandalous love triangle involving a pretty mother of two and big-city lawyer at the center of the brutal murder of Olivia Kravis in her own home?*). But this case was different. This was the daughter of the network's founder we were talking about, and because of that, the bar for us was higher than normal. One screwup and I could be taken off the story or, worse, fired. FirstNews had to be the network of record on this case. Anything less would be considered a failure.

"What's your next step?"

"I'm going to find out everything that's public on Rachel Rockwell and her husband."

"Good."

"I need someone to case Rachel Rockwell's neighborhood for sources."

"You can have as many APs as you need." *AP* stood for *assistant producer*. They were the lowest on the totem pole and made slave wages. I'd spent my four years in the job, running last-minute script changes between the producers in the control room and on-air talent in the studio and picking the cashews out of our ten o'clock anchor's kung pao chicken. I'd also spent those four years drowning my troubles in tequila and rum.

"I just need one. The new girl, Sabine," I said, recalling the handful of interactions I'd had with her in the office and on set. Twice she'd saved us from bungling facts on the air with her thorough research, and about a month ago she'd clued us into some online chatter about an alleged cannibal/porn star who may have killed as many as three people in the United States and Canada. We were one of the first major news shows to start following the case, thanks to her. Sabine had smarts, good instincts, and ambition. I could use all of that on my team.

"The newbie? You sure?"

"Why not? She's up for the task. This'll be a good learning experience for her."

"She's all yours if you want her. I'll let the assignment desk know."

"Great."

"One more thing. How are you holding up?"

"It's a shock, but I'm fine."

"The truth, girl."

"That is."

"You have someone to call if you get—"

I cut her off. "Yes. OK? Stop worrying."


I felt the beginnings of a massive headache as I made my way back to the Haverford. The afternoon sun had warmed the air and burned off the clouds, revealing what could only be described as the perfect fall day: bright blue sky, temperature in the upper sixties, a gentle wind rustling the leaves in the trees overhead. But with the good weather came the spectators. Now, in addition to the PD, media, and paparazzi congregated around the Haverford, there were about a hundred onlookers crowding my way back to the van.

Unbuttoning my coat, I got out my elbows. A few minutes later, I had my head in the door of the van, where Alex and Dino sat talking football. There was a big game on that night—Redskins versus Giants. Alex liked the Skins, Dino the Giants, and I had to break it to them that they probably wouldn't be home in time to watch even the highlights.

"You got a new lead?" Jen asked from the back of the van, hopeful. None of us liked being on a losing team.

"Better." I filled them in on Rachel Rockwell.

Alex offered me his hand for a high five. I hesitated, and then decided to go for it, smacking him hard on the palm.

He gripped his hand. "You hit hard for a girl."

"I'll take that as a compliment."

"The girl part? Or the hitting hard?"

"Considering I haven't been a girl since the eighth grade?"

Dino rolled his eyes at both of us. "My wife's making souv-laki and dolmathakia tonight," he complained from the front seat. Sunday hours were usually easy; he'd banked on getting home early.

"We'll order Greek." I opened a bottle of water and slugged down three Excedrin from the pill bottle I'd dug out of my red messenger. "And by the way, Alex, this is New York. You'd better be a Giants fan."

"No way. I'm a loyal man." He winked at me as I crept past him in the van to sit next to Jen.

"Does it ever stop?" she muttered in my ear.

"We'll find out eventually," I replied, not bothering to whisper while I waited for my laptop to power up. As it did, I dialed Sabine, and gave her detailed instructions about the kind of visuals I wanted her to find for Olivia and Rachel Rockwell. Next she had to pull Michael Rockwell's divorce filing and take a news van and team out to Greenwich to start gathering footage of the Rockwell home and neighborhood, then start casing for neighbors and parents of classmates of the Rockwell kids to put on air during that evening's *Topical Tonight.* "It shouldn't be hard. Tell them we'll do hair and makeup and arrange free transport there and back. I'll do the pre-interviews over the phone."

"Consider it done," she said.

I liked her attitude. If Sabine delivered for me, I'd make sure Georgia knew it. Of course, there were a lot of ifs between now and then, including most pressingly, whether my latest scoop would hold until our broadcast.

In the meantime, I needed to know more about Rachel. Everything I knew about her had come directly from Olivia, and it wasn't much. I hadn't known she was from South Dakota, for example. But I did know she was a mother of two, devoted to her kids, and in the midst of a divorce. The husband was apparently a workaholic and a bully, and he liked his wife to play the part of the perfect Greenwich housewife. I'd start my search with him.

My first hit on Google was a wedding announcement in the *New York Times* from 2003. According to the piece, Rachel Rockwell, née Hart, had graduated with honors from SUNY Albany and New York University School of Law, after placing as first runner-up in the 1995 Miss South Dakota beauty pageant. Her mother was listed as Roseanna, a homemaker, and her stepfather, Vernal, a mechanic, both from the Pine Ridge Reservation in South Dakota. Michael Rockwell had attended Dartmouth, and made law review at NYU Law, after which he worked as an associate for a multinational firm with offices in London, Dubai, and New York. He was the son of Joan, an elementary-school teacher, and Peter, a neurosurgeon based in Saddle River, New Jersey. The announcement made much of Rachel's Sioux heritage and her work for an American Indian legal foundation, less of Michael Rockwell's upper-middle-class roots and promising career.

Another hit, this one more recent, detailed Michael's role brokering a big M&A deal, and yet another revealed a picture of the couple dressed in coordinating pastels at what looked like a country-club event. Rachel had a heart-shaped face, high cheekbones, and shiny long brown hair. Rockwell stood a good foot taller and about a hundred pounds heavier. He was holding a pair of beautiful toddler-aged boys. A few more clicks and I had the number of his firm, Bennett & Wayne. It was a long shot that he would be in his office on a Sunday, but from what Olivia had told me, it sounded like he rarely took a day off.

I got lucky. Rockwell was in, and because it was the weekend he answered his own phone. I introduced myself quickly; before he could hang up, I asked him the last time he'd seen his wife.

"You mean my soon-to-be ex-wife," he corrected me. "And I already told the police everything I know."

"Which is?"

"None of your business."

"Fair enough," I said, pausing briefly. "How about we talk on background for now? Could you tell me how Rachel knew Olivia Kravis?" If Rockwell wasn't willing to tell me what he did know, maybe I could get him to tell me what he didn't.

He didn't respond.

I restated the question. "Was your wife friends with the murder victim?"

"We're done here," he gritted out. "You have any questions? Talk to my lawyer, Frank Uffizo."

"Is Uffizo also representing Rachel?"

"I said we're done."

Michael Rockwell was locked up like a box, but I wasn't giving up so easy. It was time to try another approach, shake things up by saying something crazy, something that was not likely to be true and that might get him talking. "Is it true you were sleeping with Olivia Kravis?" I asked.

"Fuck you."

At least he hadn't hung up.

I took a deep breath. "Mr. Rockwell, I can understand why you don't want to talk to me. But whether you do or don't, a lot of things are about to happen to your family. In a few hours, the American public is going to find out about Rachel's involvement in this case, and starting from that very moment, the public will be forming opinions, opinions about Rachel's guilt or innocence. Think about how this is going to affect your children. If their mother is branded a murderer, that's probably going to have some kind of impact. It would be good if there were someone speaking up on Rachel's behalf."

Rockwell cut me down with a series of curse words.

"How about you take a few minutes to think about it?"

"Not necessary. The answer is no. Not now, not in ten minutes, not tomorrow. I'm not interested." And then he finally did hang up.

Rockwell never called me back. No surprise there. But he did call Frank Uffizo, who in turn called Hiro Itzushi, our chief legal counsel, to threaten legal action if we uttered one word about Rachel in connection to the Kravis case. Itzushi went into a tailspin, insisting we pull the Rachel angle from *Topical Tonight* until the police confirmed her involvement in the case on the record. But cooler heads prevailed. Georgia made it known that cowering to Uffizo's demands was not only ridiculous but also contrary to our mission as members of the press.

Diskin gave us the green light, signing off on our copy at thirty minutes to air. By the end of the show, the e-mails and phone calls were pouring in by the hundreds. Exactly as I'd anticipated, the armchair detectives in our audience had latched on to Rachel's wardrobe choice of purple fur. They tweeted. They blogged. They sent our ratings through the roof. Then came the news that *People* was writing a cover story on the case.

In less than twenty-four hours, Olivia Kravis's murder had become the biggest crime story of the year.

# Monday

# eight

I woke up at 6:00 a.m. fully clothed and reeking of garlic.

The phone was ringing. I croaked hello as the caller ID registered. It was Olivia's work line at the foundation. "Who is this?" I rasped, now fully awake, scrambling out of bed. There was a brief moment of silence before I heard a click. The caller had hung up. I dialed Olivia's number, my fingers shaking, and listened as the line rang and rang. When the foundation's answering service finally kicked in, the sound of Olivia's voice rendered my adrenaline to tears faster than I would have thought possible. I got back in bed and sobbed into my pillow, then got up again, gulped down two Excedrin with a mouthful of lukewarm instant coffee. What I really needed was three hours' more sleep and a week of therapy to get over the shock of losing my best friend. Neither was going to happen. I was due at work in an hour.

Stumbling toward the bathroom, I made a pit stop at the linen closet for a fresh bath towel. By New York standards, my apartment was a respectable size. Everywhere else it would have been called a shoebox. It suited me just fine. At the entrance was a small foyer outfitted with a wood console, a lamp, and a painted ceramic bowl I dumped all my mail and keys into every night when I got home.

On the left was a kitchen, just big enough for a café-style table and a pair of iron chairs. The butcher-block countertop held the main attractions: the coffeemaker, microwave, and a small wine fridge that I used to store bottles of mineral water. Beyond the kitchen was a den, decorated with an antique rug, a couch I'd bought online, a flat-screen television mounted on the steamer trunk I'd taken with me to college, and a treadmill I'd used maybe twice. Then the bathroom—nothing exciting there—and my bedroom, where I kept my desk, computer, a queen-size bed, and a side table, on which stood a stack of non-crime-related books I aspired to read one day.

After a quick shower, I brushed my teeth and got dressed before spending another few minutes trying to deflate the inner tubes under my eyes. It was a lost cause. I grabbed a pair of dark sunglasses and headed out the door.

I was almost at the FirstNews building when my phone rang again. It was my father. He'd seen the news. "Why didn't you call me?"

Eight years ago, after I moved out, my father sold our old apartment in the city and bought a house upstate, about two hours north of Manhattan. It was a sweet hundred-year-old colonial with exposed wood beams, stone fireplaces, and a kitchen overlooking a cornfield. I visited him as much as work would allow, which wasn't often enough as far as he was concerned. "I was busy," I said. "They put me on the story."

"Do you want me to come down? I'm worried about you." I could hear his dog, Milton, yapping in the background, and the concern lacing his voice. He knew Olivia was my rock, and was probably worried that her death would cause me to fall back on some old bad habits. That wasn't going to happen.

"Dad, I'm fine. Or I will be. But I wouldn't be able to see you anyway. I'm going to be working this case twenty-four/seven."

"I don't mind if you're out all day. I can keep myself busy during the day and just be there for you when you get home." There was a long pause before Dad sighed. "All right, Cornelia. Let me know if you change your mind. E-mail me when I can expect to see you again. I want to see my daughter. And princess," he said, pausing briefly, "promise not to make this about your mom."

"OK, Dad, I promise," I said before saying good-bye.

My father's not-so-secret opinion was that I'd chosen my profession because I was still determined to solve the unsolvable. In a way he was right, because here I was, once again looking for clues I'd probably never find. The first time was thirty years ago.

My mother never picked me up after my first day of kindergarten. She'd gone home that day, run a few errands, and killed herself by jumping off the fire escape. A neighbor found her body on the concrete slab in our building's courtyard and called the police. I'd arrived home before they'd had a chance to remove her body and, barreling through a sea of adults, thrown myself on top of her.

Several weeks after her funeral, once time had worn down the sharpest edges of my grief and I'd finally grasped that she hadn't fallen, but deliberately thrown herself off our building, I started asking questions. I wanted to know how people could kill themselves, knowing what pain they were causing the people they left behind, and why my mother would possibly do that to us, to me. Nothing my father said satisfied me, and the counselor at school was no better, so I began going through my mother's drawers and papers, hoping to figure out why she'd done what she had. Why she'd hated her life, why I hadn't been enough to keep her happy, why plunging to her death seemed like the only or best option. If my mother had left a note, it would have been easier to accept her choice. But she hadn't, and all I was left with was a succession of horrifically clear memories: the sight of all those police cars outside my building, the feel of her still-warm hand—chafed and red—in mine, the look on my father's face when he pried me off her dead body.

What ended up haunting me most about my mother's death were not these things, but the afternoons I spent alone in her room, turning every pocket inside out, emptying every drawer, and always, without fail, coming away with nothing. At some point I must have realized she'd left us no answers, just aching loss and the vicious anger I'd eventually turn on myself.

Despite what I'd just promised my father, I wasn't going to let that happen with Olivia.


The Monday-morning meeting was the bane of my existence. I slumped down in my chair and did my best to get comfortable for what was sure to be another hour-long confab in the cheerless chamber that was Conference Room B. The room was barely big enough to accommodate the oval Formica table and twelve chairs it held within, and it had no windows, just a pair of sputtering vents and a strip of fluorescent lights hugging the ceiling tiles. Conference Room A, on the other hand, was a spacious, window-lined room outfitted in leather and glossed mahogany furniture. It was reserved for meetings with important advertisers, network heads, and skittish guests who needed a little hand-holding before they agreed to go on camera.

I should have been listening, but my mind was on who might have called me from Olivia's office that morning. Fred Wallace— Georgia's executive producer, who went by his last name—pointed at me, snapping his meaty fingers impatiently. "Earth to Clyde. Could you be so kind as to honor us with a rundown of the Kravis story?" He was well aware of my feelings about the Monday-morning meeting, and apparently not inclined to cut me any slack for being the victim's best friend.

I recounted to the group everything that we'd learned so far. Some crime-scene info, a few leads. A lot of questions.

"We'll want a couple in-house guests. A prosecutor and a family member," Wallace said.

"We're getting Delphine Lamont, Olivia's stepsister. I'm waiting on confirmation from legal that we're a go for tonight," I replied, my eyes not lifting from my notebook paper. "As for Rachel Rockwell's side of it, her husband's a definite no and Frank Uffizo, the Rockwells' attorney, is a long shot. I've already called him a few times."

"He's talking to *Today*," piped up Barton Oberlink, one of our senior bookers. "Word is Lauer's interviewing him tomorrow a.m."

"I knew it," I said, swearing under my breath. Aside from being able to identify Rachel Rockwell before anyone else, we weren't as far ahead of the competition on the story as my bosses would have liked. GSBC had scooped us on purple fur, CNN on the number of blows Olivia had sustained—twenty-seven—and now *Today* was landing Uffizo.

Wallace leaned back in his chair, his arms spread wide. "Well, anyone got any other ideas?"

I looked up. "The Kravis Foundation. Olivia's assistant might give us an interview, help establish a timeline for Friday."

Wallace rubbed the stubble on his chin. "Who's got the timeline?"

"I'm working on it," I replied.

"What else we got?"

The team debated our strategy while I marked the time on the wall. I was itching to hit the pavement, but, as much as I didn't want to be holed up in an airless conference room, meetings were an important part of my job. I couldn't afford to be cast as anything but a team player.

I'd worked my way up over the years, cultivating sources inside the New York, Chicago, LA, San Francisco, and Washington, DC, police forces, plus a Rolodex full of the best private investigators, psychologists, and medical examiners. I'd landed exclusive interviews in the investigation of Natalee Holloway's disappearance, the Laci Peterson and Caylee Anthony stories, and countless other national crime sagas. If I was ever going to move my career to the next level, I needed to show my worth beyond landing the occasional blockbuster interview. I was on the wrong side of thirty-five, and even for those of us behind the camera, you can only be young and hot for so long.

Sabine Weller was both. Diskin's most recent hire, she was twentysomething and curvaceous, with a face that looked camera-ready at every angle. Suddenly she was in the doorway in a form-fitting sweaterdress, her cheeks flushed. "Alex just called," she said to me. "He's got a woman who says she saw Rachel arguing on Friday night with a man."

"What time did she spot them?" I questioned.

Sabine shook her head. "Alex didn't say."

"Take a camera," Wallace said to me, standing up. "Meeting adjourned."

I ran out the door and grabbed my bag and jacket from my desk, then met my team—minus Alex, who was already waiting for us at the scene—in the van. A few minutes later we'd gotten around the snarl of west Midtown traffic and were sailing uptown. I took advantage of the drive time to make a call. The neighbors Sabine had managed to corral for our show last night weren't friends of Rachel and Michael Rockwell. They'd provided good sound bites, but little in the way of useful information. What we needed was a real Greenwich insider—or close friend—who could give us the skinny on the couple's relationship. Why did they break up? Was he mean? Was she a drunk? Did they fight over money or sex or both? And did those fights ever get out of control?

I dialed Sutton Danziger. She was the alumni-relations officer for my class at Livingston. Her husband did something arcane and extraordinarily lucrative in finance, and they lived in one of those gigantic homes you see listed in real-estate advertisements with an asking price equal to the GDP of a small country. Knowing Sutton, she belonged to the same posh Connecticut country club as Rachel and Michael Rockwell.

Sutton answered her cell phone after a few rings. She asked me four questions within the space of ten seconds: *Can you believe it? How are you doing? How is her family taking it? Have you spoken to Delphine?*

"Not yet," I said.

Diskin had just texted that Delphine was confirmed for a taped interview in one of our studios at three o'clock that afternoon. Alex was conducting the interview, which would then be edited in time to air during *Topical*'s broadcast at nine.

"The school should do something in her memory." Sutton sighed. "The alumni association will send a wreath for the funeral, but we should do something more substantial. I'm thinking a dedication during graduation ceremonies."

"I'm sure the Kravises would like that," I said.

"Would you be willing to give a speech?"

I demurred. Most people assumed I was a natural public speaker because of what I did, but it actually terrified me to say more than three words in front of a large group.

"Olivia and you were inseparable. You have to do this."

Sutton wasn't going to take no for an answer, so I told her I'd do it if she'd answer a few of my questions.

"What kind of questions?" she asked.

"Did you see last night's broadcast?"

She hesitated before apologizing. "I watch Greta."

At least she was honest. "Well, then you probably already know that Olivia entertained a guest at her apartment the night she was murdered. A woman named Rachel Rockwell, who lives in Greenwich. Do you know Rachel?"

There was a long pause. "I'm afraid I don't know her personally," Sutton began. "But I know who she is and I have a friend who knows her quite well." The way Sutton said *quite*, I knew I'd hit pay dirt. "This friend of mine will be at a dinner I'm hosting tonight. If you want, I could ask her if she's interested in speaking with you, and get back to you tomorrow."

Although a dinner party in Greenwich wasn't how I wanted to spend my evening, I couldn't rely on Sutton to land me an interview with Rachel's friend. The stakes were too high.

"Would it be possible if I came by and asked her myself? I don't have to stay for dinner."

There was another pause as Sutton considered my request. I couldn't blame her. The last time she saw me was about five years ago. I was thirty-one, sloshed out of my mind, wearing a face of smeared makeup and a dress that showed more than it should. I'd also just had sex on her bed with her twenty-year-old baby brother.

"Sutton, I'll be coming from work," I said. "And on my best behavior."

She relented with a weary sigh. "As it happens, my numbers are off. One of my husband's friends is recently divorced. You can sit next to him."

"Sounds great," I lied.

"We're here," Aaron announced from the front seat. The van pulled into an open spot. I told Sutton I had to go and hung up.

Alex opened the door from the outside. "What took you so long?" His face split into a wide grin. Damn, he was handsome.

I looked up at the woman's building. It was a five-story walk-up. "Which floor?"

"Fifth."

"Of course it is," Dino grumbled.

We all helped carry the equipment upstairs. Her apartment was one of those railroad units, a narrow row of rooms, front to back. High ceilings, old creaky floors, the stench of yesterday's fish dinner mingling with the neighbor's cigarette smoke. "Can someone open a window?" I asked, narrowly sidestepping a little dog that was yapping at my feet.

"Bad Riley." A woman, fortyish, with short brown hair and a slender figure, scooped up the dog in her arms and held out her hand. "I was taking Riley for a walk when I saw that woman. I saw her picture on your show."

"Rachel Rockwell." I motioned to the couch. We both sat down. "You sure it was her?"

The woman nodded.

"The man she was with. What did he look like?"

"He was tall. Good-looking. Reminded me of that actor. The one on *Sex and the City*?"

"Chris Noth?"

She furrowed her brow.

"He played Mr. Big?" Michael Rockwell bore a small resemblance to him, especially in the dark and at a distance.

"No, the other one. Aidan." The dog leaped off the woman's lap and onto the floor. He sprinted toward the woman's bedroom, at the back end of the apartment where Dino was setting up a shot with Jen and Alex.

"What time was it?" I asked. I was reasonably sure I could get time of death from Panda. If this lady had seen Rachel after Olivia was killed, that could be significant.

"Around eleven thirty."

"You told my colleague they were arguing."

She shrugged. "I couldn't really hear. It was late. I honestly just wanted to get home. I'm a nurse at a hospital and I'd been on my feet since five."

"How are you sure it was Rachel you saw?"

"It looked like her."

"Do you remember what she was wearing?"

She shook her head. "She wasn't wearing that coat, if that's what you want to know. Bet she ditched that at the crime scene."

She was a fan, one of our armchair detectives who watched every night and dreamed of meeting Georgia face to face. I raised my eyebrow. "Have you talked to the police?"

Her chin lifted an inch. "Not yet. I got up late this morning and saw that woman's picture. First thing I did was call your hotline."

"You probably should go ahead and call the police after we're done here," I told her.

"We're all set," Dino called from the other room. The woman stood, excitement flashing across her face. My gut told me she had convinced herself she saw something she hadn't. For the network's purposes, that didn't matter. For mine, it sure as hell did. Either way, I needed to find out Olivia's time of death.


An hour later we were out the door. Another half hour and I was back at my desk, waiting for Panda to get back to me, chicken-salad sandwich in hand. I was about to unwrap it when a man appeared in my cubicle. He was dressed in a navy Windbreaker and rumpled khakis. He had a buzz cut and a beefy build.

"May I help you?"

"Clyde Shaw?" he asked in reply.

I scanned his jacket and hands for one of the stick-on visitors' passes security would have given him downstairs. My posture stiffened when I realized he didn't have one. "Who let you in here?"

He unzipped his jacket. I clutched the sides of my chair, preparing to hurl myself out of it. There were plenty of nut jobs who blamed the media for everything wrong in our world, and a scary number of those would like nothing more than to gun a few of us down.

The man produced a police badge. "Detective Tom Ehlers. We have a friend in common."

Ehlers. Panda's partner. I'd never met him in person. My shoulders relaxed away from my ears. "So we do."

"There a place we can talk?"

I led him to Conference Room A. It was located along a hall that didn't get a lot of foot traffic. With any luck, my tête-à-tête with the detective would go unnoticed. I offered him a bottle of water and took a seat at the table. Ehlers chose to remain standing next to the window, looking out at the view over Seventh Avenue. "I understand you knew Olivia Kravis," he said in a heavy Long Island accent. Panda had once told me that Ehlers was passionate about two things, sailing and dogs, and that he was the youngest of eight, most of whom worked in civil service or on the force. They were a tight-knit, community-minded big family—the kind I'd always dreamed of having.

"I did know Olivia," I said.

"She sent you a message the night she was murdered."

"What?" My hand reflexively went to the pearls at my neck. "No she didn't."

He repeated himself.

"Are you talking about the voice mail she left me?"

Ehlers shook his head. "She sent you a text. May I see your phone, Ms. Shaw?" It was more command than question.

Normally I wouldn't let a police officer within ten feet of my phone—freedom of the press and all—but this was Olivia's case, and Ehlers was my ally for as long as he was trying to find her murderer.

I took my phone out of my jacket, entered in the security code, and slid it across the table. Ehlers sat down, picked up my phone, and began tapping and dragging his finger down the screen. He was looking through either my texts or e-mails.

"When did it come in?" I asked.

"How about you let me go first with the questions?"

I spread my arms. "Be my guest."

His fingers stopped moving. He slid the phone back across the table. "Can you explain that?" There was a text from Olivia. The hair on the back of my neck stood on end as I read her message:

WE NEED TO TALK. IT'S TIME YOU KNOW THE TRUTH.

I read it again, noting the time stamp—6:05 on Friday evening, about twenty minutes after she'd tried calling me. *It's time you know the truth.* What truth? What did she want to tell me? I looked up at Ehlers. He had a small notebook open and a pen poised to write. "I didn't get the text," I said, my hands trembling so hard the phone slipped from them and skidded across the table. "I didn't get it."

"Are you in the habit of ignoring texts from friends?"

"No, of course not," I replied, flustered and defensive. "But sometimes they get buried under a bunch of other texts and I miss them. I didn't ignore her text. I didn't see it," I said, repeating myself.

"And you didn't think to check your phone after you found out your friend was murdered?"

"What? No." I shook my head. I was still trying to wrap my mind around the fact that Olivia had wanted to tell me something before she died.

"What does that text mean, Ms. Shaw?"

"I don't know. Obviously she had something to tell me. It sounds like it was something important. How am I supposed to know what it was when she never got the chance?"

"You have no idea?" He sounded dubious.

I scoured my memory for answers, for a clue, and came up with nothing. I thought I'd known all of Olivia's deepest, darkest secrets. Clearly I hadn't. "No," I said at last.

He nudged the phone closer to me. "Read it again."

I did, trying this time to set aside my emotions and think analytically. I read the whole thing aloud again to Ehlers.

"Anything?"

"It sounds urgent. *We need to talk.* That's urgent, right? And the words *it's time* make it sound like this thing she wanted to tell me wasn't something brand-new, like she'd been keeping something from me for a while. My God, do you think this has something to do with why she was killed?" A chill shot down my spine. This was too much of a coincidence.

"We have to investigate everything."

I felt the world bob and shift around me, my vision darkening. I was going to faint. *Breathe,* I told myself. *Breathe.*

Ehlers didn't give me long to find my equilibrium. "Did you recently have a fight with Ms. Kravis?"

"No."

"When was the last time you saw her?"

"Two Wednesdays ago. I went to her apartment. We ordered in from an organic soup place and drank wine. I went home close to midnight. Everything was fine."

He wrote down what I said. "Was Ms. Kravis in a relationship?" he asked without looking up from his notebook.

I froze. *What do they know?* "Not that I'm aware of," I said plainly, keeping my tone in check.

He sucked his teeth. "You sure?"

"Olivia's life, like mine, revolved around work. Her priority was the foundation, like mine is this network." It wasn't a lie.

Ehlers got up. "Thanks for your time."

"Wait." I jumped out of my chair, blocking the exit. "What about the time of death?"

"It'll be in the ME's report later."

"That's not fair. I just gave you information—now how about you return the favor?"

"Actually, you didn't tell me much I already didn't know." He zipped up his Windbreaker.

"What do you guys know about Rachel's whereabouts? Has she fled the country?"

He answered me with an annoyed glare.

"Is she the only suspect?"

Again, silence.

"Where on the head was Olivia hit? Do the wounds indicate that the person who murdered Olivia was taller than she is, or the same height? Because Rachel is small, five five, five four, max. If the wounds are higher, there's no way she could have committed this crime by herself."

Ehlers pushed my chair gently aside. "I'd ask if you ever heard of high heels, Ms. Shaw, but I can see that you're wearing some."

I shut my mouth.

"The department thanks you for your cooperation. I'll let you know if I have any further questions."

# nine

Three p.m. I was in the lobby of the FirstNews building waiting for Delphine Lamont.

Back at Livingston, I'd remembered my best friend's older stepsister as one of the all-stars. She was an A student and a born competitor, a star athlete who excelled in every sport she tried. She had every gift known to mankind except for, perhaps, good looks, having inherited a prominent nose and diminished chin from her natural father, a French playboy who had died in a powerboat accident when Delphine was just a baby. Both the nose and chin had been fixed by the time she left high school, although neither seemed to impede her ascent to the top rung of Livingston's student hierarchy. At sixteen, however, Delphine had showed enough promise as a skier to be sent to a Swiss boarding school, where she could train all winter long. Olivia, it was decided, was to be sent with her to keep her company, although I never understood why. They had never been particularly close, and Delphine wasn't the type to get homesick.

I, on the other hand, was rudderless without my best friend. I'd developed early, getting breasts and hips before anyone else in my class. The girls teased and alienated me and made me feel ashamed of my body. The boys had the opposite reaction. They loved my curves and gave me the attention I craved. I took to my role of sex object with gusto. At fourteen, I gave a boy a blow job in the bathroom of the Ziegfeld Theater. At fifteen, I met Ethan Wilcox.

He was a senior at Collegiate with a fringe of dirty-blond hair and a tall, athletic build that his school put to good use on the basketball court. His parents lived in an apartment on Park Avenue, a duplex with a grand staircase and long hallways paneled in dark wood. When he called—out of the blue—he said his parents were going to be gone for the night or out of town, I can't remember which. What I do remember is that Ethan had invited a friend over, and that we played pool and drank something syrupy and potent from heavy glass mugs, and that midway through the game Ethan lifted the hem of my skirt with the end of his cue.

"I see London, I see France," he said, setting down his pool stick to lift me on the green-felt-covered table. Off went my sweater, down came my skirt. Ethan snaked his fingers beneath the pink lace of my bra, his head traveling lower, his tongue swirling between my legs. It wasn't until he was inside of me, my legs straddling the air, that I remembered his friend. He was standing at the end of the table, dick in hand, waiting his turn.

Later, I convinced myself that I'd been drunk; that's why I'd done it, why I'd let them do what they did to me. But alcohol wasn't solely to blame, and I'd hardly been a passive participant once things got going. In fact, it was the opposite—the power and control I felt, that spurred me on and gave me a high no drug could match. It was only afterward, once I was home, and in the days to come, when the other girls inevitably found out, that I felt dirty, slutty, and worthless. But that didn't stop me from screwing around, and it sure as hell didn't stop me from drinking. In a cute boy's arms, both of us shit-faced on Hawaiian Punch and rum, I found a reprieve, however brief, from the loneliness and despair that dogged me every other second of the day. Sex and alcohol. Alcohol and sex.

When it came time for me to apply to college, even my father—not the most perceptive man on the planet—could see that the farther away I got from Manhattan, the better. He'd tried talking to me, enforcing a curfew, then therapy that cost him an arm and a leg and made no difference in my behavior. My grades slipped even further; I couldn't sleep without taking a Tylenol PM and a nip of Benadryl. By some miracle I scored well on my SATs—which my father took as evidence I still had a brain inside my head, despite all my efforts to prove the contrary—and had my pick of Midwestern colleges. In August, we drove west in a rented Honda packed with my belongings. "Go get your fresh start," Dad told me at the gates of Macalester. "Everyone deserves at least one."

Except I failed to turn over a new leaf in Minnesota, my home for four frigid years, and failed again in Washington, DC, where I earned a graduate degree in journalism by the skin of my teeth. I returned to my dad much the same as I had left, and God help him, he loved me anyway. I don't know how. Because all I ever saw in the mirror was trouble.

Then Olivia stepped back in to my life. She got me that FirstNews job, and then she lent me the money to get my own apartment. But the news business isn't the best place for a person with my kind of tendencies. People party. People fuck. For the first four years at the network, I was able to keep my work and partying mostly separate, but then I got promoted to segment producer and started pulling longer hours and going on the road with my colleagues, plenty of whom were cokeheads or big drinkers like me. I started having trouble drawing the line between blowing off a little steam on a Friday night and going on a twelve-hour bender that left me incapacitated for an entire weekend. I was spinning out of control, worse than ever before. It wasn't until Georgia Jacobs finally gave me an ultimatum—get help or get out—that I left the worst of it behind. I'd been sober for two and a half years.

I had just broken up with Jack Slane. It was late March, still cold enough to snow. My crew and I had been covering a child-abduction case in Maine and had been stressed to our eyeballs, going on four hours of sleep a night for ten days straight. We'd flown home that morning, put on a huge show, and adjourned to Coyote Cinco's en masse, ready to drink the place into the ground. I did a few shots with Doug, one of our cameramen, a big guy with about five tattoos on his body. Around midnight, we screwed in the alley behind the bar; then I went back inside, kept drinking, and asked one of my underage interns—a college girl doing her semester-at-work—for a couple of the OxyContin I knew she was carrying. I swallowed two, maybe more, and the next thing I remembered I was on my kitchen floor. Georgia at my side, kneeling on the floor, a phone pressed to her ear.

Later I'd learn that there had been a break in the case we'd been covering—the police had found the girl's body buried beneath a blanket of snow in an icy ravine less than a mile from the strip mall where she'd been abducted—and Georgia hadn't been able to reach me. She'd taken a car to my place on her way to the airport, persuaded my landlord to let her in, and found me on the floor, passed out in a pool of my own urine. She threw a bucket of cold water on my face and made a call to Hilltop, a recovery center in Connecticut. "They're expecting us in a couple of hours," she said. "You have ten minutes to shower the stink off your body. I'll pack a bag."

With effort, I managed to lift myself to a sitting position. "I overdid it last night. That doesn't mean I need to go to rehab."

She shook her head. "Girl, we both know this isn't the first time."

Georgia was referring to the last time I'd passed out. It was nine months earlier. I was in a bar on the Bowery, knee-deep in vodka tonics, a couple of codeines working their way through my system. I came to in the emergency room of St. Vincent's. After the doctor pumped my stomach, I got a visit from the psychiatrist on call. She sent me on my way with a baggie of pamphlets on alcohol abuse, once she figured out I hadn't been trying to kill myself. Not intentionally, anyway.

I pushed the hair off my face. "Georgia, I'm not going."

"Then you're fired."

"You can't do that. You can't just fire me," I sputtered.

"I absolutely can and will, if you don't get your ass moving this instant." She pulled me to my feet, ushered me to my bathroom, and put me in a cold-water shower fully clothed. When we finally were in her car, she gave her driver a new set of directions. "Change of plans." I slept most of the way and woke up as we were pulling into the facility, a redbrick building sitting on a high hill, overlooking a glassy pond and plenty of snow-covered acres. Georgia sat next to me in the waiting room, ignoring all the calls and messages that must have been coming in on her phone. She was missing a breaking news story, and that's when I realized she really cared about me, and that I owed it to her and everyone else who had tried, unsuccessfully, to help me, to make myself better. I started to cry. Georgia put an arm around my hunched-over back. "Stay here as long as you need. Don't even worry about work. All that will be waiting for you when you're ready."

I stayed at Hilltop for three weeks. Georgia, I later learned, footed the whole bill. My roommate was a forty-year-old recovering meth addict from Ohio who read romance novels and looked like a PTA president. I wore hospital-issued sweats, took showers in a communal bathroom, and had twice-daily sessions with a therapist named Elaine.

Elaine had gray spiky hair, and an office decorated in half-dead plants and Russian nesting dolls. Within the first week she looked me square in the eye and said, "You're not borderline and you're not bipolar, so what are you?"

I shrugged. "Why don't you tell me?"

"An alcoholic?"

"No."

"You realize that's what every alcoholic says."

"I slipped down a bad slope, but that's over with now."

"When you say over with, does that mean you're never going to drink alcohol again?"

"I can have one drink and stop myself."

"What about the times when you don't? What's happening then?"

I spent much of the next few weeks in Elaine's office trying to figure out the answer to that question. We started with my childhood, and more specifically my mother, Tipsy, who had earned her nickname in gin and vodka and who had passed down to me a love of both. Tipsy, who had left me abandoned and bereft, with low self-esteem and too many questions, all of which led me to seek comfort in the arms of boys and, later on in life, to make risky choices, like screwing strangers I met in dark bars. I drank and slept around, and hated myself for it.

"Tell me about the scars," Elaine said, pointing at the thin white lines etched across my wrists. They were barely visible now, but in the right light you could still see them.

"I wasn't trying to kill myself."

"Just punish yourself?"

I shifted in my seat.

"When was the last time you cut yourself?"

It was after a trip to Guatemala with Olivia. "Six years ago."

"Good," she said. "That tells me something."

"What?"

"That you are capable of recovery. You stopped that behavior. You can stop this one."

By the end of my stay at Hilltop, Elaine and I had agreed that once I returned to the real world, I needed to go to AA meetings, find a sponsor, and do the whole twelve steps to help maintain my sobriety. I also needed to continue my work on the couch.

Back in New York, I had good intentions. I saw a shrink on Fifty-Seventh Street and went to beginners' AA meetings at a church on East Forty-Third. But my new psychologist was a jerk, and the meetings, with my hectic schedule, were hard to make on a regular basis. I quit them all after a few months. I was convinced I had a handle on my issues—which I had, for two and a half years and counting—and that I was better off leaving my past where it belonged.

I stood waiting in the lobby of the FirstNews building. Delphine pushed through the rotating door, accompanied by a man. She was wearing a charcoal skirt suit that flattered her tall, athletic frame; a navy silk blouse; and no makeup. Her thick, chestnut-brown hair was pushed back with a headband and fell in a heavy curtain to just above her collarbone. A gold bracelet with a diamond-studded clasp encircled her strong wrist, and two large diamond stud earrings twinkled at each ear. She saw me standing by the reception desk and walked straight over.

"Cornelia Shaw, it's been a long time." Up close, I could see that her hazel eyes were red, and that she wasn't entirely makeup-free. A thick coat of pigment did its best to conceal the dark circles beneath her eyes.

"Delphine, I'm so sorry. I know how you must—"

She held up her hand. "Don't, really, or I'll just start up again."

*That's right, save it for the camera,* the producer in me thought.

The man next to her shifted his weight in his shoes. He was mostly bald and short. He also looked familiar. "This is Prentice Maldone," Delphine said, introducing us.

I shook hands with the head of Maldone Enterprises, a fast-growing conglomerate that owned and operated a string of newspapers and television stations in second-tier cities. I'd read an article on Bloomberg that said Maldone was planning on giving the Tribune Company—which had a similar business model—a run for its money. The article hadn't named any of Maldone's acquisition targets, but it was fairly obvious he wasn't hanging around our lobby to offer his condolences.

"Nice to meet you," Maldone said. He had a flat Midwestern accent—if I had to guess, I'd say from Iowa or Illinois—and small blue eyes that probably missed nothing. "Are you with the network?" he asked.

"I'm a segment producer for *Topical Tonight*."

"Very good," Maldone said.

Delphine grabbed the gold chain strap of her handbag and looked at me. "How long has it . . ." Her voice trailed off as she worked the math.

"Two years." We said it at the same time. The last time had been at a birthday party for Olivia at Orsay, a popular Upper East Side restaurant. I'd been sober half a year.

Maldone touched Delphine's arm lightly. "I'll see you soon." Then he nodded good-bye to me and entered one of the elevators on his own.

"Shall we?" I said, cocking my head in the same direction.

She pressed her lips together tightly and nodded.

While Delphine went through makeup and hair, I went in search of Alex to make sure he was prepped for his interview. He wasn't at his desk, or in the studio. I was about to call him on his cell when I spotted him in the kitchenette, chatting up Sabine. She was leaning into him, her pretty face lit up like Fifth Avenue on Christmas. I knew that if I didn't break them up then and there, he'd have her legs in the air by the end of the week—maybe sooner.

"Hey, Alex." I stepped between them. "Any more scoops from Pump-Me-Hard?"

He laughed it off, but his cheeks had turned beet red. "Penny Harlich's covering the Kravis story for GSBC. Clyde thinks because I talk to the competition, I must be sleeping with it," he told Sabine.

I planted my hands on my hips. "All the more reason for you to stay as far away from her as possible. I don't like the idea of you swapping tips with her. Saliva, that's your business. But that's where the reciprocity should end until this story is over. *Capisce?*" I turned back to Sabine and left her with one parting comment. "You'd better watch it, dear. This one has an appetite for fresh meat."

"You know, Clyde, I wouldn't have pegged you for a rumor-monger," Alex called from behind me.

"You know you love me," I yelled back, circling my way back to the green room.

Delphine was still in makeup, so I went back to my desk and dialed Panda. This time he picked up. "How'd you like Ehlers?" he asked.

"I would have liked him better if he gave me time of death."

Panda chuckled. "I bet you would have."

"Please, Neal. I need to know it."

He sighed. "ME says ten twenty-five, but you didn't hear it from me."

That was a little more than four hours after she sent my text, and about twenty-five minutes after Olivia arrived back at the Haverford with Rachel. It was also an hour before that lady said she spotted Rachel on the street arguing with a man. "Pastrami's on me next time," I said before hanging up.

Delphine sat on a lumpy love seat in *Topical Tonight*'s so-called green room. No green here, just beige wall coverings, some worse-for-wear seating options, a coffee table covered with ancient issues of *New York* and *Time* and three near-empty candy bowls, plus a machine that spat out coffee, hot chocolate, and hot and cold water. "Would you like anything?" I asked, gesturing toward the machine. "Water, tea?"

She'd removed her jacket, and her sleeveless navy blouse exposed a pair of muscular arms. "Nothing, thanks."

Delphine looked away, her hands balled up in her lap. I could tell she didn't feel like talking, but I had questions I couldn't ask her while anyone else was present and certainly not while we were being taped.

I sat on the cushion next to hers. "What do you think happened?"

She angled her body back toward mine. "Clyde, don't make me do this with you. I'm here because someone has to be. Please don't make this any harder for me."

"You know you're the only one I can talk to," I said, lowering my voice to a whisper.

"Please, Clyde," she repeated, her nostrils flaring as she grabbed both my hands in hers. "I can't."

I set my jaw, soldiering on. "Have you told the police?"

"Why would I?" she asked.

"Because of Rachel. Someone's going to figure it out if they haven't already."

She released my hands, looking away again. "I doubt that."

"What about when the police find Rachel? You don't think she's going to talk?"

She pressed her lips together. "There's nothing I can do about that."

"Delphine, I was visited by one of the detectives. He asked me if Olivia was in a relationship. I was thinking that now might be the perfect opportunity to get it out there." I paused to give her a chance to respond, but none came. After a long silence, I ventured, "Isn't it better coming from you, a family member, than someone else? And on our network?"

She jerked her head toward me, her body language freshly combative. "How? No one knew."

"Plenty of people knew. Olivia respected your family's wishes, given their political leanings and how this could affect her father's alliances, but she didn't live in a tower a thousand feet in the air. She had lovers. I'm telling you, you can't keep something like this a secret."

"Well, we can try, can't we?" she said crisply. "And if you truly cared about her, you'll do the same. This isn't your decision to make, Cornelia."

There were two knocks on the door. Sabine stuck her head around it. "Everything's set," she said, her bright tone cutting through the tension like a knife. "Would you ladies care to follow me?"

The interview lasted fifteen minutes. There were tears, tissues, and lots of usable footage, all of which would be proprietary to our network and help us get back on top of the competition. On any other story, I would have felt relieved. But on this one as soon as we wrapped I was out the door, more determined than ever to find my best friend's killer. I kept thinking about that cryptic text she'd sent me. *It's time you know the truth.* My gut told me it had to have something to do with her murder.

# ten

Sutton Danziger lived on a stretch of prized waterfront property in one of Greenwich's most exclusive neighborhoods. Her home, a massive gray stone structure, was situated between two equally gargantuan homes, neither of which were marked by mailboxes or numbers—for security reasons, no doubt—and had it not been for the row of Aston Martins and Bentleys parked in Sutton's circular pebbled drive, I wouldn't have known at which of the three mansions I was expected for dinner.

The door opened before I stepped out of my taxi. Before me stood a large black man dressed in khakis and a denim shirt. There was a cell phone clipped on one side of his belt, on the other, a gun holster. "Your name?"

I gave it to him. Then he gave it to someone else over the phone, and five minutes later, after subjecting my bag to a quick search, I was escorted through vast marble halls into a vaulted-ceiling living room. The sleek, custom-made furniture was seemingly designed to complement but not compete with the art on the wall, as was the quartet of stiff-backed women perched on the room's silk-velvet couches. The four of them were dressed in neutral tones like taupe and bisque, and I wondered which of them I was going to have to sweet-talk into giving me information on Rachel Rockwell. The men, apparently, were elsewhere in the cavernous house.

Eyeing me in the doorway, Sutton moved to the arm of her couch, patting the seat next to her. I took her place, accepting a glass of champagne one of the servers proffered from a white lacquered tray. The women were introduced one by one, but their names blended into each other, much like their voices. I endured a good twenty minutes of banter—a reminder of why I stayed away from school-related functions—before asking Sutton for a tour of her home.

A few minutes later, we were standing on a pair of zebra rugs in Sutton's study, a vast distance from the living room. She lifted her gaze to the wall behind her desk. "Rauschenberg," she said in a whisper, though her point had come across loud and clear: Sutton, like almost everyone else at the Livingston School, came from money, but nothing like what she had now, and she wanted to make sure I'd noted the difference.

"Lovely." I pretended to admire her painting before asking which of her friends knew Rachel Rockwell. "Vanessa Cox, the blonde," Sutton said, repositioning a penholder on her desk.

"They were all blond, Sutton."

She rolled her eyes. "She was sitting right next to you."

"Oh."

"You're not going to be rude, are you?"

"Oh jeez, Sutton. No."

She tucked a strand of pin-straight hair behind her ear. "No talk about blood, semen, or child molesters."

"What about feces?"

She scowled. "You know what I mean. Nothing gross. And easy on the booze. OK?" She gave me a knowing look that told me she hadn't forgotten about her thirtieth birthday party, the one where I'd gotten plastered and screwed her twenty-year-old brother.

I crossed my heart. "You have my word."

My dinner companion had recently divorced and was a master golfer and successful businessman. He also had wandering eyes and, as the night wore on, hands. Thankfully Sutton had also seated Rachel Rockwell's friend across from me, at a distance from which I was able to watch her get progressively more hammered with each glass of Château-something. By the end of dinner, Vanessa Cox was, as they say, well into her cups. She excused herself from the table during dessert, and I followed, catching her on her way out of the guest bathroom. It didn't take long to get her talking.

"I heard you know Rachel Rockwell." We stood side by side at a mirror in the hallway, reapplying lipstick. Hers was designer red, mine drugstore pink. "Everyone must be talking about her now," I said.

"Greenwich is a small town. People talk if you misbutton your raincoat."

I wondered if she was speaking from personal experience. In her current condition, I could imagine her having trouble dressing herself. "How do you know her?"

"Like I said, Greenwich is small. We belong to the same country club and our kids go to the same school. My youngest is friends with her oldest."

"So you know her well?" I asked.

She swayed beside me. "Pretty well. You got kids?"

I shook my head. "Nope. My job's pretty intense."

She gave me a look that was half pity, half envy.

"Rachel's the mom who makes the rest of us look bad. She does a million things for the school—carpools, bake sales, fundraising—all while maintaining a perfect house and full social calendar. And on top of that, she always looks impeccable. If there's any chink in that armor, it's that she tends to be a bit more flashy than most of us Greenwich girls."

I inched closer, lowering my voice a fraction. "What about the DUI?"

"Oh that." Vanessa looked down. "I'm not sure how that happened. Rachel doesn't drink. I think she said someone in her family was an alcoholic. Really, it surprised all of us when that happened."

"And her husband? Michael? What's he like?"

"Oh, you know." She shoved her lipstick into a sparkly clutch before dropping both at her feet.

"No, I don't." I picked up the bag and handed it to her.

"He's controlling," she said, taking the bag. "Like a lot of the alpha males out here. But Michael took it a step further. He put a lot of pressure on her, and he liked to know where she was at all times. He was always texting her. And Rachel told me once she thought he'd put a tracer on her car. Truth is, none of us blame Rachel for what she did. Not one bit."

"What did she do?"

Vanessa locked eyes with me in the mirror. "Rachel had an affair with her trainer."

"When?"

"I guess it was about a year ago that it started. Michael suspected something was up—and when he found out the truth he went nuts. He got the guy fired and kicked her out of the house. Then he filed for divorce."

Murderers often display violent tendencies—frequently domestic battery or sex abuse—long before they commit homicide. Most of the time, warning signs go overlooked and unreported. Michael hadn't been busted for beating up or raping Rachel—I'd already checked—but that didn't mean he wasn't guilty of it. And this certainly helped establish him as a jealous spouse. "Do you know if Michael ever laid a hand on Rachel while they were married?"

"Rachel and Michael are still married, even though they've been living apart for almost a year. The divorce isn't final, and at this rate, it won't be for a while. In the meantime, Rachel has the house again and the kids most of the time, but Michael is suing for full custody."

She hadn't answered my question, so I repeated it. "While Rachel and Michael were still living together, did he ever hurt her?"

She shook her head. "I saw Rachel changing in the locker room at the club on a pretty regular basis. I would have seen a bruise if she'd had one."

I looked at my watch. It was 11:10 and I was suddenly exhausted. There was a train that left at 11:47 and if I hoped to make it, I needed to wrap things up with Vanessa in the next few minutes. "One more question: The trainer you mentioned, the one Rachel was sleeping with, is she still seeing him?"

Vanessa leaned against the wall. "I don't know. I haven't seen Rachel in a while."

"She's been missing since Friday."

"I meant before that. She hasn't been to the club in months."

"Do you happen to know the trainer's name?" I asked.

She put a manicured finger to the center of her forehead and closed her eyes. "Something European," she said at last.

"Do you remember anything about him?"

Vanessa opened her eyes. "He was hot. Blondish. Young. Killer body. That's probably what pissed Michael off more than anything else. He's used to being the tough guy in the room."

"Anything else?"

She thought a bit. "He had a tattoo on his arm. A green dragon. Or maybe it was a snake."

# Tuesday

# eleven

I was in Diskin's office, competing for attention with the four monitors on the back wall. They were all tuned to the *Today* show. Diskin, along with the FirstNews target audience, had just watched Matt Lauer's interview with Frank Uffizo, the lawyer Michael Rockwell had hired to represent him and his wife. Diskin had called me into his office to tear me a new one, but I'd stopped him short with what Vanessa Cox had told me about Rachel and her personal trainer, a man with a tattoo on his arm who fit the description of the doorman from Olivia's building. Except the doorman we'd put on camera went by Andrew, not André Kaminski, as he'd been known at the Greenwich country club before he was fired. That much at least checked out. It could all be yet another coincidence, but I didn't think so.

Diskin tapped his bottom lip with his pen. "Do you think the affair really happened?"

"I haven't made up my mind about that yet. There's a chance it could all be town gossip," I said.

"What's your plan?"

"I'm going to ask Andrew or André or whatever his name is if he was having an affair with Rachel Rockwell."

Diskin nodded. "Ask him where the hell he thinks she is. And bring the crew."

I hadn't planned on bringing a cameraman. People tend to freeze up as soon as they see one, and I needed Andrew—or André—to talk. "Are you sure that's a good idea?"

"Yes, I'm sure." Diskin rapped his pen against his desk. "You're going to go out there and catch that SOB in a lie on tape, and we're going to put it on air and make news. That's what people tune in for." He turned his gaze back to the four monitors. "You should have had Uffizo. Rachel Rockwell is the police's only suspect. And since she's MIA, he's the next best thing."

"Person of interest. Rachel isn't a suspect yet. And we always lose Uffizo to Lauer."

"Screw that. You should have had him. Rachel's going to be arrested, and MSNBC is going to cream us. Christ, Clyde. Georgia's counting on you. So is Alex. Do you know what it will do to ratings if Lauer gets Uffizo every morning?" He shook his head. "Goddamn it, what do you have to say for yourself?"

"With all due respect, Mitchell, I think you're overreacting."

Diskin laughed. "Oh really?"

"There's a possibility Rachel didn't do it. There's Michael Rockwell."

"Uffizo's his lawyer too."

"Well, what about the doorman?"

His face turned grim. "Stop playing detective and get to work. Your job isn't to solve the case but to cover it. Show me I was right to trust you with this assignment and land me an exclusive."

"What do you think I'm out there trying to do?"

"Get out of my office."

When I had one foot out the door, Diskin dragged his eyes away from the monitors and announced, "I'm going to put in a call to Naomi Zell to let the family know where the story is heading."

I stepped back into his office and shut the door. "Why her?" Naomi was the chair of the company and Charles Kravis's hand-picked successor. She also had a seat on the board. That was the extent of what I knew about her.

"Naomi is now acting as the family's liaison with the press on this matter. Charles, Monica, and Delphine are grieving. They've decided to delegate the responsibilities to Naomi in the interim."

"Still, are you sure about reaching out to her? Don't we have a protocol against this sort of thing?"

"Oh please, Shaw," he said peevishly.

"Mitchell, I'm serious. This sets a dangerous precedent, giving a representative of the Kravis family inside information about our coverage plans. Naomi's obviously not going to care whether we report that Rachel Rockwell was screwing her trainer, but what if something else comes to our attention, something the family won't want made public?" My thoughts ran to my frustrating conversation with Delphine in the green room. "Are you going to put in a call to her then? Give her the opportunity to ask us to kill it?"

"Why do you presume she'd want to kill anything we dig up?"

I gave him a look. "You must be joking."

"The Kravises are used to being in the public eye."

"All that means is that they are used to doing what it takes to kill stories that don't suit their personal interests."

He let out an exasperated sigh. "Let's just say for argument's sake we do end up with a scenario like the one you're envisioning—Naomi knows how this business works, and she has an allegiance to the network. She also knows that we'll spin the story to make it sound better than it would coming from any other network."

"I can see we're not going to agree about this." I was still uneasy about consulting someone with ties to the Kravis clan about our coverage. The family had its own agenda, one that involved keeping certain facts about Olivia's life secret.

"Here's the thing, Clyde. Nobody here wants to be accused of a cover-up, but the tawdrier this case gets, the stickier things are for us. Do me a favor and stop worrying about hypotheticals. Focus on your job. Find out what people are saying, and get them on air. And if what they have to say makes our founder's daughter look like anything but the victim of a heinous crime, be 110 percent sure they're not lying."

I pulled my cardigan closed, wrapping my arms around my torso. Diskin kept his office the temperature of a meat locker. "Are we talking about Kaminski now? Because my working hypothesis is that he was having an affair with Rachel Rockwell, not Olivia."

"You sure about that?"

I nodded, but the truth was I didn't feel sure of anything at that moment. Olivia had died with a secret, and I still couldn't even fathom a guess as to what it was.

Kaminski's shift didn't start until eleven that night, which left me a whole day to start digging into Michael Rockwell's background. My first move was to call Rachel's parents in South Dakota. Maybe Rachel had complained to them about Michael hitting her; maybe she'd confided other things in them too. And maybe that's where she'd gone into hiding, a cave somewhere deep inside the Black Hills. But that couldn't be the case, because the woman who answered my call told me Rachel's parents had already flown to Connecticut to be with the family.

Damn it. I pressed my face into my hands. Behind me, I heard Sabine's small voice. "You OK?" She stood in the doorway of my cubicle, holding a small cream envelope. "Clyde?"

"I'm fine," I muttered, taking the envelope from her and tossing it into my inbox.

"It's from Diskin," she said, eyeing it. "I think you're supposed to open it now."

I tore it open and tipped it over. A card sailed to the floor. It was an invitation to the upcoming benefit for the Charles S. Kravis Foundation. Stuck on it was a yellow Post-it note bearing Mitchell Diskin's steeply slanted script. "The network gets a table every year. Be prompt and bring someone," he'd written.

"What is it?" she asked.

"Another headache." I tossed the invitation aside and turned back around to face my computer.

Sabine left me to fret alone at my desk. As if I didn't have enough on my plate, now I had to worry about finding a date in six days' time. And not just any date, but a man I wouldn't be embarrassed introducing to the president of the network and a smattering of my most esteemed colleagues.

I'd deal with the date problem later. Right now, it was time to get a face-to-face with Michael Rockwell. Unfortunately, I could think of only one way into his law firm.

I'd met Jack Slane at the Oyster Bar in Grand Central. I was thirty-three and not yet sober. It was a Friday in September and I was thirsty. Jack was tall and lean, with brown hair that curled at his ears and blue eyes that glimmered with mischief. Jack bought me a martini and we shared a dozen bluepoints while comparing workday horror stories. At a quarter to ten, he asked if he could walk me home. I knew that what I was supposed to do was hand him my business card and say good night. And if I hadn't had three martinis and only a handful of oysters sloshing around in my stomach, I might have done just that. But I was drunk and he was cute, and I didn't feel like calling it a night.

On the sidewalk, Jack clapped a hand to his forehead. "I forgot some paperwork at the office. Do you mind coming up? It'll only take a second."

I didn't mind. Five minutes later we were up in Jack's office at Bennett & Wayne, his hand inside the lace cup of my bra, his mouth on my neck. "I want to fuck you here," he breathed into my ear, pushing me onto his desk, dipping his head between my thighs, his hands and mouth doing the work of three men.

We continued to see each other, on and off, for the next six months. Then one night, after a particularly athletic session on Jack's king-size bed, with my left breast exposed and a damp spot on the sheets between us, he broke the news that he'd met someone else. "She's amazing," he'd said, his hand reaching for my nipple. I wish I could say I handled the news with dignity.

Pushing aside my memories, I dialed Gloria, Jack's assistant, and pretended to have found a sweater Jack had forgotten long ago at my apartment. I could drop it off while I was in the area. "Mr. Slane isn't in yet," she said, her voice barely concealing her disapproval. Apparently Gloria remembered me.

"That's fine. I don't need to see him. Like I said, I just want to drop off a sweater."

She sighed wearily. "You are aware that Mr. Slane is engaged now."

"It's a sweater, Gloria."

Twenty minutes later, I was in the elegant brown and cream lobby of Bennett & Wayne, carrying the oversize cardigan I kept in the office for summer days when the AC was on full blast. It was possible that Michael Rockwell had taken the day off, in which case my whole lost-sweater charade would have been for nothing, but I was willing to take the chance. Rockwell wasn't returning my calls, and even if I did manage to get him on the phone, he'd probably just hang up on me. It would be far harder to kick me out of his office if I was threatening to make a scene.

The receptionist buzzed Gloria to come get me, and Gloria told her to send me back. Without an escort, I had a brief window during which I could find Rockwell's office and confront him without raising too much suspicion. After taking the internal elevator to Jack's floor, I took off my visitor's tag and asked a harried-looking associate where I could find the corporate department.

The woman stopped, readjusted the box of files she was carrying on her hip. "Who are you looking for?"

"Michael Rockwell."

"Oh." Her face screwed up a little at the sound of his name. "He's in M and A, down that hall; take a left at the bathroom. Third door down. Names are on the doors."

Sure enough, his office was marked with his name in brass letters. His door had been left slightly ajar, which allowed me to hear that he was inside, alone, and typing at his computer. I knocked once, went in, and closed the door behind me.

"Can I help you?" He was tall and brawny, with thick dark hair, slicked back from his forehead. His pinstriped suit looked custom-made, and two gold-and-onyx cufflinks flashed from each of his starched, white cuffs.

I took a seat in one of the two grommet-studded armchairs facing his desk. "Hi, Michael. I'm Clyde Shaw. We spoke on the phone the other day."

He furrowed his brow, not immediately connecting the dots.

"I'm a producer for FirstNews."

Swiveling in his chair, he picked up the phone and began to dial what I assumed was building security.

"I wouldn't do that if I were you."

"How did you get in here?" he demanded.

I could hear the line ringing on the other end of his call. "Did you really get your wife's trainer fired from his job?"

His face turned white. "This may come as a shock to you, but I didn't return your calls for a reason. I have nothing to say, and I know nothing about this case."

"Where is Rachel, Michael?"

"I don't know."

"When was the last time you spoke to her or saw her?"

He slammed the phone back down, booming at me, "I already told the police! She called me Saturday morning, but the call went to voice mail. And she didn't leave a message."

"Is there a record of that call coming in?"

"That's a question for the police. Now, could you kindly get the hell out of my office?"

"You're leaving me no choice but to reveal some unsavory things about your marriage."

"My marriage is already over," he blustered, picking up his phone again.

I had to think quickly, buy myself some more time. "What about your career? I bet the partners here will love hearing about how you put a tracer on Rachel's car. Let me tell you, once that stuff is out there, it's out for good." I stood up and took a few steps toward the door. "News cycles may come and go, but the Internet never forgets. You'll never live that shit down."

"Wait." Rockwell picked up his phone and hit a button. "Ruby, move my eleven o'clock to five. Then bump the five to tomorrow at ten. Thanks."

I slipped my business card across the hand-tooled leather of his desktop and took my seat again.

He studied my card. "Any relation to Bronson Shaw?"

"He's a distant cousin," I said, neglecting to mention that Bronson, a successful agribusiness lobbyist down in DC, was part of the Shaw clan that liked to pretend I didn't exist.

"I went to Harvard Law with him. Shall I tell him we met?"

"That's entirely up to you." If Rockwell was trying to intimidate or impress me with his ties to society—and my own distant kin—he'd pegged me dead wrong.

He removed a small voice recorder from his desk drawer and turned it on. "With your permission, I'd like to tape this interview and also have you state your name, media affiliation, and job title, and that this is an off-the-record interview, meaning that nothing that is said or suggested during the course of our discussion can be used in your reporting."

"Actually, I do mind. I thought we were having a casual conversation."

"I record *all* my meetings, Miss Shaw. If you have an issue with this, or any of my terms, you are free to leave."

I had to hand it to him; the guy had his bases covered. Typical lawyer. I repeated the information he requested and then asked my first question. "What does the name André Kaminski mean to you?"

He gritted his teeth.

"When did you find out he and your wife were sleeping together?"

Rockwell's eyes lit up with anger, but he kept his voice steady. "It seems to me you already know the answer to that question."

"The harder you make this, the longer it's going to take. I've got all morning, but it sounds like you don't need me tying up your schedule any longer than necessary." I let that sit with him for a second before plunging forward. "Did you know that after you had André fired from the gym, Rachel found a job for him at the Haverford—the building where Olivia Kravis lived? And that he was working the night Olivia was murdered and your wife disappeared?"

He didn't say anything for a long time. "That is news to me," he finally said. It sounded like he was telling the truth.

"How would you describe Rachel's relationship with Olivia?"

"They were social friends."

"Can you elaborate on that?"

"They traveled in similar circles, had similar interests."

"Can you be more specific?"

"No, I can't."

"Can't or won't?"

Again, silence. Rockwell was either completely stonewalling me or he really did have no idea what his wife was up to with Olivia. Recalling one of Georgia's favorite sayings—*If the front door's locked, throw a rock through a window*—I took a more direct approach. "Were you at Olivia Kravis's apartment the night of her murder?"

Rockwell gripped the edge of his desk, and when he spoke again his voice was stern and full of malice. "This interview is over, Ms. Shaw, and if you do make the mistake of slandering or libeling me or any of the members of my family, rest assured I will not hesitate for one second to ruin you." He stood to his full height. "I can be very, very nasty when I want to be."

I smiled sweetly. "If I had a dollar for every time someone threatened me with a lawsuit, I'd be richer than, well, you, Mr. Rockwell. You'll have to try a hell of a lot harder than that to scare me." Then I gathered my things and left. Behind me, I heard Rockwell's door slam shut.

I was almost at the elevator when I felt a tap on my shoulder. I jumped, thinking it was Jack Slane or his mean-spirited secretary, but it was a man with a sweater in his hands. "You dropped this," he said, handing it over with a lopsided grin. The man was on the short side, with a blond beard and thick black glasses—geeky but attractive in his own way.

Before I could say anything, I heard Jack Slane's voice carry around the corner. He was looking for me. I needed to get out of there. "Is there another way out of here?" I asked the man.

"You in a hurry?"

"I need a place to hide. I promise I didn't steal anything."

He motioned for me to follow him. A couple seconds later, I was in his office, the door closed. He introduced himself as Philip Drucker, and offered me water, coffee, and a muffin, all of which I declined. Then he sat on his desk and crossed his arms. "What's your story?"

I picked up a paperweight on his desk. "Actually, that's why I'm here. For a story. I'm a journalist."

He waited a beat for me to elaborate. I didn't. "Can I at least have a name? Number?" he asked, his eyes crinkling in the corners. "I can't ask you out on a date without one."

A hard knock on the door interrupted us. Phil excused himself and opened the door a crack, and then, seeing who was on the other side of it, he stepped outside and closed the door behind him. There were muffled voices, a crackle that sounded like it was coming from a walkie-talkie, and then a man's voice escalating to almost a shout. Suddenly the door opened.

On the other side stood two security guards and Jack Slane. He pointed a finger at me. "There she is, guys."

# twelve

He was fatter than I remembered—a nice big spare tire where his six-pack used to be—and he had less hair. Most everything else was the same: wide shoulders, narrow eyes, smug, pretty-boy face. Looking at him now, I couldn't believe I'd wasted one moment of my life pining for him and berating myself for losing him to another woman.

"Is there a problem?" I asked, playing dumb. I was on his turf, but I also had the upper hand.

"She's trespassing!" Jack yelled. "She lied and she's up to something. Get her out of here."

One of the guards coughed and, with an apologetic glow in his eye, turned to address me. "Mr. Slane says you have a sweater of his in your possession."

"This is my fault," Philip Drucker said, his hand encircling my waist. "She wanted to surprise me. It's my birthday today."

The second guard took a step back. He looked flustered. "Happy birthday, sir."

Jack glared at Philip.

"OK, Mr. Slane," the first guard said. "Mystery solved. Sir. Ma'am. Sorry for the trouble."

"I'm so sorry, Jack," I cooed, unable to resist the opportunity. "I didn't mean to disrupt your day."

His eyes flashed to me before he turned to leave. "The fuck you didn't, you whore."

"Are you OK?" Philip asked, closing his door.

"I'll be fine," I said, looking down at my shaking hands. "Thanks very much for covering for me."

"It's none of my business, but what happened between you and him?"

"Once upon a time I did a little damage to his apartment. Would you believe me if I said he had it coming?"

Philip laughed. "He is a prick."

I cocked my head. "It's not really your birthday, is it?"

"Actually, it is. Do you have plans tonight?"

I think I may have blushed. "I do. Work. I'm a producer for FirstNews. But if you aren't busy next Monday, there's a fund-raiser at the Mandarin Oriental I have to attend. Black tie. I know it's short notice."

He rubbed his hands together. "Lucky for you, I'm free *and* I just got my tuxedo back from the dry cleaners. What time do the festivities commence?"

"Seven, and we have to be there on time. No showing up half-way through the salad course."

"It's not a problem. I'll change into my tux here. May I arrange a car for the evening?"

"Please don't go to the trouble."

"But it's no trouble."

"OK, then." We exchanged phone numbers and he walked me back to the elevator, pressing the button for the lobby once it arrived.

"See you next week," he said as the doors slid closed.

I spent the rest of the day at the office tracking down and talking to a few of Olivia's coworkers at the foundation. All of them told me basically the same thing, which was that Olivia didn't have any enemies, and that she hadn't been acting differently in the months and weeks before her death. There had been no strange meetings, unexplained days off, or other red flags. No money had randomly disappeared from the foundation's coffers, and none of the grant recipients had shown up on the trust's doorstep with complaints. I didn't come away totally empty-handed, however. After some pestering, Olivia's assistant, Emma Reiter, a recent college grad with blue shock hair and multiple facial piercings, said she'd let me into Olivia's office if I came by after everyone else went home.

Emma called me at six o'clock. I walked over to their offices on Thirty-Seventh and Madison, right across from the Morgan Library. I handed my identification to the security guard, got a building pass, and rode the elevator up twenty floors to the foundation's offices. Emma was waiting for me behind a pair of glass doors. "You'll be quick, right?" she asked with an anxious frown.

I sailed past her, making a beeline for Olivia's office. "As quick as I can."

One wall of Olivia's office was covered with awards she'd received on behalf of the foundation, the other of photographs she'd taken of the children the foundation had helped over the years. Her desktop was crowded with framed art and pottery kids had made for her, but something was missing. "Where's the laptop?"

"The police took it."

"Were they in here early yesterday morning? Like around seven?"

"No. Why do you ask?"

"I got a call from her line."

"From here?"

"Yes."

Emma was quiet before responding. "I got here at maybe five past eight. Doors were locked. The police hadn't arrived yet."

"Does anyone else have keys?"

"Sure. Lots of people. But nobody was in yesterday besides me and a couple other folks later on. I was here alone most of the day."

I could tell she was spooked. "I'm sure it was a mistake," I said, trying to assure her. "Maybe the cleaners came in and mistakenly hit redial. Can we check the last calls that came in to her phone on Friday?"

"Oh g-gosh," Emma stammered. "The system only stores a limited number of calls, and I've been fielding calls from donors at her desk since yesterday."

I pulled open the top drawer. "Where's her agenda?"

Emma looked at me like she didn't know what I was talking about. "I keep track of her schedule electronically."

"Olivia keeps a date book at work. It's green. Leather. Did the police take that too?"

She shook her head. "I don't know."

I rifled through Olivia's desk drawers and file cabinets. There was no agenda anywhere. "I give up," I finally said, throwing my hands in the air.

Emma offered to e-mail me Olivia's work schedule from the past weeks. With it, I'd be able to see everyone she'd met with recently, and start cold-calling the ones that seemed out of the ordinary.

"You have my e-mail address?" I confirmed.

"I think so."

"I'll give it to you again, just in case." I opened the top drawer of Olivia's desk and found a pen and a pad of paper. I flipped through it, looking for a clean sheet. Midway through, a piece of paper fell to the floor. I bent over to pick it up and froze. It was a xeroxed copy of a birth certificate. *My* birth certificate. *How did she get it?*

I'd never given it to her. The only copy I had was in a lockbox in my apartment, along with my mother's death certificate and other important documents. My heart pounded as I wrote out my e-mail address for Emma and handed the pad to her. Then I slipped my birth certificate in my purse without her noticing. *Why, Olivia, did you have this?* First the text and now this. Exactly how many secrets were you hiding from me?

I had dinner at my desk, watched Georgia's show from the control room, and piled into the van with Aaron and Dino to go ambush André, otherwise known as Andrew Kaminski. We planted our van around the corner at half past ten. I spotted him about ten minutes later, coming down the street on foot, from the direction of the subway. This time he was dressed in a plaid flannel shirt, jeans, and a beat-up brown leather jacket. As he came near us, two thoughts popped into my mind. The first was that André Kaminski was sexy enough to lure an unhappy Connecticut housewife away from her husband. The second was that our viewers would love him, no matter what he had to say—or what he'd done. A sick fact about the American viewing public: good looks trump all. Take Scott Peterson, for example. He received two marriage proposals and bags of love letters *after* he was convicted of killing Laci, his pregnant wife.

I jumped out of the van, a mike gripped in my left hand. Dino slid out on the other side of the van, waiting for my signal.

"Hey," Kaminski said, slowing to a stop. "I was hoping I might see you again."

I motioned to Dino, who came out, the camera hoisted on his shoulder. He gave me the thumbs-up sign with his free hand. Kaminski shaded his eyes from the bright light of the camera. "What the hell? What's going on?"

"You don't mind if I ask you a few questions, do you?"

He glanced toward the Haverford. "I thought I told you. I'm not supposed to talk to the press anymore." His voice was low and edged with panic. "You're gonna get me fired."

"Is it true that you were sleeping with Rachel Rockwell?"

He glanced at the camera. If it hadn't been there, I might have had a shot at hearing the truth. Instead Kaminski dug his hands in the front pocket of his jeans and tried to shoulder past me.

I moved to the side, blocking his path, and tried again. "I heard you used to train Rachel Rockwell in Connecticut. Is it true that you two were having an affair?" He pivoted, stumbling into the street. Two taxis screeched to a halt, the first nearly knocking him down. Once he'd made it safely to the other side, I called out to him, "I know your name isn't Andrew." He turned to look at me, just for an instant, but I knew I had him. He jogged the rest of the distance to the Haverford.

I turned to Dino. "You get that?"

"Sure did."

"Good," I said. "Sit tight in the van for a few minutes, will you?"

Dino lowered the camera off his shoulder. "He's not going to talk, Clyde."

Eyeing the front of the Haverford, I checked my watch. "We'll see about that."

Fifteen minutes later, Kaminski appeared at the Haverford's front door. I scuttled across the street and under the building's awning before he could head me off. The pristine marble lobby glistened through the gilt and glass doors. "Not here," he said gruffly, gripping my arm. "I need this job."

"Then tell me the truth. Were you sleeping with Rachel?"

A fortysomething woman with a fluffy white dog appeared behind the door. She rapped on the glass twice, her thin lips displaying her displeasure. "Sorry, Mrs. Himmel," Kaminski muttered as she walked past us, disappearing into the night. "Go now. I mean it," he said into my ear.

"I'm not leaving until you tell me what you know."

A vein surfaced beneath the skin of his neck. "I get off at seven. There's a diner on Lexington a few blocks south."

I knew the place, a diner on a busy corner.

"I'll meet you there at seven thirty."

"And when I see you there, what will I call you? Andrew or André?"

"It's Andrey. With a *y* instead of a *w*. They got it wrong at the uniform shop."

# Wednesday

# thirteen

On Wednesday morning, Andrey Kaminski was seated at a red-leather booth at the back of the diner, dressed in the same street clothes he had been wearing the night before.

I threw my bag in the booth. "Have you ordered yet?"

He nodded at his coffee. Even tired and disheveled he was hot.

I reached for my scarf. Suddenly he was out of his seat, helping me out of my jacket, lifting my hair gently at the nape. The gesture sent chills down my spine—the kind I shouldn't have been feeling. *No*, I told myself, *this is totally inappropriate.*

He motioned to the waitress behind the countertop. She came over with a pot of coffee, leaning over our table to treat Andrey to a glimpse of her cleavage as she refilled his mug and splashed some in mine. "What ya want?" she asked, not even bothering to look at me. I went with my usual eggs and sausage. "Yours will be out soon," she almost cooed to Andrey, evidently in no rush to get my order in.

I shook my sugar packets together loudly. She got the picture and skulked off. "Am I really supposed to buy that your name change is all because of a mix-up at the uniform shop?" I asked, pouring a generous amount of cream in my coffee.

He shrugged. "Yeah."

"Then why didn't you correct me before I put you on TV?"

"Seemed like you were in a hurry."

It was true I had been in a rush to get him on camera. "So why not correct me later, when we talked on the street?"

"I didn't want to embarrass you."

"I wouldn't have been embarrassed."

He scratched the back of his neck. His sleeves, this time, revealed more of the green tattoo. "Are you going to use that footage from last night?"

"I have to. Unless you agree to sit down for us."

"Not gonna happen."

"You did it Sunday morning."

He shrugged again. "That was a mistake."

"Well, there's no camera on you now, and all this is off the record." I was giving him the highest amount of protection possible, but he had to give me something in return. "I need to know everything you know. Everything. Tell me something I don't already know, Andrey, and I promise, I'll make it up to you. Believe me when I tell you I can be a very powerful ally."

"Everyone's got to answer to somebody." He stared at the paper napkin he was twisting in his hands. "Who's your boss?"

It was a strange question, but sometimes sources liked to be coddled and indulged. One source of mine would only meet in the housewares section of a department store; another source required a lobster salad and porterhouse to get him talking. Andrey apparently needed to know who my boss was before he would give me what I wanted. "Georgia Jacobs is my immediate boss," I told him. "But I have others, including the bureau chief and the network president. Anything that goes to air, especially on a story as high-profile as this one, has to be approved by one of those three people, plus a slew of lawyers from our legal team."

Our food arrived. Andrey had ordered pancakes and bacon. The waitress, who had applied a fresh and very unnecessary coat of lip gloss in the interim, lingered once again over our table. "Let me know if you want more maple syrup, or anything else," she said, flirting with all the subtlety of a lap dancer.

"I think she likes you," I said after she left.

Andrey cut into his pancakes and ate without further comment, his head down and focused on his food. His manner reminded me of a little boy sitting at his mother's table. All that was missing were the flannel pajamas. I ate a few bites of my eggs and bacon, my appetite still not what it used to be, and pushed my plate to the center of the table to make way for my spiral notebook. Andrey finished his food, took a slug of coffee, and planted his elbows on the table. "She was a referral," he said finally.

I picked up my pen. "I assume we're talking about Rachel Rockwell?"

"Rachel has a great body, but she wanted to be more toned. She came to me in the spring, about two years ago. Her second child was about a year old. We started working out in the gym, but then we worked out a deal where I would come to her house a couple days a week. It was easier for her, and I didn't have to give half my fee to the club. I trained Rachel Mondays and Fridays at the club, Wednesdays and Saturdays at her home. Her husband built a huge gym in their basement, so we had everything we could ever need."

"She's in good physical shape?"

"That woman is 115 pounds of pure muscle."

I had to rethink my previous assumption that Rachel Rockwell might not be strong enough to kill Olivia on her own.

Andrey moved his plate to the side. "We were friends at first. That's how it started. After we trained together, she'd invite me to stay for coffee or breakfast and we'd talk. Then one day one thing led to another."

"How long did it go on like that?"

"A year," he said.

"And then what happened?"

"Her husband found out and had me fired. The club had a rule—not against sleeping with your clients, because they'd have no trainers left—but against working with clients on the side." He paused, threw his napkin on the table. "Then she dumped me."

"Rachel broke up with you?"

"She said she had to put the kids first. Michael had served her with papers. Her lawyer said it wouldn't look good if she was shacking up with me."

"Were you in love with her?"

"At the time, yeah. I guess."

"But that was the end of it?"

Andrey looked down into his coffee cup, his shoulders sagging beneath his flannel shirt. "It's what she wanted."

His sudden vulnerability reignited my attraction to him, but I couldn't afford to get distracted. Not now when I was finally getting somewhere. "Tell me how you got the job at the Haverford," I said.

"After I got fired from the club, I trained a few clients at their homes, but mostly I was sitting on my couch for three months pissing away my savings. Rachel knew I was hard up for cash. She offered to try and help me find something."

"As a building worker?"

He nodded once. "I'd worked as a doorman before. Right out of high school I was a porter at a building downtown. I became a trainer because I wanted to leave that shit behind. The life sucks, but the money ain't bad."

"How did that work? Aren't there unions involved?"

"I was part of the union already. All Rachel had to do was get me on the interview list."

Our check arrived. It was time to stop circling around the question. "When did you realize that Olivia and Rachel were sleeping together?"

He reached for the check, pulled out his wallet. "I've got to go."

"No you don't."

Andrey climbed out of the booth.

I reached for his forearm. It felt warm and strong, and for the briefest of moments I let myself imagine what his body looked like beneath his plaid shirt and worn jeans. "Put your money away and sit back down."

He ignored me, throwing a ten and a twenty on the table.

I stood up and faced him square. "Then you give me no choice. I'm reporting that you and Rachel had an affair," I said. "People are going to assume you are still carrying a torch for Rachel and that you killed Olivia out of jealousy. Do you know where Rachel is, Andrey?"

He leaned forward, his handsome face mere inches from mine. "I'm not a saint, Clyde. But I didn't kill your friend and I have no idea where Rachel is."

He grabbed his leather jacket and left.


I was pissed as hell, cursing myself for being attracted to him, cursing myself for not getting closer to the truth. I grabbed my bag and trench coat and filed out onto the street. It was a quarter to eight, the sky still cloaked in gray. The sidewalks were crowded with school kids in backpacks and uniforms, the streets with rush-hour traffic. I inhaled the cool autumn air and tried to tell myself that I was making progress, even though it felt like I was spinning my wheels. I had Rockwell in my sights, Andrey on the run. One of them was bound to slip up and tell me something useful.

I hailed a cab and directed it to the FirstNews building. As we inched down Lex, I looked out the window and bit down hard on my bottom lip to keep from crying. I'd made a bargain with myself: I could cry as much as I wanted in the privacy of my own home, but come daylight, the pain had to go back in the box. I had a job to do and a murderer to catch, and doing anything less than that would be failing Olivia. "Get it together," I hissed at myself, my hands balled in my lap.

*Get it together.* Olivia's voice was in my head as I recalled a memory I'd pushed out of my consciousness for good reason. It was four years after I'd started at FirstNews. I was thirty. I had my act together at work—Georgia had just promoted me from assistant to segment producer—but after-hours I was still drinking too much, too often, and with men who were less than honorable. Olivia, meanwhile, had taken over her father's foundation, and recently bestowed a grant to a group of American plastic and reconstructive surgeons to travel to Guatemala to help children suffering from various disfigurements. She invited me to come down on the charter with them and assist the team.

Believe me, I tried to weasel out of it. I had two weeks of vacation, one of which would be spent upstate with my father at Christmas. The other I'd reserved for a hedonistic retreat by myself to someplace warm, like Jamaica. I'd always wanted to go there.

Olivia kept pestering me, though. Every day for a week she e-mailed me pictures of the kids and their parents, with little blurbs about each. "We'll be changing these people's lives forever," she wrote in the last e-mail. "Don't you want to help?" I wrote back that what I really wanted to do was drink a piña colada on a white-sand beach. Five minutes later, she called. "Seeing such a profound sense of joy on a mother's face. It's like a high, Clyde, and no drug can come near it."

"You're clearly taking the wrong drugs," I told her.

But I ended up going.

On the first morning of our trip, Olivia took me to the clinic where the surgeries were going to be performed. I held Magdalena, a baby with a cleft palate who cooed into my ear when I held her against my chest, and played checkers with Avril, a five-year-old with a tumor the size of a grapefruit growing out of her face. I met their parents, saw the hope in their eyes, and finally understood why Olivia had wanted me there. In the van home that night, she turned to me and said, "I knew you'd get it."

"Yeah," I'd merely replied, because by then I'd already made up my mind about what I was going to do next. Seeing those mothers who would do anything for their children had reminded me of my own mother. I'd never know her or understand how she could do what she did.

That night, after Olivia went to bed, I stole off to the bar, got wasted on rum and Cokes with one of the doctors—the very married, fifty-year-old plastics man from Iowa City. Olivia found me next to him the next morning, naked, condom wrappers and empty minibar bottles strewn about my room. She let him leave before she started slamming doors and banging into anything that made noise. I clutched my ears in pain. "Stop, OK. Just stop."

She stood panting in the middle of the room, glowering down at me. "You're thirty years old, and life—real life—is passing you by. When are you going to grow up?"

"I fucked up, Olivia. What else can I say besides I'm sorry?"

"Don't apologize to me. I don't want apologies and I don't want excuses. This was for your benefit, Clyde. I did this for you."

I put my head back down on the bed. It hurt too much to be held upright. "I don't need your help."

"Oh really? Who got you your job? Who cosigned for your apartment?"

I lifted myself back up. "Don't be a bitch."

Olivia walked two steps to the end of my bed, her nostrils flaring, but when she spoke again the thunder was gone, and in its place, disappointment. "Don't you want to get married, start a family?"

"You really think I should get married? Have a kid? Could you imagine *me* with a kid?" Of course I wanted to have a normal life, to come home to a handsome, adoring husband and a kid or two every night instead of my empty apartment and a box of takeout. But I knew myself well enough to know I'd be a terrible wife and an even worse mother. Just the idea made me nervous, made me itch for my next drink. I'd come to terms with what was in the realm of possibility and what wasn't. Why'd she have to stir that shit up in me? Show me a bunch of saintly mothers loving their poor, disfigured children?

I peered up at her, my voice like ice. "Come on, Olivia. Have a family? We both know it's not going to happen—for either of us." By then Olivia had come out to me but none of her other friends or family members, and my comment was designed to make her feel as bad as I did.

She crossed her arms. "No, we don't. I have every intention of having kids one day."

"How's that going to work? You going to marry a man and stay in the closet forever? That sounds like a great life."

"Now who's the bitch?"

"You pretend to be so perfect, so much better than me, but you're living a lie, Olivia. Your whole goddamn life is a lie. What are you so afraid of? Charles disowning you? Losing the foundation? You're a coward. I may be a drunk and a slut, but at least I don't pretend to be someone I'm not."

She left after that, slamming the door on her way out. I ordered some hair of the dog, packed my bags, and hailed a taxi for the Guatemala City airport. I didn't leave a note.

Olivia wouldn't talk to me for almost a year after that, and when we did finally begin seeing each other again, our friendship was never quite the same. After Guatemala, Olivia rarely confided in me about her love life. If I tried asking questions, she made it clear she didn't want me prying. Rachel was just one of a string of girlfriends about whom I'd known embarrassingly little. Yet as upsetting as it was to be frozen out of such an important part of my best friend's life, I had no choice other than to respect Olivia's boundaries. It was only now, after reading the text on my phone, that I realized she might have been keeping other—potentially bigger—secrets from me.

Five blocks from the office, my cab wasn't moving. I killed time checking my e-mail and found at the top of my inbox a message from my dad asking me to come up for the weekend. I wrote him back that as much as I wanted to, I doubted I'd be able to get away. He was worried about me, but I wasn't going to solve Olivia's murder moping around my father's house. I needed to be here, in the city. "Sorry, Dad," I tapped out with my thumbs. "I'll come up as soon as things get more settled at work."

When I clicked back to my inbox, there was a new e-mail from Georgia. "Deep shit," read the subject line, and in the body of the message: "You're in it, girl. Call me as soon as you get this."

I dialed her cell. No answer. So I dialed Alex. Also no answer.

This wasn't good.

I had the cab pull over and ran the rest of the way to the bureau.


Georgia was waiting at my desk. I was surprised to see her. "What happened?" I asked, panting.

She looked grim. "Let's go. Everyone's waiting."

"For me?" I dumped my bag under my desk. "Where are we going? What happened?"

"Diskin's office. GSBC landed an interview with Olivia's housekeeper."

"Ilsa Chavez?" I'd had the woman's name but never followed up with Sabine to see if she'd tracked down her number. "What did she have to say?"

"She found the body."

"I know that. So what?"

Georgia pressed the elevator button. "It's a fucking barn burner, Clyde. GSBC is way out in front now. You'll have to see for yourself."

In network news, you're only as good as your last scoop, especially when it came to stories like these. It's not enough to land one big interview; you have to land them all. Get out in front and stay there. Dominate the competition. This is what we do, and anything less will earn you a pink slip and one-way ticket to Des Moines. "How pissed is Diskin?" I asked.

"On a scale of one to ten, he's an eleven."

Alex was already in Diskin's office when we got there. So was Hiro Itzushi, our chief legal counsel. I wasn't quite clear why he was there other than that he'd been personally vetting everything we reported on Olivia's murder and was, for better or worse, a member of the team covering her case.

"Glad you could fit us into your schedule," Diskin said to me as I took my seat facing the wall of monitors. He hit the play button on his remote, and Harlich's perfectly symmetrical face filled the screen. As the camera panned back, I could see that she was in one of GSBC's studios. Sitting across from her was a shapely Latina dressed in a black-and-white-striped blouse and black knee-length skirt.

"I'm here with the woman who discovered the body of slain heiress Olivia Kravis. Her name is Ilsa Jimenez Chavez," Penny said. "She's here to tell us about what she saw."

The interview started out innocuously enough, with Ilsa explaining in heavily accented and broken English why she'd gone to Olivia's apartment on a Sunday morning. Apparently, she'd missed a day of work because of a family emergency and was making up for lost hours. Then Penny said, "I know it must be hard for you, but can you tell us exactly what you saw on Sunday morning, Ms. Chavez?"

Ilsa described the murder scene in detail, explaining how she dropped her coffee when she discovered Olivia's body and dialed the police. Penny squinted her eyes Couric-style. "How long had you worked for Ms. Kravis?"

"Nine year."

I glanced over at Georgia. I didn't understand what all the fuss was about.

"Here it comes," she mouthed at me.

Penny uncrossed her mile-long legs and leaned forward. "What was Olivia Kravis like?"

"She was good boss. She work hard. I no see her that much."

"Was she in a relationship?"

"I no think so. But one day I come in, regular time and she still home. I usually start by cleaning the sheets on the bed. But the bedroom door is locked. I wait, clean the kitchen. Finally Miss Kravis, she come out. And there was someone else with her. A woman. And she say, 'Ilsa, I like you to meet my girlfriend.'"

# fourteen

Deep down, I knew this would happen.

Olivia was a lesbian, and now everyone knew.

Georgia snapped her fingers, directing my attention to the television monitor and the fact that GSBC—and God help me, Penny Ho-stick—had scooped us yet again. I had a lump the size of Alex's ego in my throat. But it wasn't over. Ilsa Jimenez Chavez had another bombshell to drop.

"What was the name of the woman who came out of the bedroom?" Penny asked.

"Rachel."

"Rachel Rockwell?"

The housekeeper nodded. "Yes."

Diskin stopped the tape. "Shaw, goddamn it, we should have had this."

I crossed my arms. "You're telling me you would have let me report that our right-wing founder's daughter was a lesbian? Hiro, back me up. There's no way this would have made it to air."

Hiro cleared his throat. "I'm sure there would have been a discussion."

"Moot point." Diskin ripped off his glasses. "How could you let GSBC scoop us? It's *GSBC* for crying out loud."

Not just GSBC, but Ho-stick.

"You have no other job at this moment than getting this story. Not to mention, Olivia Kravis was your friend," Diskin continued. "How could you have not known this about her?"

"I thought our policy was pretty clear on this stuff," I replied, sidestepping his question. "I think what we should really be talking about is where GSBC gets off outing Olivia and Rachel's relationship. Since when is it OK for a news organization to do that to a private citizen?"

"I'll tell you when," Diskin said, his voice growing louder than I'd ever heard it. "When that private citizen is no longer living and at the center of a major news story."

I knew that. But I also knew that as recently as a day ago Diskin was warning me off reporting on Rachel Rockwell's rumored affair with the doorman—in case it led to an unpalatable discovery about Olivia. Welcome to the news business, where prerogatives changed by the hour. "Stop me if I'm wrong," I said. "But I was under the impression you wanted to keep our coverage of the Kravis case PG."

"I never said that. What I said is that we have to have corroboration before going public with anything that is remotely scandalous. All the information you've brought me so far is secondhand. This is *your* story. You're supposed to own it. You should have had the housekeeper, just like you should have had Uffizo. That's two strikes, Clyde."

He was right, and nothing I could say could change the fact that I'd been beat. I shouldn't have delegated the housekeeper lead to Sabine. I should have known that other networks would be gunning for her and that she might have known about Olivia and Rachel's relationship. In that regard, I'd let down not only Alex and

Georgia, but Olivia as well. My anger disappeared, and now all I felt was shame and resignation. *I could have prevented this.*

"The rules of the game have changed," Alex said gently. "It's hardball now. Go after every lead, Clyde. I know Olivia was a friend of yours, but we can't protect her anymore."

The disappointment was written on my face. "Can you handle that?" Georgia asked me.

"If you can't, I can put someone else on the story," Diskin added. "I still think you're the right person for this job, but if you're not willing to pursue this story through all possible means, you need to let me know now."

And lose my chance at decoding what Olivia meant in her text? My shot at catching her killer? "I can do this," I said, mustering every bit of conviction I had left in me.

"Good." Diskin pinched the bridge of his nose. "Now go find me Rachel Rockwell. Dead, alive, figure out what happened in that apartment."

Alex and I exchanged nervous glances. We had our work cut out for us.

"And one more thing, before you all go," Diskin continued. "We're about to come under even more scrutiny. In about an hour, the network is going to make an announcement. You might as well learn it from me. FirstNews is merging with Maldone Enterprises. Pending government approval, we will be part of their network of companies beginning on January 1."

Georgia grabbed me by the elbow as we all filed out of the meeting. "My office."

Facing Seventh Avenue and boasting one of the best views on our floor, Georgia's office would have been an impressive space if it weren't for all the clutter—empty Diet Coke cans, half-eaten bags of Chex Mix, and old newspapers piled high on every available surface. Not that Georgia was trying to impress anyone. She did things her way and if someone didn't like it, it was their problem. At five two and 130 pounds, she wasn't physically intimidating. But factor in her wit, her penchant for swearing, and her delight in reducing two-hundred-pound cameramen to tears on a regular basis, and you had a force to be reckoned with.

Georgia sat at her desk and grabbed a can of Diet Coke from the mini-fridge under her desk. "Close the door behind you," she clucked.

I did as asked and took a seat in the one chair facing her desk that wasn't already filled with a week's worth of St. John suits in Easter-egg colors. After her last divorce, the network brought in an image consultant, who'd managed to convince Georgia that hers needed significant softening. A month later, Georgia was back at work with a ladylike wardrobe and highlighted hair. The media made a fuss over the makeover, which only served to boost ratings.

Popping open her soda with a diamond-ringed finger, Georgia studied me closely. Dressed in jeans with her blond hair piled in a messy ponytail at the top of her head, she hardly looked like one of the network's top-earning on-air personalities. The only clues to her monstrous success were swinging from her fingers and twinkling from each of her earlobes. Diamonds, that's what Georgia loved— that, and nailing rapists, murderers, and child molesters to the wall.

"Girl," she said in her oft-parodied twang, "what in the hell were you thinking?"

I cleared my throat. "About what?"

"You knew Olivia Kravis was a carpet muncher, didn't you?"

"What?"

She took a swig of her soda straight from the can. "Don't you dare lie to me. You may be able to get past a blowhard like Diskin, but I know you inside and out. Surer than shit, I do."

I bit my lip. "Georgia, I made a promise."

"Well, I figured," she conceded. "But you could have mentioned it. Say, 'Hey, heads up, you old bag. I'm keeping a secret about Olivia and it's gonna get me in some deep doo-doo, but I gotta do it.'"

"Georgia—"

"I could have protected you up there. Now your job's on the line and there's not one fucking thing I can do about it." She shook her blond curls. "Diskin's mad as a pig in a bathtub, Clyde, and if things don't get better real quick, he's gonna can your ass."

"I don't care about my job."

"That's a bunch of bullcrap." She wagged her finger at me. "Need I remind you of how far you've come? Where you were when I got to this godforsaken place years ago? You were running scripts, Clyde. In skirts so short my five-year-old niece would have the sense not to wear them. No one took you seriously. The fucking interns got more respect. And why? Because you were letting assholes like Mike Fischer have their way with you in the bathroom of Coyote Cinco's."

I winced at the memory. Mike anchored our three o'clock news hour. He was married with three kids, teenagers by now, and kept a big bitch Lab named Daisy that he—swear to God—sometimes used to let lick his balls. I'd messed around with him at least a dozen times over a one-year period, mostly at my apartment but, yes, sometimes in places like the bathroom of our closest Mexican cantina, and in all that time he never once said hello to me at the office. He wouldn't acknowledge me in public, and yet somehow everyone at the office knew exactly what the two of us were doing behind closed doors. "It's been a long time since I engaged in that sort of behavior," I said.

"Two and a half years," she said, "is not that long a time."

"Give me some credit, Georgia."

"I love you, kid, but you still wouldn't know a worm if it were staring at you from the end of a fishing pole."

"What?"

"Alex Amori. Admit that you're attracted to him."

"That's crazy. He's a great guy. Fun and smart and, yes, pretty damn cute. I'll give you that. But he's also a total hound. I know that. And I know enough to stay away."

"Who do you think you're talking to? Do I *look* retarded? Because maybe my plastic surgeon messed up my face real bad and I ought to be suing Diskin for making me get that shit done."

I would have laughed if Georgia hadn't been glaring at me like I'd just poured her Diet Coke on her head.

"Listen up, smarty-pants. I know you better than you know your own self. I'm giving you one more chance to get off this train. I can go right now and tell Diskin I need you on another project."

I uncrossed my legs and straightened my posture. "No, Georgia."

She sighed. "Don't blame me when you're crying your eyes out and drowning your sorrows again in booze."

"Thanks for having so much faith in me," I said, crossing my arms at my chest.

Georgia narrowed her eyes. "How much you drinking every night?"

"Nothing, Georgia. Not a drop."

"But you've wanted to. Don't tell me you haven't."

"I wouldn't be what I am if I hadn't."

"I tell you once, I tell you a thousand goddamn times: the road to hell is slick with gin."

"Georgia, my best friend just died. I think I'm doing pretty fucking great considering the circumstances. How about some positive reinforcement for a change?"

"OK, how's this? Good job for not losing your shit so far. Now let's get you some counseling and pull you off this case."

"No."

She threw her hands in the air, her bangles clanging against one another. "Best-case scenario, we ride this Kravis case out and you somehow stay off the hooch. You're going to be working long hours with Alex, side by side, alone, in dark rooms, sometimes in hotel rooms. Honey, we all know how this is gonna end. You fall for him. He breaks your heart. You drink yourself back to rehab. Don't put yourself in a situation you can't handle."

"Now you're being ridiculous. And frankly I don't have time for this. Alex has no interest in me and I have no interest in him."

She rolled her eyes.

"It's true. When he's not taking out Penny Harlich, he's putting the moves on one of my PAs."

"Let me guess, it's what's-her-name?" Georgia snapped her fingers three times. "You know, eraser nipples?"

"You're thinking of Sabine Weller. She's doing research for me."

She rolled her eyes again. "Whatever."

"The point is you've got nothing to worry about."

Georgia selected a newspaper from the stack on her desk. "Guess I'll have to take your word for it."

"You do."

"Fine, smarty-pants. Let's talk Kravis case. What's your next move?"

I slumped back down in my chair. "I'm not convinced Rachel Rockwell did it, but that's where the coverage is headed. I'm taking the team out to her house in Connecticut as soon as I leave here. We can go live from there for *Topical Tonight*."

"Along with every other network. What are we going to say that the others aren't?"

"They're all going with Rachel as the prime suspect. We take a different tack. Use our exclusive video of Andrey running away from our cameras and the affair he was having with Rachel that got him fired from his job. We then spin out the scenarios, and motives: sex, jealousy, money. The other networks will be focusing on one suspect; we'll have three: Rachel, Michael, and Andrey."

"That's good, Clyde. We can promo the shit out of that."

"Right."

"But I'll need a studio guest."

"Olivia's stepsister, Delphine Lamont. Maybe she'll want to respond to the lesbian stuff."

Georgia knew that was a long shot. "Who else?"

"My source on Rachel's affair with her trainer. Her name is Vanessa Cox. She's the picture of a Greenwich trophy wife. I could try to wrangle her for tonight's show."

"Keep me posted." Georgia scratched her skull with a pencil tip. "We need to nail it tonight. This isn't just about you, you know. The show is on the line, Clyde. Golden boy's half hour is gonna come out of somebody's time."

"What? What are you talking about?"

"Surely you've heard the rumors about Alex getting his own show?"

I shrugged. I had.

"Well?"

"They can't cut *Topical*." I stood up and began pacing the room.

"They will if ratings don't pick up."

I stopped midstride. "What will you do?"

"Don't worry about me. I've got a pretty little offer from HLN sitting on the table."

I covered my hand with my mouth. "Georgia, I had no idea," I said between my fingers.

"Shit, I'll be fine. I just want you to remember, there's a lot riding on this story. You hear me?"

"Loud and clear," I said.

"All right, now get on out there." She pointed to her door.

I made my exit. "Stay off the fucking sauce!" she yelled after me.


By the time I got back to the bull pen, someone had turned up the volume on a television monitor. CNBC was on, announcing Maldone Enterprises' pending acquisition of the FirstNews Network in a cash-for-stock deal valued at $4.6 billion. The anchor was talking about the underlying fundamentals of the deal and the unlikelihood of antitrust officials trying to scuttle the merger. Wall Street liked the news too: Maldone Enterprises' share price had spiked following the announcement. A guest analyst likened FirstNews to the missing jewel in the Maldone crown and predicted that the stock would continue to see big gains, thanks to considerable synergies. My coworkers let out a collective groan. Synergies meant redundancies and more layoffs. Before the anchor transitioned to another subject, he made a passing comment about Olivia's murder, and how the companies had opted to announce the deal via a press release instead of a news conference out of respect for the Kravis family's recent loss.

I picked up the phone and told the troops to meet me at the van in five. Then I popped a few Tums from my purse and dialed Delphine's number from my cell. Predictably, it went straight to voice mail. After the beep, I began speaking. "Delphine, it's Clyde Shaw. I know you don't want to do any more press, but when you feel up to it, please call me." I paused to search for the right words. "I think I can help with how everything is playing out in the media. And I can assure you, I am committed to reporting on Olivia's death with not only accuracy but also the utmost degree of sensitivity. You can call me anytime." Then I left all my various numbers and hung up.

Rachel Rockwell's home was another mob scene. There were satellite trucks from GSBC, CNN, and ABC News lining the length of the street, news helicopters flying overhead. Ever since the news of Rachel's affair with Olivia had broken, the feeding frenzy had reached a new level, with ABC reporting a rumor that the police knew where Rachel was, and CNN positing that her arrest was imminent. While Aaron and Dino set up their equipment, I sent Jen and Alex to Vanessa Cox's house. I figured if anyone could coax her into repeating some of what she said to me on camera, Alex could. "Be charming," I told him.

He threw up his hands. "Flirt. Don't flirt. You know I'm not some light switch you can turn off and on."

"Oh please." I rolled my eyes. "Just go over there and do that thing you do."

His forehead wrinkled. "What are you talking about?"

"You know, that squinty, glittery-eye thing."

He laughed. "I have no idea what you're talking about."

Jen caught my eye. "Do you think?"

"No way, he totally knows what he's doing." I dug a roll of breath mints out of my bag and tossed it to Alex.

"What are these for?"

"Just in case."

He gave me an incredulous look.

"I'm just kidding," I said. "But we do need this one."

He pocketed the mints and took a step toward me. "You got a date for Monday?"

"You're doing the eye thing right now."

He wiped away a grin and took another step closer. "Well, do you?"

I pushed him away. "Quit clowning around and go get us an interview."

About fifteen minutes after they left, I made a call to Panda to see if there was any truth to ABC's report. Panda picked up on the first ring.

"What's the deal with Rachel Rockwell?" I asked. "Have you guys upgraded her to suspect yet?"

"Can you meet?" Panda asked.

I explained that I was in Connecticut, staking out Rachel's house with virtually every other news outlet on the face of the earth. We made a plan to meet for breakfast the following morning, but before he hung up I asked Panda if the PD had any clue where Rachel could be hiding.

"She's missing, Clyde." His voice was serious.

"Missing as in she's on some yacht in the Caribbean or missing as in she's dead in a ditch off the New Jersey Turnpike?"

He hesitated. "I can't comment further."

"Can't you give me something?"

"What do you think I just did?"

"I need more than that."

Panda heard the desperation in my voice. "You OK?"

"I'm hanging on by a thread."

There was a long pause. "Frank Uffizo just filed a missing-person report on behalf of the family. You didn't hear it from me."

I showered Panda with a million thanks and hung up.

I texted my team to meet back at the van after they were done with Vanessa; then I e-mailed Georgia's executive producer and Diskin to let them know we had to alter our game plan.

The missing-person report was a good start. But I wasn't done yet. First I called the task force's information officer and told them what I'd heard. Predictably, they refused to help. Since Rachel Rockwell wasn't under twenty-one, they didn't have to abide by federal laws and report the case to the National Crime Information Center, nor did they have to confirm to me, or any other network, that the family had indeed filed such a report.

No problem. If there was one thing I knew about missing-person cases, it was that family members welcomed media attention. I found Frank Uffizo's number in my call history and pressed send. Michael Rockwell wouldn't go on air, but Rachel's parents might. Especially if they knew media pressure could get their daughter reclassified from person of interest to missing person. Uffizo didn't pick up, so I left a message. "All I want is to provide Rachel's family with a public forum so that they can get the word out about her as quickly as possible." And because I knew how Uffizo's mind worked, I added, "They can still do the *Today* show tomorrow morning. No one over there is going to fault them for wanting to get a jump on the coverage, and Georgia's the best you can do in her time slot." Then I told him I was going to report the missing-person angle whether he confirmed it or not. "You've got a sympathetic producer, here, Frank. If I were you, I'd jump on this."

I stuck my phone back in my bag and gazed up at Rachel's home. It was made of limestone, with an inward-curving façade divided by three Corinthian columns. Like the other homes on the street, it was secured behind ten foot hedges and wrought-iron gates. The B-roll of the neighborhood would illustrate the high level of wealth of its inhabitants; we'd let schadenfreude do the rest.

All the other networks would be doing the same regurgitation, but thanks to Panda, and barring a massive double-cross from Uffizo, we'd have an exclusive on the missing-person report filed by

Rachel's parents. I grabbed a pen, banged out a script for Alex, and waited for him and Jen to call in from Vanessa's house.

Fifteen minutes later, I had him on the line. "She's on her way in to the studio," he said. "No breath mints required."

I updated him on the missing-person report and read him his new script. He didn't say anything. No thank you. No good job, Clyde. "Well?" I asked.

"Well what?"

"If you have something to get off your chest, just say it," I huffed.

He sighed. "I'm just wondering which network is going to get to interview Rachel's parents."

I knew what he was saying—that my scoop was meaningless, that the real coup of the day was landing her parents' first interview and that I was incapable of delivering it.

"I don't like being on a losing team, Clyde."

"Neither do I, Alex."

I slammed open the van's door. It was ten past five and there were still several hours before we were due to go on air. I headed down the street, hoping to hook up with Jen and work the streets with her. I walked about a quarter of a mile before I came around a bend and realized there was a large, undeveloped parcel of land situated directly behind Rachel's house.

I called Dino and asked him to meet me where I stood. We'd go together, get some footage of the backyard, and maybe knock on the back door. With any luck, Rachel's parents were in there with the kids, and I'd be able to appeal to them directly to do an interview with Georgia. Screw Alex.

I waited for a few minutes before I started getting antsy. Through the trees, I could just make out an oversize yellow umbrella, the kind people put up poolside. I decided to move in for a closer look while there was still sunlight, and pushed away some low-hanging branches. I had to step carefully to avoid tripping on tree roots, but as I got closer to the Rockwells' house, my heels began to sink deeper into the soil.

I heard a fallen branch crack, and called out, "Dino, is that you?"

"No such luck," said the voice behind me.

# fifteen

The figure came closer, close enough that I could make out the tall, muscular build and slicked-back head of hair. "What are you doing here?"

Michael Rockwell pointed to his house. "Same thing it looks like you're doing. Trying to get in there. Only I'm not trespassing."

Perspiration beaded on my forehead and trickled down my sides. "Am I trespassing? I didn't know I stepped over the property line." I glanced behind me. There was no sign of Dino. "And if this is your house, why don't you just use the front door?' I asked Rockwell.

"Too many reporters. But I'm actually really glad to see you. It's Clyde, right? Like a man. Not Cornelia. I made a few calls after you left my office. Your cousin didn't have particularly favorable things to say about you. Jack Slane either. But he did give me some rather memorable visuals." Rockwell took a step closer.

It was darker than I realized, the sun falling fast behind the trees. I turned to run, but I was too slow. Rockwell held me by my wrist. "Let me go!" I yelled as loud as I could, trying to wrest myself free. But he was too strong.

He pulled me to him, growling into my hair. "You think just because you're a woman, I won't take you down?"

I stopped squirming. "Is that what you said to Olivia? Did you kill her?"

"Clyde!" Alex's and Dino's voices carried through the wooded lot. Rockwell let me go, and without another word, he took off for the house.

Alex and Dino reached me a second later. I could barely speak, but I managed to point to Rachel's house. "Roll tape now," I instructed Dino.

Dino aimed his camera and gave me the thumbs-up. I released the breath I didn't know I was holding and sank to the ground on my heels. Alex squatted down next to me. "Christ, Clyde. You're shaking," he said, wrapping his arms around me, hugging me tight to him, my face buried into his chest, until the trembling stopped. "Can you stand?" he asked.

I nodded, looked up at Dino. "Did you get it?"

Dino grinned. "Full three seconds. The asshole broke in through his own back door."

Back at the van, Alex poured me a cup of coffee from his thermos and told everyone what happened. Jen wanted to call the police on Rockwell, but I assured them I'd do it myself once Alex's package was done.

But then my phone rang.

It was Frank Uffizo.

Rachel's mother and stepfather were ready to talk.

I called Georgia to let her know we were going to have to once again rejigger the rundown for that night's broadcast. We finished shooting Alex's package in front of Rachel's home, then hightailed it back to the bureau to get ready for the arrival of Roseanna and Vernal Hart. I asked everyone to keep an eye out for Michael Rockwell, but none of us saw him again that night.

The interview almost didn't happen. At the eleventh hour, Uffizo demanded we keep any discussion about Rachel's sexual orientation off the table. Georgia refused and Uffizo threatened to walk, but I wasn't about to lose my exclusive to his cronies at NBC. While Georgia kept Uffizo busy in Conference Room B, I barricaded the Harts in the green room and convinced them that the *Today* show and every other network were going to demand total access, and the only difference between answering questions now or the next morning was ten hours, ten hours they didn't have to wait to tell the world about Rachel's disappearance.

Georgia pulled rank on Alex and demanded that she do the interview with the Harts; Alex was given the Vanessa Cox interview as a consolation. I overheard him grumbling a little, but he knew the score.

We opened the show with the Harts. After an intro, the camera panned wide to Roseanna, a generously shaped woman with her daughter's long black hair and wide-set eyes, and Vernal, Rachel's stepfather. He held up a picture of Rachel, tears forming in his deep-set eyes.

Georgia introduced the couple. "Ms. Hart, can you tell us why you waited this long to file a missing-person report with the police? It's been five days since anyone has seen or heard from her."

"We thought . . . hoped . . . she would come back home." Roseanna's voice was so soft, her mike barely picked it up.

In my earpiece, I could hear Fred Wallace, Georgia's EP, yelling at the sound techs in the control room to raise the volume.

Georgia's face remained placid despite the cacophony of voices in her left ear. "Has Rachel disappeared before?" she asked.

Roseanna shook her head. "She would never leave her children."

Georgia softened her expression. "I know this is such a personal question, but what can you tell us about Rachel's relationship with Olivia Kravis? Is it true they were lovers?"

"We knew nothing about what she and—" Roseanna faltered. She looked to her husband.

Vernal put down the photo of Rachel. "We love Rachel no matter what. We just want to know that she's safe," he said stoically.

Georgia glanced down at her notes. "Your daughter's husband filed for divorce amid reports of infidelity. She was, according to sources, sleeping with her personal trainer at the time. Did you know anything about that?"

Roseanna shifted in her seat. "No."

Georgia looked incredulous. "She never talked to you about another man?"

"No."

Stymied, Georgia flipped to another note card. "Did Rachel ever seem worried about her safety? Did she worry that Michael would hurt the children?"

"As far as we know, he never laid a hand on her or the boys," Roseanna replied.

Georgia leaned forward. "Did he ever threaten to?"

Roseanna opened her mouth to speak, but Vernal beat her to it. "Actually, yes. He did."

The color drained from Roseanna's round face as she turned to face her husband. Vernal had gone off-script, putting his and Roseanna's access to their grandchildren in peril. To go out on such a limb, Vernal had to believe that Michael could be responsible for Olivia's death and his stepdaughter's disappearance.

"Mr. Hart, what do you mean by that?" Georgia asked.

"Before they separated, Michael once told her that if she ever crossed him, he'd make sure she'd pay for it in blood."

Roseanna's shoulders shook as fresh tears cascaded into her lap. Vernal Hart regarded his wife sadly before turning his weathered face back to Georgia. "All we want is for Rachel to come back home."

Only time would tell if they'd ever get their wish.

Thursday

# sixteen

At eight o'clock on Thursday morning, I opened the green-painted gate to the Peter Detmold Park, narrowly missing a head-on with a golden retriever. The dog brushed against my leg instead, throwing me off balance and making me spill the two coffees I'd brought for my sit-down with Panda. He didn't have a dog of his own, but his mother, who lived in one of the condos overlooking the East River, had a ten-year-old dachshund he'd walk for her when her sciatica was acting up.

"How's Dax?" I gestured toward the little dog. He was chasing a Jack Russell with a tennis ball in his mouth.

"Forget Dax. How are you?"

"I've been worse. Did you see *Topical* last night?"

"No, but I got an earful about it this morning from Ehlers."

"He had to have known Rachel's parents were going public."

Panda jogged over to clean up after Dax. He flipped the plastic baggie into a green waste bin on his way back to me. He sat down on one of the benches and motioned for me to join him.

I handed one of my coffees to Panda and took a sip of mine. "Neal, level with me. Is Rachel missing or is she a suspect? I've had enough of this person-of-interest bullshit."

Panda removed the lid of his coffee and blew on it. "Rachel's not a suspect."

That left me with two theories. One, Rachel was dead, murdered alongside Olivia and disposed of somewhere other than the crime scene. Or two, she'd witnessed the murder, freaked out, and taken off. Maybe she was hiding from the killer, maybe the cops. Either way, what Panda had just told me confirmed that the PD didn't have enough crime-scene evidence to book her, let alone name her as a suspect. "What about the tissue you found under Olivia's nails?"

"It wasn't tissue, Clyde."

"What?"

He waited, watching my face for signs of comprehension. "Vaginal fluid," he said at last, giving up.

"Oh Jesus." This was the kind of sordid detail GSBC would be all over. I grabbed Dax's muddy tennis ball and hurled it across the park, but it did nothing to dissipate the frustration I felt building in my chest. "Why didn't you just tell me what it was?"

He set his coffee on a bench and gave me a fatherly pat on the back. "Remember what I said about the Kravises putting pressure on the PD? Well, this was something they had considerable concerns about leaking to the press. I gave you what I could, but that was completely off the table."

"What else have they taken off the table?"

"Beats me. The topic came up after we established the nature of the relationship, and once we did, the Kravises intervened to make sure certain information stayed under wraps."

I handed over a white paper bag. In it were two cream-filled beignets from a little café up the block on First Avenue. We sat on the bench, eating and watching Dax chase the Jack Russell around the dog run. I got up to toss the bag and my empty coffee cup. "What does Ehlers think? Is Rachel hiding or missing?"

"We don't know, but his money's on missing."

If she was missing—as in, abducted or dead—the woman with the yappy dog's story about seeing someone who looked like Rachel on the street the night of Olivia's murder was a bunch of bullshit. It also meant that Rachel couldn't have called Michael the next morning. "Does Ehlers think the killer used Rachel's phone to call Michael Saturday morning?"

He nodded.

"Were there any other calls made from that phone?"

"No."

"Does that make Michael seem more or less guilty to you? We've already established that he had threatened Rachel. What if he went over to Olivia's apartment to exact some revenge? He kills Olivia, abducts or kills Rachel, and then the next morning uses Rachel's phone to call himself, thinking that the call would be enough to convince the police that she'd killed Olivia and had gone into hiding?"

"It's not a bad theory, Clyde. But it's just a theory." Panda called to Dax and the little dachshund came running, his short legs carrying his body as fast as they could.

I patted the dog's smooth head as Panda clipped on his leash. "It's more than that. There's something I haven't told you yet," I said.

While we climbed the steep stairs back in the direction of the apartment building where Panda's mother lived, I told him about my run-in with Michael Rockwell in the woods behind his Connecticut house. Panda's concern was no longer about the case, but about me. "Why don't you come to the station with me and make a statement? We could get some security on you."

I had a gut feeling Rockwell had only meant to scare me. This sort of thing had happened to me a few times before, once in a Detroit parking lot by a suspect in a sex-abuse case, another time on a beach in Florida by the parent of a murder victim. It was always frightening, but I'd come to accept it as part of the job. A job I couldn't do if I was tied up filling out paperwork at the one-nine. "I don't have time to make a statement," I said.

"If that's how you feel, I can at least make sure Ehlers is up to speed," he said. "We'll keep a closer watch on Rockwell. And you, I want you to be careful. Watch your back, Clyde. I mean it."

We finished climbing the stairs from the dog run. Panda bent over to rub his left leg and catch his breath. It had been more than a week since my last workout, but I was barely winded, thanks to my regular sessions.

I hadn't always liked exercising. The gym reminded me of the worst parts of high school and singles' bars combined, and my breasts made it nearly impossible to run, no matter how many sports bras I layered on over my double Ds. But a couple of years ago, I started swimming laps at a municipal pool near my apartment to help manage my stress levels and found that it also helped me stay in pretty decent shape. I wasn't about to quit my job to become a swimsuit model, but I could clock a respectable time for a four-hundred-meter freestyle.

"How's the knee?" I asked Panda.

"Knee's old." He hauled out a handful of Bit-O-Honeys from his pocket and handed me one. Ever since he'd quit smoking, he'd developed a massive sweet tooth. He'd also packed on about twenty extra pounds.

I popped a candy in my mouth and chewed. "Rockwell got an alibi for Friday night?"

Panda lifted his arm and hailed me a taxi. "You know, it's not your job to actually solve the crime."

"So make sure your guys do it." I slid into the taxi's backseat. "The alibi?"

"I'll look into it." Panda closed the door, and I noticed his tie for the first time. This one featured rows of piano keys against a bright green background.

"Too easy." I rolled down the taxi window, nodding at his neckwear. "Key lime."

"You nailed it, kid," he said, waving me away.


At work, word had spread about my sunset encounter with Michael Rockwell in the lot behind Rachel's house, and everyone wanted to hear a firsthand account. I indulged one retelling and was at my desk, studying the overnights, preparing a new to-do list, when Georgia called. She wanted to see me in her office, pronto. Another pep talk to keep me on my toes, I assumed, waltzing into her corner digs. Georgia was seated behind her desk, reading a book, her hair in hot rollers.

"Knock, knock." I picked up a throw pillow embroidered with an old Groucho Marx quote—*Anyone who says he can see through women is missing a lot*—and took my seat.

Georgia held up the book she was reading for me to see. "It's a galley of Charles Kravis's memoir."

"Sure to be a bestseller," I said, slipping the pillow behind my back. "Are they holding the release?"

"To the contrary. They just pushed up the pub date."

"How can they?"

Georgia laughed. "You obviously know nothing about publishing."

"I know bookstores are closing, book sales are down, and everything's going digital."

"The business is in the shitter. And some asshole is into this book for $1.5 million. That was Kravis's advance. So now, you're the publisher, you've got an author who's about to croak, can't do publicity, but his daughter's murder is the biggest story of the day.

What're you going to do? The right, moral thing, or the thing that's gonna save your ass when heads start to roll?" She slammed the book shut and passed it to me across the desk. "I want Alex to do a segment on it for tonight's show."

I picked up the book and tucked it under my arm. "Is that all?"

"I heard about what happened in the field."

I felt a lecture coming on, one I didn't feel the need to hear twice in one morning. "I already told the PD about it," I said, hoping to head her off.

"Did you make a statement?" Georgia removed one of her rollers, rewrapping her hair and securing it again to her scalp.

"No."

"Why not?"

"Because the police are already keeping an eye on the guy."

Georgia studied my face. "OK, one more thing. I want you to come with me to a party Prentice Maldone is throwing tonight after the broadcast. It's in honor of the merger."

"Why do I have to go? Can't you take your husband?"

Georgia's bangles clinked as her torso shook with laughter. "Do I have to spell everything out to you?"

"Not everything."

Georgia sighed. "There will be men there, Clyde. You do realize you have about two, maybe three years left—tops—to have a baby."

"Why are we talking about this? Last time I checked, you didn't have a kid either."

"I have stepkids."

"Ex-stepkids. And they never called you mom."

She threw me one of her quit-sassing-me looks.

I crossed my arms. "Actually, Georgia, I just met someone. A lawyer, and he's coming as my plus one to the Kravis benefit next week."

"One date does not a dance card fill," Georgia snapped. "And anyway, I want to keep my eye on you."

"So that's the real reason."

"You're coming with me and that's final. So get Sasha to do something with your goddamn hair. Looks like a fucking rat's nest up there."

The party was held at a duplex gallery space in SoHo. Georgia gave her name in the lobby, and we were escorted upstairs in an elevator that opened directly into the party. At the center of the event space were two low-backed Italian sectionals and a Lucite coffee table with a huge orchid plant in an oval chrome planter at its center. Behind a glass staircase stood a large bar and a cluster of food stations serving pink rectangles of beef tenderloin and toro.

Threading through the crowd, I recognized a few faces from the FirstNews legal and corporate departments. By the floor-to-ceiling windows, Mitchell Diskin towered over one of our morning anchors, a smiley blonde. I also recognized our noon and four o'clock anchors, a couple members of Congress that contributed to FirstNews's Sunday-morning current-events talk show, and Naomi Zell, FirstNews's CEO and the Kravis family's recently appointed spokesperson.

Georgia left me to go mingle. Actually what she said was, "You look pretty. Now smile, be nice, and pretend like you don't crush testicles for a living. It should also go without saying but I'm going to say it anyway: steer clear of the hooch." Then she thrust me into a group of men dressed in expensive blue suits and Italian loafers.

I introduced myself to them and then promptly excused myself as soon as Georgia had her back turned. I was about to walk out of the party when I spotted Delphine huddled beneath the staircase, next to an Egyptian limestone bust. She was dressed modestly in a dark short-sleeved dress and mid-height heels, and was standing with a man I took to be her husband. I tapped her lightly on the shoulder.

"I'm surprised you're here," she said, looking startled to see me.

"I could say the same." The last time we spoke she seemed ready to go into hiding. What was she doing at a party celebrating Maldone's purchase of FirstNews?

"I'm only here because it's what's expected of me as a board member. We'll be making an early exit." She then introduced me to Hamish, whom she quickly dispatched to the bar to retrieve us drinks. I'd ordered a tonic water, Delphine a vodka and cranberry.

"Why haven't you returned my calls?" I asked once we were on our own.

"It's the merger," she said, lowering her voice. "No media interviews. Everything is supposed to go through Naomi. I'm sure you understand why it has to be this way."

"I do. But I'd still like to have a chat. I told you everything could be off the record."

Her eyebrows knitted together. "But your message. You said I had to go on camera if we wanted to move the focus from Olivia's personal life." She was using my words against me. I hated when people did that. "I wish I didn't have to say this," Delphine continued, "because I know Olivia thought the world of you, but with the merger, things are very delicate. Now just isn't the right time."

I touched the pearls at my neck. "I'm not just interested in talking to you for professional reasons. Personally, I feel . . . involved."

She gave me a tight smile. "Of course you do. You were her friend."

"It's more than that. There's something I haven't told you," I said. "The night Olivia was murdered, we were supposed to get together but I got stuck at work. She sent me a text I didn't see until Monday morning. I'm not sure how I missed it on Friday night."

"What did the text say?" She cocked her head.

I realized, from her reaction, that I finally had a card to play, one I wasn't going to hand over without getting something in return. "It's so loud here, I can barely hear you. How about we meet for coffee tomorrow?"

I could tell she wanted to press me further but her husband had returned, and with him, Prentice Maldone. Hamish handed me my tonic water and Delphine her vodka cranberry. "About Olivia's memorial service," Delphine said, changing the subject. It had been scheduled for the following Thursday at 10:00 a.m. "I hope you can make it."

"I'll be there," I assured her, remembering the promise I'd made to Sutton to make a speech at the service. "I've been preparing something."

Delphine shifted her weight. "I'm afraid we need to keep the ceremony brief. My stepfather's health is declining. We don't want to tax him any more than necessary."

Only part of me felt relieved. Mostly I felt snubbed. Surely the Kravises could have found a few minutes for me if they'd wanted.

"And please, Clyde, attend as a friend, not as a member of the press. We'd like to keep the details of the service private."

It wasn't an unreasonable request, but something about it stuck in my craw. "Of course," I replied, mustering a closed-mouth smile. What choice did I have?

Delphine put a hand on her husband's back, and the two of them said their good-byes. After they left I thought Prentice would excuse himself, but instead he asked if he and I could speak privately. I assented, following him up the staircase to the doorway of a heated terrace devoid of both furniture and other guests.

"Can I get you another?" He gestured to my drink, misunderstanding the reason for my reluctance to join him at the terrace's plexiglass ledge.

I lifted my glass to show him that it was still mostly full.

"Not a lightweight, are you?"

Maldone didn't know my history, or that my tonic didn't have any vodka in it. I took a few steps to the middle of the terrace. It was as far as my fear of heights would let me go. "Do I look like a lightweight?"

He smiled indulgently. "I don't think I should answer that."

"That answer wouldn't play well on TV."

"What would?"

"Changing the subject."

"I'll remember that." He took a long sip of his drink. "By the way, good show tonight."

We'd opened with a follow-up report from Connecticut and closed the hour with the editor of Charles Kravis's memoir. "You watch *Topical*?"

"Never miss it," he replied.

"Have you read the memoir?"

Prentice leaned forward, gazing out at the view. "Charles is an interesting man. Patriotic. Hardworking. Highly conservative, yes, but a dedicated newsman. Not too many of those anymore."

"What are you?"

"A businessman." He turned back around and took another sip of what looked like Scotch. "I'm sorry I didn't have much of a chance to get to know Olivia. All I know is the work she was doing with the foundation. It's interesting, though, that she didn't have a larger role at the network. Considering what I read in the memoir, Charles clearly thought the world of her."

"That was Olivia's choice. She preferred being able to help people and change lives—for the better. That's not what we always end up doing at FirstNews."

"Are the Kravises being helpful to you?"

I didn't know how to answer that. The truth was that they weren't, but it would be disloyal—not to mention unprofessional—for me to say so. "As much as can be expected. It's a rough time for them."

He set his drink down on the ledge. "May I ask you for a favor, Cornelia?"

"Sure."

"In all likelihood, Olivia's murder had nothing to do with network business—"

"Was Olivia opposed to the merger?" I asked, interrupting him.

He gave me a pointed look. "I'm sure I would be the last person to know that. A trusted friend, on the other hand . . ."

"Olivia and I didn't talk about network business. We discovered that it was better for our friendship." Just saying that aloud reminded me of the other, not-so-insignificant topic we didn't discuss. *What else was she keeping from me?* "So I didn't know about the merger, let alone how she felt about it."

He considered my response. "The timing concerns me. I'm not a fan of coincidences."

"And I don't believe in them."

"Then we understand each other." He picked up his drink and moved closer to me, closer than would have been considered appropriate in an office setting. "Cornelia, can I depend on you to do something for me?"

I nodded. Prentice was, after all, going to be my new boss.

"I'd like you to let me know if you discover any correlation between this crime and the merger. Even if it's something you can't corroborate or put on the air, I still want to know about it."

Prentice led me back downstairs to the party. At the base of the stairs, he pressed his card into my hand. "That has my direct line on it. Please do not hesitate to use it." Then he disappeared into the swarm of bodies.

The party had doubled in size while I was upstairs. Georgia was nowhere to be seen. I elbowed my way through the room to seek out a few bites of food before I called it a night. Halfway to the door, I heard a familiar voice in the crowd. It was Penny Harlich.

*What the hell is she doing here?* This was a FirstNews and Maldone Enterprises party. Was it possible that Diskin was thinking about hiring her away from GSBC? I shuddered at the thought and should have put it out of my mind, but curiosity got the better of me. I abandoned my plans to leave and found the staircase. Up a few steps, I could watch Penny easily, not that she would be hard to miss in the spiky heels and skintight cherry-red dress she was wearing.

She circulated the room, waving to some of the other on-air talent, getting a drink, but not stopping to talk to anyone. She was clearly looking for someone specific. A minute later, she spotted her prey. Downing her drink and fluffing her mane, she walked right up to Prentice, wrapping one of her tawny arms around his shoulders as she whispered something in his ear. He looked up at her and laughed. To a woman like her, a man like Prentice looked a lot taller standing on his money.

I don't know why I did it, but I took out my phone and snapped a picture. Then I ditched my tonic water and headed to the bar, where Penny was waiting for a pair of refills for her and Prentice.

"Enjoying yourself?" I asked.

She gave me an icy smile. Her perfume smelled of cloyingly sweet gardenias and vanilla, and she had long nails that had been painted the same shade of her dress. Without wanting, my mind pictured them raking across Alex's muscled chest. "I'm sorry, do I know you?" she asked.

She knew who I was, but I introduced myself anyway. "Clyde Shaw. *Topical Tonight.* We kicked your ass last night."

"So you did. And I think I do recognize you. You're the hag who works for Alex Amori." She tapped the side of her face mockingly. "Or had he called you a nag? I can't be sure. What I can be sure of is that the Hart family scoop is your last. I don't care what kind of inside track you think you have on this case, I've got better."

Her response was anything but expected. Alex was right: Penny was smart. But my network loyalty prevented me from seeing her as anything other than my sworn enemy, which is how I would have preferred Alex see her too. I took another glass of tonic from the bartender. "By the way, I don't know how it works at GSBC, but at our network it doesn't matter how much leg you're willing to show if you don't have the numbers to back you up. Yours are falling, and last I checked, you're running out of skirt."

It would have been a perfect exit, if I hadn't walked in the wrong direction of the elevator. I didn't want Penny to see me doubling back on myself, so I kept walking and carved a little space for myself on one of the sectionals. I set my glass down on a side table and found my phone in my bag. There was a new text from Phil Drucker, the lawyer I'd met at Michael Rockwell's firm. He wanted to know if he could get away with wearing his green lizard-skin cowboy boots to the Kravis benefit. I was reasonably confident he didn't own a pair. I took a few sips from my glass and texted back. "By all means."

A moment later, his reply arrived. "Good. They go with the corsage I'm getting you."

I laughed to myself, took one last sip of tonic, and slipped my phone back into my jacket pocket. Then I stood up and I started for the elevator, but with each step I grew more exhausted, the fatigue of the past two days finally catching up with me. I needed to splash some water on my face. A waiter pointed me in the direction of the bathroom, which turned out to be down a small corridor at the back of the gallery.

I barely made it. Sliding open the door to the bathroom, my legs buckled beneath me, and my head banged into the indigo tile floor. I had just enough presence of mind to realize that what I was feeling wasn't exhaustion.

Someone had drugged me.

The bathroom door opened. I discovered I couldn't move. The room grew dark, and my whole body felt like it was sinking, being pulled under by a heavy fog.

"You are treading on very dangerous ground," growled a voice in my ear. In my deadened state, I couldn't make out if it was male or female, or if it was even real.

I gasped for breath. Everything was black. Fingers dug into my cheeks. "You'll only get one warning."

# Friday

# seventeen

I woke up at a hospital, screaming, hooked up to an IV and a heart monitor. I'd been dreaming, or remembering, I wasn't sure which.

"I'm here, Clyde. You're OK. You're safe."

It was Alex. His hand took mine. I felt nauseated as I looked around the room, gathered my bearings. The clock on the wall read half past 5:00 a.m. "What are you doing here?"

A small Asian woman in blue scrubs entered the room and stood at the end of my bed. "Good to see you're awake, Ms. Shaw. I'm Dr. Cho. You've been admitted to Beth Israel hospital."

"What happened to me?"

She walked toward me and grabbed my arm, feeling for a pulse. "Your blood test confirmed you received a large amount of Ketalar, otherwise known as ketamine, or Special-K. It's sold to veterinarians as a general anesthesia and sedative, but is also used and sold illegally as a hallucinogenic and a so-called date-rape drug. Do you know how this substance may have been given to you?"

I rubbed my forehead with my free hand. I looked to Alex, hoping he could fill in the blanks. "I wasn't there," he said to the doctor. "I was told she passed out at a party."

"Are you her husband?" Dr. Cho asked.

"A friend," Alex replied.

"Colleague," I corrected.

The doctor wrote that down in my file. "Did you have anything to drink at this party?"

I nodded. "I had a couple tonic waters."

"Without anything else? No alcohol?"

"No."

She made another note. "Did you ever leave your glass unattended?"

"I can't remember."

She put the file down, sidled up next to me, and took out a small penlight, which she shined in my eyes, checking my pupils. "The effects are pretty immediate, within five and twenty minutes of drinking the substance, depending on how much food you have in your stomach."

I turned my head to Alex. "How did you know I was here?"

"Penny saw you carried out on a stretcher and called me."

"Penny? Who else saw me?"

"I think everyone there. All she said was that you were on a stretcher, passed out, and the paramedics were bringing you here."

"They just sent me here alone?"

"One of Maldone's assistants was in the waiting room when I got here at a quarter to midnight." He ran a hand down the rumpled front of his denim button-down. "Alice, Maldone's assistant, told me she found you on the bathroom floor and tried to revive you. When she couldn't, she dialed 911."

Dr. Cho opened my chart. "Would you like for me to call the police?"

I wanted to speak to Panda. If the hospital called the authorities, I didn't know whom I'd get. With my luck, it'd be some rookie who would drown me in paperwork. "I can do that. I just need my cell phone. Is my purse around here somewhere?"

Dr. Cho looked around the room. My coat was resting on a chair, but I didn't see my purse. "Did Ms. Shaw have a bag with her last night?" she asked Alex.

"It wasn't here when I got here."

My throat seized. My notebook and tape recorder, with all my notes from Olivia's case, were in there. I sat up and pawed at the tape securing the IV to my arm. "I've got to get it. I need to go."

Dr. Cho moved swiftly around the bed. "Ms. Shaw, you are in no condition."

I was about to argue with her when the room began to spin. I rested my head back down against the pillows and waited for the spinning to stop before looking back at Alex. He had my jacket in one hand, my phone in the other. "It was in here," he said, handing both to me.

"But my notes," I said, my eyes widening with urgency.

Alex grabbed his own jacket from the back of his chair. "I'll call Maldone's assistant. She left her card. They must have it." He hovered by the door. "Are you sure you don't want me to stay, Clyde? I can have someone else handle this and stay with you."

"Just go find my bag."

The door shut behind him. I turned back to Dr. Cho. "Is it normal not to be able to recall anything?"

"Memory loss is common."

"Will it ever come back?"

Dr. Cho checked my IV bag. "It may. It's hard to tell. If you've been sexually assaulted we'll be able to find evidence of that upon examination. I did a visual exam when you were admitted and I didn't see any evidence of an assault, but I would still like to do a rape kit just to be sure. Do I have your permission?"

I nodded, sickened by the thought. I wanted to call my dad, but if I did he'd only get worried and insist on taking me back upstate with him. "When can I leave here?" I asked Dr. Cho.

"After I examine you, I'd like to keep you under observation for the next few hours; then you can go home to rest. You received a rather large dose of ketamine, Ms. Shaw. The sedative effects will take some time to wear off completely."

"When can I go back to work?"

Dr. Cho poured water in a cup and handed it to me. "By tomorrow afternoon you should be able to return to your normal daily activities. But you probably won't feel like working for another forty-eight hours. I'll come back in a few minutes for your examination. In the meantime, ring the call button if you need anything."

I drank my water, wondering who at the party had seen me get carried out and whether the news had filtered to the network, specifically to Georgia and the dozen or so colleagues who had been around at the height of my drinking days. I hoped they'd give me the benefit of the doubt and not jump to any wrong conclusions.

I dialed Panda, feeling terrible for disturbing him at such an early hour. He picked up on the third ring. I could hear the grogginess in his voice, his wife murmuring next to him in bed as he turned on his bedside lamp and listened to me explain as concisely as I could what had happened. It took some time; my brain was still a bit foggy.

"I'd come over myself but I think you're better off talking to my partner in case the two crimes are linked. Call the precinct in a few hours and ask to be put through to Ehlers. He and Detective Restivo from North Homicide will come pay you a visit. I know they want to talk to you again. Call me after they leave and we'll figure out a time to meet."

"Is everything OK, Neal?" Panda's wife asked in the background.

"Go back to sleep, Bess. Everything's fine."

"I'm sorry I woke you," I mumbled into the phone.

170

"It's OK. I was going to call you this morning, actually. There's been a development in the case. I'll swing by your apartment later with bagels and coffee."

"I'll be at work."

"Like hell you will. Ketamine is a serious drug. Your body needs a chance to recuperate."

"And miss out on the scoop you've got for me?"

He sighed grumpily. "Now I'm sorry I told you. Get some rest, kid."

I fell asleep sometime after Dr. Cho was done administering the rape kit. When I woke up, it was with a start, breathing hard, my hands gripping the rails on either side of my hospital bed. I'd been dreaming. Someone was chasing me through a dark forest. I hid behind a fallen tree, only to find I was standing in a bloody bog, a pair of soft white hands just visible through a clump of leaves. Suddenly they came alive, reaching for me, the fingers just inches from my face before I came to.

Dr. Cho had warned me I might be haunted by flashbacks for a while as my body finished processing the drugs in my system and my mind dealt with the trauma of being attacked, but it still took me a good three minutes to get my pulse back down to normal.

The clock on the wall read 9:45 a.m. Dragging my IV line, I managed to change back into my own clothes. Back in bed I placed a call to the police department, eventually getting patched through to Detective Tom Ehlers. He arrived with Detective John Restivo as I was downing the tepid, watery cup of coffee on my hospital-issued breakfast tray.

I raked a hand through my hair and invited them to sit.

"I'll stand." Restivo was tall, dark-haired, and craggy-faced, with even less interest in small talk than Ehlers. He might have been considered the bigger dog on the case, but Ehlers was the better "get." He was more attractive and had more energy.

Ehlers planted himself in the same chair Alex had spent half the night in. "How's the noggin?"

The headache had subsided but I still felt disoriented and foggy-brained. "Been better." My speech might have been a little slurred.

Restivo tossed the remainder of his Starbucks in the plastic-lined bin by my bed. "Why don't you tell us what happened last night?"

I told them everything, ending with the ominous warning I'd received in the gallery's bathroom. Ehlers brought out his notebook and took down all the names of the people I'd seen at the party as well as all the names of the people I'd interviewed so far and the address of the gallery. "What about your encounter in those woods behind the Rockwell house?"

I repeated what I'd told Panda. The detectives exchanged glances. Restivo leaned against the door frame. "How was Mr. Rockwell's demeanor?"

"Threatening. Angry. But I think he just wanted to scare me."

Ehlers put his notebook away. "Mr. Rockwell has a known history of violence, Ms. Shaw. I suggest you stay as far away from him as possible."

My reporter instincts kicked in. "What do you mean *known history of violence*? We checked police records. He has no priors, no restraining orders either."

Restivo took a step closer. "This is not for your show."

"He threatened me, detective. I have a right to know."

Ehlers looked to his partner, who gave him a slight nod. "Off the record, date rape. She said, he said, and then she decided he didn't. Whole thing was swept under the table, but most everyone agreed he'd done it."

"When did this happen?"

Ehlers glanced again to Restivo, who this time shook his head. "Who's your source?" I pressed.

Restivo moved toward the door; two strides on his long legs were all it took to get there. "Isn't that your job, to find sources?" His tone was heavy with sarcasm.

There were two kinds of cops in this world: those who thought all newspeople were the devil's spawn and those who didn't. My guess was that Restivo had been double-crossed by a reporter early on in his career, and was hell-bent on punishing the rest of us for the hack's misdeeds.

Ehlers slipped his notebook back into his pocket and gave me a sympathetic smile. "We'll see if we can pinpoint who slipped the ketamine into your drink. But I have to tell you, these cases are pretty hard to crack without eyewitnesses or surveillance video."

"There's another thing. I'm missing my handbag," I said.

Ehlers pitched forward in the chair. "What was in there?"

"My notebook with my interview notes. It's extremely important it doesn't fall into the wrong hands."

"Like your competitors' at GSBC?" Restivo quipped, his hand back on the door frame.

I clenched my molars.

He opened the door, holding it ajar with his foot. Ehlers got up, zipped up his Windbreaker. "We'll look for your purse and do our best to figure out who drugged you, but in the meantime, get your locks changed, Ms. Shaw."

My apartment keys. I hadn't thought of them. I kept spares in my desk at work. The super also had a set. He'd have to let me in so I could shower and get back to the office.

"You'll call me as soon as you know something?"

"Just take it easy, Ms. Shaw. And get those locks changed. We'll check in with you soon." Ehlers joined his partner in the hall, closing my door swiftly behind him.

In the cab home, I dialed Alex's cell. "Don't tell me you left the hospital already," he said.

"Like you would have stayed if it were you on that bed. Did you find my bag?"

I heard him open a desk drawer. "Maldone's assistant had it and brought it to the office."

I rolled down the taxi's window and lay down on the backseat. "What's in there? Anything missing?"

"Not that I can tell. Wallet, keys, tape recorder, a roll of Tums, a notebook, a few takeout menus, powder compact, lipstick—that's all here. Do you want me to count the cash in the wallet?"

I breathed a sigh of relief. My notes and tape recorder weren't gone. "It sounds like everything's there. I'll be back in an hour. Can you keep it for me until then?"

"No problem. But are you sure you should be coming in? I can have someone take it to your apartment."

"No, I'm coming in."


At my apartment, the super let me in so I could shower and change. I was about to blow-dry my hair when I noticed some papers sticking out of one of the file drawers of my desk. I wasn't the tidiest person on the planet, but I was fastidious about my files.

I carefully canvassed my apartment, but nothing else was missing or out of place. Was I being paranoid? Dr. Cho had warned me the ketamine could have that effect, and Alex had confirmed that my keys were in my bag. I opened my desk drawer, returned the papers to the correct file, and then got the hell out of there. Crazy or not, I couldn't shake the feeling that someone had been in my apartment while I was gone.

Half an hour later, I lumbered through Georgia Jacobs's office door. "I was about to send out a search mission," she said, spearing a salad crouton with a plastic fork. It was a quarter to one and she and Wallace were having a desk-side lunch. "You look like hell."

"Feel like it too," I said.

Wallace's spoon hovered midair over what looked like cheese-covered chili. "Alex filled us in. Why aren't you still at the hospital?"

I threw myself into the only vacant chair and grabbed a packet of oyster crackers from Georgia's desktop. I split the wrapper open with my front teeth and dumped the whole thing in my mouth. "I'm fine," I said, almost believing myself.

Georgia didn't buy it. She wanted to force-march me back to Beth Israel herself, while Wallace tried bargaining with me, hoping to get me to go home for the day. They were taking turns yelling at me when my phone buzzed in my hand.

It was Panda. I'd tried him twice already that morning, without any luck. I held up my hand, motioning for them to be quiet.

"I can't talk long," he said.

"What's going on?"

"We found Rachel's body."

# eighteen

"The Haverford. Basement storage. Another resident complained of a smell and the super called it in last night. Parents identified the body this morning."

"God, that's awful."

"This is a game changer," Panda remarked. We were no longer dealing with a crime of passion but a deliberate, calculated killer. This also meant that Olivia's case had gone from homicide to double homicide. Bodies were stacking up. So were the stakes and so were the potential ratings. I wondered if GSBC knew about the body too. Penny Harlich clearly had her own inside source. She couldn't have landed the housekeeper interview without one.

"When is the PD going to announce it?" I asked.

"Soon."

"Do we know how long she's been dead?" At that, Georgia began waving her hands frantically. I held my finger up to my mouth and moved into the hall for some privacy.

"Don't know," Panda exhaled. "We're way past rigor mortis."

I shut myself into an empty conference room. "Cadaver dog?"

"Yep, but not that necessary."

When a body dies, muscles relax, including intestinal muscles. I'd been around enough crime scenes to know that what the resident smelled probably wasn't decaying flesh but excrement and urine. "Cause of death?"

"Not bludgeoning. Looks like asphyxiation."

From a killer's perspective, suffocation was a smart choice. No blood splatter, and if done right, virtually noiseless. Plus, it fit the killer's profile in that it was intimate—like bludgeoning, you really had to get up close and personal to do it—and it took a good amount of strength, especially if the victim wasn't tied up. "Ligature marks around the wrists?"

"Yes. She was cuffed behind her back."

That sounded sexual to me. "Autoerotic?"

There was a long pause.

"What is it?"

"This is all I can give you."

"No way, Neal. I need everything this time. The rest can be off the record, but you've got to give it to me. Whoever killed Olivia and Rachel probably just drugged me."

Panda expelled a breath. "Off the record, ME said Rachel had recently had sexual intercourse."

I was confused. "We know that already because Olivia had vaginal fluid under her nails."

"No, Clyde." He cleared his throat. "I'm talking *intercourse*. The ME found ejaculate in her vagina."

"How old?"

"Premortem."

"But not rape?" The wheels of my mind spun to Michael Rockwell and his date-rape past. What if he'd gone to Olivia's apartment, killed Olivia, and then raped and killed Rachel before smuggling her down to the basement?

"No sign of it."

So much for that scenario. It took me a few seconds to come up with another. "Three-way, then?"

"Possibly."

I thought of Alex's comment in Diskin's office, back on the first day of the case. "So much for no sex play." I thanked Panda for the heads-up and hung up. Then I sat down on the floor of the hall, a fresh wave of nausea roiling my stomach. Olivia was dead. Rachel was dead, and someone had drugged me. Taking a long, deep breath, I girded myself for the hours ahead. I needed to do my job and get the story out there. Then I could get some rest.

I got up and let myself back into Georgia's office and announced the news. "They found Rachel's body."

"I got that, Sherlock." Georgia looked at her watch. "How fast can we take this to air?"

"An hour if we want to go live from the scene. I'd also like to get confirmation from the information officer first."

Wallace shook his head in disagreement. "If they won't confirm, just go to air with the speculation. We are not gonna lose this one."

Georgia threw the rest of her lunch in the trash. "Get the van, take your crew, get them set up, and then get your ass home. I don't want to see your sorry mug anywhere near this building until Monday morning."

"What about the weekend shows?" I crossed my arms in defiance. The news wasn't a Monday-through-Friday gig. When you were on a big story, you worked twenty-four/seven, weekends, nights, whatever it took.

"Save it," Georgia barked. "It's either go home now or go home in a few hours. We can handle the weekend shows without you."

I picked up Georgia's desk phone to buzz Alex and bring him up to speed. Then I e-mailed Diskin and the two o'clock news hour director from my phone to tell him to make some room for us at the top of the hour.

Ten minutes later, I was back in the satellite truck with Alex and the team heading uptown to the Haverford. My head ached and the stop-and-go traffic wasn't helping the nausea. Alex took one look at me bent over, my head between my legs, and tried to hand me half his sandwich. "You need it more than I do," he said. "It's homemade. Even the bread."

I lifted my head an inch. "I'm not taking your lunch."

Dino, our cameraman, whipped his head around from the front passenger seat. "I'll take it, man. I'm starving."

"You're always starving, man." Alex pushed Dino's hand away and patted me on the back. "C'mon, Clyde, you look like you're about to faint. I need you in form when we get out there."

"Jennifer can get me pizza."

"This is much healthier than a greasy slice of pepperoni."

"I get the sausage and pepper."

"Even worse." He pulled me up to sitting and unwrapped his lunch. "Now eat."

I reluctantly took a bite. Then I handed it to Dino.

"Clyde, what?" Alex yelped, pawing at Dino for his sandwich half.

Too late. Dino held it out of his reach. "Is that Camembert I taste?" he asked with a full mouth, taunting Alex.

"Yes," Alex groaned, giving up. "And fresh roasted turkey, avocado, romaine, and this mustard I picked up in Paris. Can't get it here."

Aaron eyed Dino's windfall from behind the wheel. "You really make the bread too?"

Alex nodded glumly. "Organic split wheat."

Jen and I looked at each other. This was a side of Alex neither of us would have guessed existed. "I'll get us some slices as soon as we get a break," she said.

We pulled up around the corner of the Haverford. I stayed inside the van and let the sound and truck engineers set up the shot as I continued working on the script with Alex. My phone rang and I stepped outside to take the call from the very irate IO, who first hassled me about where I'd gotten my information and then refused to confirm the tip. He also declined to give me any additional crime-scene details, like the name of the resident who smelled the body, or how the killer had hidden the body.

I slipped in my earpiece and stepped outside, gathering my team and the remainder of my energy. "Let's go live, people!" Jen called the studio, Dino hoisted his camera, and I counted down from three. It was go time.

"We're standing here back at the Haverford, the exclusive Manhattan building where Olivia Kravis, daughter of media baron Charles S. Kravis, was found brutally murdered in her own home," Alex began before jumping into the scoop about Rachel. A fast five minutes later, he wound up his report, and our team piled back into the van. Our work wasn't over yet. We still needed to put together a package that could be aired that evening during *Topical Tonight*.

While Alex and I worked on a script, Dino grabbed some fresh B-roll of the building and Jen finally made the pizza run. Once we had three minutes of television gold hashed out, I sprawled out on the last row of seats in the van and shut my eyes.

"You got a date for the fund-raiser?" Alex asked.

"I've got someone," I mumbled in reply. The fund-raiser was truly the last thing on my mind.

He sat up and peered at me over the seat. "Who?"

I opened my eyes. "Who are you taking?"

"I asked first."

Aaron came to life in the front seat of the van. "If you're taking Hardlick, you're making a massive mistake, bro."

Alex took a swig of water as he leaned back against the van's vinyl-coated seating, facing away from me. "You guys really don't like her, do you?"

"Forget what we think," I said. "You can't have a correspondent from a rival network sit at our company's table. It would be totally inappropriate."

"Relax. I know I can't bring Penny. I was going to ask if you wanted to come with me."

I bit my bottom lip. Did he really just ask me to be his date? Surely he didn't think it was a good idea for us to turn up at a work function for our first outing together? He'd probably just thought it made sense for us to go together since we'd be working the case together all day before the event began. "Alex, I'm—"

"Don't worry," he said, cutting me off. "I got a plan B."

"Lucky girl, your plan B," Aaron quipped sarcastically from the front seat.

I was about to tell our sound guy to go easy on Alex when my phone buzzed with a text from Panda. "I've got more for you," was all that the message said. It was enough.

I typed out a location for us to meet and put my phone back in my pocket. "I need to go meet a source," I told Alex.

"Want me to come with you?"

He was trying to be helpful, but I couldn't take him. I climbed out of the van to the sidewalk. "I need to handle this one alone."

Walking west to Central Park, I followed the path to the reflecting pond. Little kids stood around the edges, some operating remote-control boats, others watching and wishing their mom or dad would spring for a rental. Panda sat on a bench with a can of soda. "You should be at home," he said by way of greeting.

I sank down onto the bench next to him. "I know."

He gestured to my bag. "I see you got it back."

"Maldone's assistant found it and had it sent over to Alex. Everything's still there." I stopped talking, remembering something. I pawed through my bag until I was sure I couldn't find it: my birth certificate. "It's gone."

"What's gone?" Panda asked.

I told him about how I'd found my birth certificate in Olivia's office desk. "You sure you left it in there?"

"Yes, I'm sure."

He scrubbed his forehead with the heel of his hand. "Why didn't you tell me about this before?"

"I didn't think it was important."

"I ran a search for crimes involving ketamine in the last twelve months. Almost all of the cases were your standard date-rape scenarios."

"Any of the perps work for GSBC?" I asked, elbowing him playfully.

"This is serious, Shaw."

He didn't have to tell me that. "You heard about Michael Rockwell's date-rape past?"

"Never proven, but yeah."

"You said you had more for me."

He pulled open his khaki parka to reveal a blue tie printed with stalks of corn. "First you must guess correctly."

"Neal, I don't think I have enough brain power today."

"C'mon. It's an easy one." He took a sip of his soda.

I gave it another look and shook my head.

He pulled on an earlobe. "All ears."

"I should've gotten that."

"I'll give you a pass today, kid." He patted my back.

"That's generous of you," I said, teasing.

He chuckled. "What does Globe-Trotter mean to you?"

"The suitcase brand?" They were fashionable and expensive. They were also built like the old steamer trunks, with roomy insides and hard exteriors made from fiberboard and leather. I only knew all that because Olivia had them. "Rachel?"

"The killer stuffed her body inside one and then hid it in the storage space. Probably used the elevator to get it down to the basement and everything."

"Can I take this to air?"

He nodded. "You didn't hear it from me. Body was wrapped in a garbage bag, then locked inside a suitcase."

We sat there in silence, both gazing out over the pond. Finally, I turned to Panda. "So what's the latest theory?"

"It looked like a lovers' quarrel—neighbors' account of two women yelling in the residence, no forced entry, and a murder weapon indicating an unplanned crime. But now we got another body and some semen, which suggests a wholly different scenario. Maybe a three-way, or maybe Rachel was doing a guy behind Olivia's back."

"Andrey Kaminski. He had access."

Panda bobbed his head. "But no motive."

I gnawed on that for a second. What could Andrey's motive be? Money? Sex? Killing Rachel and Olivia wouldn't give him more of either. "The only person I can think of who has one is Michael Rockwell. But why would Rachel sleep with him if they were divorcing?"

The mention of Michael's name jogged Panda's memory. "By the way, I asked about his alibi. Rockwell said he was on a train back to Connecticut."

"Was he?"

"He bought the ticket. No way to know if he was actually on the train."

"He couldn't name a witness?"

"Not a one."

"Is he a suspect?"

"Ask me that tomorrow. In the meantime, keep your distance from him. Send someone else to ask the questions this time."

This was why Panda wanted to see me. The Globe-Trotter tip was just the bait. He could have told me earlier, or over the phone, but he'd held on to that little nugget to lure me to the park in person, so he could make sure I'd gotten the message about Rockwell.

He drained the rest of his Sprite. "I mean it, Shaw. Stay away."

I left Panda in the park and returned to the Haverford, where our satellite truck had been joined by vans from every other major network, plus crews from the syndicated entertainment-news shows, *Extra, Inside Edition*, and *TMZ*. I even spotted a few reporters from the *Times* of London and the *International New York Times* milling around the police barricade.

I wanted to stay to make sure everything went off as planned, but I was exhausted. I'd hit a wall and felt like I was going to collapse if I didn't get home soon. I passed on to the crew what Panda had told me about Rachel's body being stuffed into a suitcase, then put in another two calls to the bureau. One to Sabine, to ask her to find pictures of Globe-Trotter suitcases we could use on air, and one to Barton Oberlink, one of *Topical Tonight*'s guest bookers, to ask him to try to get ahold of the Harts to book them for that night's broadcast. Then I walked over to Lexington and called a twenty-four-hour locksmith to come meet me at my apartment. It was one of those bright, brisk fall afternoons—nearly cloudless sky, golden sun, and the smell of sidewalk vendors roasting chestnuts in the air—that made living in a city like New York a real joy. But all I could think about was my bed, fresh sheets, and the shades drawn. I hailed a cab for home.

# nineteen

*Click, click.*

I heard a key scraping in the lock, the doorknob rattle.

"I had the locks changed!" I yelled from my bed, bolting up from my bed. "And I'm calling the police."

I felt for my phone and dialed 911 as panic sluiced through my veins. The clock on my dresser read 10:00 p.m. I'd been asleep for almost six hours. Not long enough, not by a long shot, but I had more immediate concerns at hand.

"Someone's trying to break into my house," I said into the phone. "My name is Clyde Shaw and I've been covering the Olivia Kravis murder investigation. Please send someone quick. Find Detective Tom Ehlers." I gave my address and stayed on the line as I felt for the knife at the back of my nightstand.

A few years earlier, I'd produced a segment about a woman who had successfully fought off a rapist who'd attacked her in bed. The perp had already raped and killed three other women in her Indianapolis neighborhood, and he would have done the same to her if she hadn't been able to arm herself quickly. She stabbed him three times, twice in the shoulder and once in the neck, killing him almost instantly. Three days after my report aired, the knife arrived via FedEx with a note from my dad. "Just in case," it read.

I sat down on the edge of my bed, knife in hand, and waited. Five minutes later, I heard pounding on my front door. "Police!" yelled a male voice from the other side. I slipped on a robe and looked through the peephole to confirm that it was indeed a pair of uniformed officers before I let them in. "Did you see anyone out there?" I asked.

The tall one looked at the blade in my trembling hand. "You mind putting that down, ma'am?"

I put the knife down on the tiny table in my entryway and began to explain what had happened. The shorter officer unclipped the handheld transceiver from his belt. "I'll check the perimeter." He let himself out the front door as the tall officer told me to take a seat. "You sure you heard someone?"

I rubbed my temples, mentally spent. Had I dreamed it? Was this yet another hallucination? I didn't think so, but I couldn't be sure.

There was another knock as Ehlers popped his head around the door frame. "We seem to be making a habit of this," he said to me, not unkindly.

I smiled, relieved that I'd gotten him instead of Restivo.

He took out his pen and notebook. "From the top, Ms. Shaw."

I repeated my story. Ehlers wrote everything down and told me they'd be keeping a unit outside my apartment building that night in case the perp came back. "I'm glad you changed the locks," he said, closing his notebook.

I cinched my robe closed and studied him. "You look beat," I told him. "You ever get any time off?"

"Probably as much as you do," he replied, showing himself to the front door. "Call me if anything else happens."

After the two patrolmen left, I bolted my door and went back to bed only to find that I was completely wired. I peeked out my window and saw the squad car parked just outside, watching the front door to my building, but I still felt freaked-out. A pot of chamomile tea didn't do much to calm my nerves, so I gave in to temptation and started checking the messages on my cell. There were forty. Most of them came from Georgia, Alex, and Jen. While I was asleep, the medical examiner had released Olivia's preliminary autopsy—it wouldn't be complete until the toxicology reports came in, and those would take at least another two weeks—and the ME had granted his first interview to GSBC, confirming Olivia's manner of death as homicide and cause of death as bludgeoning. "Whore-on-My-Dick managed to level another shocker," Jen said on the voice mail she'd left me. "Rachel Rockwell was pregnant."

I fired up my desktop computer. There was already a smattering of articles online about Rachel's pregnancy. Many speculated on how far along she was, who the father was, and whether this mystery man was also the killer. ABC News had an online piece referencing a study that said murder accounted for 20 percent of deaths among pregnant women. Almost every article linked to the video of Whorelick interviewing the medical examiner. He had confirmed that Rachel was with child at her time of death and refused to make any further comments on her case. I kicked the wall in frustration. We'd gotten creamed.

But worse than that, Rachel's autopsy—the semen, her pregnancy—threw doubt on what Andrey Kaminski had told me. He'd claimed it had been over between them for a long time, but now that it was apparent that Rachel had indeed been sleeping with a man while she was dating Olivia, I no longer bought it. It was possible that Rachel and Michael had slept together in the midst of their divorce battle—that sort of thing sometimes happened—or that Rachel had a more active and varied sex life than any of us realized, but Andrey as the father seemed like the most plausible explanation. Could their rekindled affair be the reason Olivia and Rachel had been arguing that night?

I picked up my phone and dialed Kaminski. "You have a whole lot of explaining to do," I said into the receiver.

"I'm at work."

That was a surprise. "They haven't fired you yet?"

"No."

"I take it you've seen the news."

He sighed. "We should probably talk in person. I got tomorrow night off."

"Saturday night?" I couldn't help myself. I pictured Andrey at my stove, his shirtsleeves rolled up to reveal that tattoo. Hell, his shirt off. A bottle of red open on the table. Dave Matthews on the stereo. There were worse ways to spend an evening—if I hadn't also suspected him of impregnating a murder victim. "Tell me something: Did you get Rachel pregnant? The baby's obviously not Olivia's. And I'm guessing it's not Michael's either."

"I can't talk about that now."

His deep voice rolled over me, awakening something it shouldn't. What was it about this guy? Why was I so damn attracted to him? "Fine. Tomorrow. When and where?"

"Seven." He named a pub on First Avenue. Then there was silence. He'd hung up on me.

The bastard stood me up. Saturday at seven, he was nowhere to be seen and not answering his cell. I was two cranberry and seltzers in by the time I gave up. I walked home and nuked a frozen Marie Callender's for dinner. I went to sleep pissed as hell, and woke up even angrier. I went swimming at a pool near my apartment and ate a Belgian waffle smothered in maple syrup and butter for brunch. By Sunday midafternoon, I was ready to get back in the game. Georgia had barred me from the FirstNews building, but she couldn't stop me from getting back to work.

First thing I did was work up a new timeline. Rachel and Olivia came back to the Haverford around 10:00 p.m. The neighbors heard them arguing shortly thereafter. Olivia probably retreated to her office, Rachel the bedroom or living room. That's when the killer made his move, and my guess is he went for Rachel first. Olivia's death was messy and quick, whereas Rachel's killing seemed more methodical and clean, almost clinical. The killer had also taken the time to wrap Rachel's body in a garbage bag, which I knew could be significant, because of a case we'd covered about five years ago.

The remains of a young Denver mom had been found in a nature preserve fifteen miles from their two-story Tudor. The killer turned out to be her husband, who had been having an affair with a twenty-two-year-old he'd met while taking his kids out for hot-fudge sundaes at a local ice-cream shop. He'd slit his wife's throat, sawed her body into pieces in their toddler's bathroom, bagged her body (minus the head, which he tossed into the Arkansas, according to a later confession), and buried the whole thing six feet underground. We'd had a forensic psychologist on the show say the use of garbage bags was telling, because it meant that the killer wanted to literally dispose of his wife.

Assuming Rachel had been attacked first, the killer had to incapacitate Rachel—tie her up, knock her over the head, maybe suffocate her—before going after Olivia, because it would have been too risky to spring on Olivia with someone else moving around in the apartment. That was my theory, anyway. Killer was there when the women got back at ten. He waited for them to separate, then went to work. No cleanup for Olivia, but Rachel was carted off to the basement and locked away in Olivia's storage space so it would look like she was the murderer. That would at least buy him a few days to get his story straight. Olivia had been killed for loving Rachel, but Rachel was the killer's real prize.

There was only one problem with this theory. It didn't explain why Olivia had texted me that night that she needed to tell me something. *It's time you know the truth.* The truth about Rachel? Or about something else?

I called up the schedule that Olivia's assistant, Emma, had e-mailed over to me and looked again for anything out of the ordinary. There was nothing, but then again, if Olivia was doing something she didn't want others to know about, it wouldn't be on her official schedule. I started looking for big holes in her calendar. There were maybe a dozen total, but few were recent. In August and the first two weeks of September, it looked like she left the office every Tuesday and Thursday at three, and didn't come back until the next day. October she was back into work mode, with the exception of one Friday, which was just a holiday—a trip to a spa in the Berkshires, if memory served me correctly. Then, the week she was killed, she was also out of the office without explanation on a Wednesday. I flagged all these dates and times and sent an e-mail to Emma, asking her to try to remember what Olivia might have said she was doing on those days.

Though it was a Sunday, she called me back in less than an hour. "The Tuesdays and Thursdays in August were spent at her father's place. She was helping Charles's ghostwriter go through some of his old boxes of memorabilia for pictures and handwritten letters they could print alongside text in his memoir."

"And the days in October?"

"That Friday was a vacation day. The Wednesday she said she had a meeting, but she didn't tell me who she met with or where she was going."

"Was that unusual?"

"I assumed it was a doctor visit."

"Why? Was she going to the doctor frequently?"

Emma hesitated. "No. Not that I know of. I only said that because she usually told me where she was going, so I figured this was something private, like a—you know—gyno visit."

"Did she take a company car to this meeting?"

"I'll have to check on that for you."

After our call, I broke for a cranberry seltzer and handful of salted cashews. Then I called Detective Ehlers under the guise of wanting to know if they'd found out who'd spiked my drink, although what I really wanted to know was how far along Rachel was and whether they thought her pregnancy had anything to do with the double—make that now triple—homicide. Ehlers didn't get back to me, but Restivo did and not until I was halfway through another Marie Callender's.

"Good news first?" he asked.

"Give me the bad."

There was virtually no way of telling who had drugged me. The surveillance cameras weren't positioned to catch someone spiking my drink or following me into the bathroom, and no one from the catering company had been busted for anything more serious than petty larceny. There also weren't any surveillance cameras outside my building, which was contrary to what the super had told me, but not entirely surprising. The cops had no idea who had tried to break into my apartment the previous night.

I felt frustrated, but it wasn't Restivo's fault they had nothing. "What's the good?"

"You're alive."

That much was true, but I wanted to shift the discussion to the case. "Can you answer something for me?"

"Have you figured out what Olivia's text message meant?" he asked.

"No, but I'm working on it." I pressed my temples, feeling another headache coming on. "Andrey Kaminski was in the building. He's knowledgeable enough about the building's storage facilities and security cameras, and was presumably having an affair with one of the murder victims, who, it turns out, was pregnant. Why aren't you taking a closer look at him?"

"Who says we're not?"

In the background I could hear the sounds of a busy precinct. People calling to each other, chairs scraping across the floor. It was Sunday night and there was another big football game on ESPN, Jets versus Patriots. But these guys were putting in hours. Even if Restivo was being tight-lipped, he was putting up with my questions. That meant he was in a good mood. It all added up to something: they had a lead. I popped open my Excedrin bottle and dry-swallowed two pills.

"Is the baby Kaminski's or the husband's?" I was convinced Andrey was the baby's father. The question was why he'd lied to me about being dumped by Rachel. If he was the killer, he would know that it was only a matter of time before Rachel's body was found and her pregnancy revealed. He would also know that there would be physical evidence on her corpse disproving what he'd told me—and presumably the cops—about the status of their relationship.

"You know I can't answer that," Restivo said.

"Well, how far along was Rachel?"

Restivo gave a low chuckle into the receiver. "That will be in the autopsy, Ms. Shaw."

"Which is not currently available."

"Correct."

"When will it be?" I pounded on my chest to help the pills on their way.

"Can't say. Why don't you ask the ME?"

"You'll call me as soon as it comes in?"

"You got it, lady. Because I got nothing better to do."

# Monday

# twenty

Monday got off to a rough start. Diskin reamed me out for losing the Rockwell pregnancy scoop to GSBC. Then Fred Wallace yelled at me. And then Alex. None of them seemed to remember or care that all this had happened after I'd been drugged at a company function and explicitly banned from the office by Georgia. I was almost grateful once it was time for our weekly storyboard meeting, which was preceded by a morning of making phone calls that were never returned and putting together a package that was entirely made up of regurgitated news and too many question marks. That got me to lunch.

In the afternoon we taped an interview with Olivia's housekeeper, Ilsa Chavez, but she was old news, and basically had nothing to add except that she hadn't noticed that Rachel was pregnant. Alex dug a little, and the housekeeper revealed that Rachel had been wearing an oversize pajama top that could have easily concealed a nascent baby mound when she'd been introduced to her at Olivia's apartment. Not my—or the network's—finest hour, but we wouldn't pitch it that way to our viewers. *Shocking new information in the Kravis murder case* was how we'd sell it. Our audience deserved better than a nightshirt that revealed nothing.

I checked my watch. It was already 6:00 p.m. Time to get rolling if I was going to make it to the fund-raiser on time. "You going home first?" I asked Alex, who was sitting next to me in the editing room.

He leaned back in his chair, stretching his arms overhead. "Gonna change in the bathroom. You?"

I got up from the desk. "Same."

He gave me another one of his quarterback smiles. "Holler if you need help with a zipper."

"Don't hold your breath," I said lightly. Letting myself out of the tiny room with my stack of papers tucked up against my chest, I marched my sorry mood into the ladies' room, where I slipped on a black knee-length column that displayed just the right amount of cleavage and did some sort of voodoo on my waist to make it look half its usual size. Last, I strapped on the sparkly black stilettos I'd purchased at Olivia's insistence; she believed every woman should own at least one pair of leg-lengthening, confidence-boosting shoes, no matter how much they cost or how much they hurt. These were sheer torture after fifteen minutes of standing, which explained why I barely ever wore them.

I might consider wearing them more often, though, if Phil Drucker's reaction to seeing me was what I could expect every time I slipped them on. He picked me up outside the FirstNews building in a hired Town Car and whistled. "That dress looks like it was made for you."

I touched my chignon. It had taken about twenty bobby pins and half a can of hair spray, but the results were better than expected. "I clean up all right," I said, blushing a little.

He held open the car door for me. "That's a whopping understatement."

In the car, Phil asked me how work was going. He and I had corresponded a few times over the weekend—he'd actually asked me out for a drink on Sunday afternoon, a "pregame warm-up" for our big date night—and I'd begged off, using work as an excuse to stay home and finish recuperating in sweatpants. "Could be better, could be worse," I said.

He tapped his fingers on the faux-wood paneling on the car door. "Well, tonight should be interesting."

Our car pulled up outside the Time Warner Center at Columbus Circle. We checked our coats in the lobby of the Mandarin Oriental and rode an elevator up to the thirty-sixth floor to the hotel's ballroom. The space boasted eighteen-foot ceilings, three massive crystal chandeliers, and floor-to-ceiling windows offering sweeping views of Central Park and the twinkling Manhattan skyline. But other than the magnificent view, and despite the best efforts of the event planner's decorator and florist, the space couldn't shake its sterile feel. We might as well have been dining in one of the FirstNews conference rooms.

I found our table assignment while Phil hit the bar. He returned with a glass of champagne for himself and a Coke for me. He looked sweet in his tuxedo, but if there had been any spark between us the other day, it was long gone. The day I'd met him at his office I'd been high on adrenaline, just coming from meeting Rockwell and trying to escape an old flame. Now, with the moment of danger well behind us, I saw Phil for what he was: a nice lawyer with a better-than-average sense of humor. Olivia would have loved him. I was pretty sure I couldn't. What was wrong with me? Why couldn't I fall for a good guy?

He held out my Coke. "I just met Georgia Jacobs."

"Starstruck?" I asked, taking my soda.

He flubbed his lips. "Who me? Not at all."

I laughed at his self-deprecating humor. "What was she ordering?"

"A martini, three olives. She also told me to take good care of you tonight."

"What did you say?"

He took a sip of his champagne. "I told her that you were more than capable of looking after yourself."

"Georgia has a habit of forgetting that."

"Here's to not forgetting anything." He clinked his glass against mine and took a second sip. I hesitated, remembering the ketamine that had been slipped into my drink at the Maldone party.

"Something the matter?" Phil asked.

I shook off my paranoia and took a sip of Coke, scanning the room for potential sources and interview subjects.

Phil peered over my shoulder. "I see one of my partners."

I turned around to find an overweight Persian man waving politely at us.

"Let's go say hello. I'll introduce you." Phil dragged me by the hand across the reception area. The man made a short bow and proffered a big white smile, but his dark eyes looked distracted. "How's your wife? Is she here tonight?" Phil asked.

"She is." The man arched his back, his stomach straining the gold studs of his shirt. "In fact, I must find her before the dinner starts. Enjoy your night."

"You as well." Phil waited a few moments before murmuring low into my ear that Reza was usually a far more affable sort of man. "It must be because he's worried about losing his client," he said.

"What client?"

"The Kravis Foundation is a firm client. I thought you knew."

I took a step back. "How would I know that?" It came out sounding harsher than intended.

Phil set his glass down and took my hand once again, leading me to a table at the front entrance where invitations and foundation materials were laid out in neat fans. Selecting a booklet filled with pictures of smiling children—recipients of the foundation's largesse—he flipped to the last page. "We're listed as one of the main sponsors," he said, pointing to his firm's name.

"So you are." I couldn't believe I'd missed such a connection. Michael Rockwell worked for Bennett & Wayne, which worked for the Kravis family and their foundation. I'd bet anything Rachel had met Olivia through Michael, and I could only imagine how that made him feel. To a status-obsessed man like Michael, Andrey didn't really pose much of a threat, but Olivia, with all her millions, sure did.

"What kind of work does the firm do for the Kravises?" I asked Phil.

"I suppose it's public knowledge we represent the foundation. Much of the work is pro bono. We used to represent the corporate entity that controls the family's holdings, but not anymore."

"Why not?"

He shook his head at me. "You don't give up easy, do you?"

I repeated my question. "Why did the Kravises dump Bennett and Wayne?"

"I don't know for sure, since it's not my department. But my understanding is that changes were made as Charles stepped away from management of the family's assets. That's not entirely unusual."

"If they fired the firm from doing the revenue-generating stuff, why keep working pro bono?"

He shrugged. "Different relationships."

"Did Michael Rockwell work for Kravis?"

He hesitated.

"Phil, this could be important."

"He worked on a couple of acquisitions for them."

"Do the police know about this?"

"I have no idea, Clyde, but I'd assume so. None of this is classified information."

The dinner gong sounded, clearing out most of the room. Out of the corner of my eye, I saw Monica Kravis, Olivia's stepmother, walking into the main dining room. Her platinum hair was pulled into a low ponytail, and she wore a conservative navy taffeta gown. Even after all these years she was still a great beauty. Charles Kravis had written in his memoir that he'd fallen in love with her at first sight, across a crowded table somewhere in the South of France. At the time, he was still full of ambition and energy, eager to experience everything, conquer everything—including women. And while the book was surprisingly candid about Charles's roving eye and "romantic nature" prior to meeting Monica, it led readers to believe that the affairs had ended with the start of his second marriage. I'd heard too many rumors over the years to believe that to be true, but if this woman hadn't been able to tame the infamous hound, I doubt anyone could.

Phil and I entered the main dining room, snaking around a dozen round tables to find Alex seated alone at ours. He was dressed in a well-cut tux, looking almost unfairly handsome. He got up and gave me a kiss on the cheek, pulling back the chair next to his. "Keep me company."

I gestured at all the other empty seats as I sat down. "Where is everyone?"

"Diskin's making the rounds with Georgia."

"And the rest?"

"No clue."

Phil sat down next to me as Diskin and Georgia and their respective spouses arrived at the table. I got up and walked around the table to greet Georgia, who, in a floor-length raspberry dress and matching eyeglasses, was wearing enough perfume to kill a small dog. My eyes watered as I leaned into the cloud of her canary-colored hair. "Rockwell's law firm used to do corporate work for the Kravis family. Rockwell, specifically, handled their account."

"You think that's how they met?" Georgia turned to me, not bothering to lower her voice. The noise around us prevented anyone from overhearing what we were saying.

"I'd bet my job on it," I replied, but Georgia wasn't listening. She was looking across the table at my twenty-four-year-old assistant. Sabine. Sabine, who was Alex's date. She looked incredible. Swallowing hard, I returned to my seat.

"Great dress," she said to me, leaning across Alex's lap, her silky brown hair dangling into his groin. Her abbreviated black frock exposed a generous amount of creamy thigh.

"Sabine, I'd like you to meet Philip Drucker," I said.

Sabine waved at Phil, who gave her a polite but disinterested nod. Alex put his hand on Phil's shoulder. "He's her dinner companion." The way he'd said *companion*, I knew he'd already pumped Phil for a backstory, which was as short as Sabine's skirt.

Diskin fluffed out his napkin and addressed Phil. "My apologies in advance. Shaw needs to work this thing tonight. I'm afraid you two aren't going to be seeing much of each other."

Phil shrugged good-naturedly. "That's OK by me. As long as I'm the guy who gets to take her home tonight."

"Shaw, as soon as the speeches are over, I want you to go make the rounds." Diskin gestured at the two unoccupied seats at our table. "Where's Mike?"

I'd thought the night couldn't get any more awkward. Mike Fischer hosted the political show that led into *Topical Tonight*. He was also the reason I could never show my face at Coyote Cinco's again. I'd had two margaritas and five shots of tequila the first time we hooked up in the men's room; the second time, I can't even remember. My only consolation was that Mike would be seated next to Sabine, and knowing him, he'd have a hell of a time keeping his eyes off all the skin on display.

"I made the seating arrangements," Georgia announced, winking at me.

"Cheers," I said, lifting my water glass to her. At least someone had my back.

Diskin looked at his watch as Mike and his wife finally arrived. She was painfully thin and pale, with short auburn hair and a brittle smile. Mike sat down, forgetting to pull out his wife's chair. "Sorry I'm late, Mitchell. Linda forgot to order a car."

Phil hopped up to help Linda into her seat. "So nice to see you again," I said to her across the table. She held her wineglass up to be filled, ignoring me.

With everyone seated, we could all dig into the starter course, a cheese soufflé and salad plate that was remarkable only in its near-total lack of flavor. I gave up after a few bites. Alex nudged me and nodded toward the stage, where Delphine Kravis was standing behind a plexiglass podium. She was dressed in a brown-lace, knee-length gown, her thick hair pulled back in a coordinating headband. "Good evening and thank you all for coming," she said into the microphone. Her voice was clear and assured.

Public speaking was one thing I'd never come close to mastering. I'd tried going in front of the camera once, early in my career, and it had been a disaster. I'd stuttered, broke out in a cold sweat, and forgot my own name. The producer who had given me the on-air shot avoided me like the plague from then on, and it took the better part of a year for my colleagues to forget the incident. Personally, I'd never gotten over it.

Delphine, by contrast, sounded like an old pro thanking the crowd for their charitable donations, which, she informed the crowd, had totaled over $2 million and would go to feed, clothe, and educate underprivileged children in the poorest communities in the United States and around the world. She stepped away from the podium, waiting for the applause to die down before continuing.

"As some of you may know, my stepsister, Olivia, was going to speak this evening. I know Olivia was very much looking forward to tonight, to telling you all about the good works the Charles S. Kravis Foundation has helped fund this year through your generosity and support. Many of you know that for the last ten years my sister played an integral and tireless role at the foundation, directing grants and helping organize tonight's event and other fund-raising efforts throughout the year. But what many of you may not know is that Olivia was also personally involved in many of our missions, accompanying our volunteer doctors, relief workers, and teachers on several trips each year. She was a shining light, a role model, and a loving friend to all who had the privilege of knowing her. In her memory, we have created the Olivia Kravis Grant, which will be awarded annually to an individual or group working with children in need in Central America."

Delphine paused again for applause as the entire room rose for an ovation. My thoughts ran to Olivia, and how much I wished she could be here to see this. As I pushed away a tear with my forefinger, two white cotton handkerchiefs appeared in front of me. One from Alex and one from Phil. I waved them both off as we all returned to our seats.

"Now I would like to introduce Naomi Zell. As one of the foundation's board members, she has intimate knowledge of everything that we do, and is, as my sister was, a passionate advocate for children's rights. This year she testified along with Olivia on Capitol Hill on behalf of Senator Epstein's child-poverty bill; together they were lauded as a clear yet impassioned voice for underprivileged youth. I'd like for you to join me in welcoming Naomi here tonight."

Naomi took the stage, acknowledging Delphine with a quick nod before looking out over the podium and beginning her speech. She was of medium height and dressed in a black knit suit significantly enlivened by a large diamond-and-pearl flower-shaped brooch. Her dark hair was coiffed in a shoulder-grazing bob and pulled away from her face with a pair of diamond combs. Everything about her was business, from her sensible mid-height heels to the tenor of her voice as she delivered a ten-minute speech that was about as forgettable as the starter course. By the time she left the stage, most of us had checked our e-mail half a dozen times.

Phil excused himself to go to the men's room. A second later Alex leaned toward my ear. "Gee, I'm glad that's over," he whispered into my neck.

"Stop doing that. It's rude," I said, admonishing him.

"You're no fun, Shaw. And not very nice either."

"What's that supposed to mean?"

He put his finger on the wrinkle between my eyes. "Your date. He's clearly in over his head."

I batted his hand away and nodded at Sabine. "If anyone's over their head, it's her."

We both looked at her. She'd spent the dinner listening to Mike Fischer brag about his recently released drivel on the state of American politics, drivel that had spent eighteen weeks on the *New York Times* hardcover bestseller list. Fischer's wife, meanwhile, had passed the hour staring at her husband with silent fury. "You haven't said more than five words to her since we sat down."

Alex grinned wryly. "She'll have my full attention later."

I held my hand up. "Spare me the details."

A fleet of waiters descended on the table, depositing platters of filet mignon and filling my red-wine glass before I could tell them not to. The food was awful, and the wine was calling to me. Just one sip wouldn't be the end of the world, would it? Everyone else seemed to be enjoying it. Sabine was on her third. I picked up my glass when I thought no one was looking, but apparently I was wrong. Georgia's fingers snapped at me from across the table.

"Having a good time?"

We both knew what she meant. I set my glass down, hot with shame. "Best Monday-night gala I've attended in years. How about you? Are you having fun?"

She barked at me from behind her water glass: "Girl, the night is long, and so is my memory."

Diskin was oblivious to the subtext of my exchange with Georgia, but he had more of his own for me. "Speeches are over, Clyde," he said. In other words: get to work.

Alex stood as I pushed my chair away from the table. Grabbing my evening bag, which was stocked with my phone, tape recorder, business cards, and a safety pin in case of a wardrobe emergency, I crossed the empty dance floor, glancing at the Kravis table. Charles Kravis was in a wheelchair, a nurse hovering behind him. Monica, his wife, sat next to him, clutching his hand. Delphine and her husband and Naomi Zell and her husband were also seated at the table. I jotted a quick note on a napkin, asking Delphine to come meet me in one of the meeting rooms behind the bank of elevators at the entrance, and handed it to a waiter along with a twenty-dollar bill. "For the woman in brown," I said. "Delphine Kravis."

But it was Naomi Zell who waltzed into the meeting room five minutes later, waving my scribbled-on napkin in the air. She took a chair at the conference-room table and folded her hands in her lap. "I'm as close as you're going to get to the Kravises tonight, Clyde. As I know you've been told, any press inquiries related to Olivia's death come through me. I'm the family spokesperson. Now take a seat."

I stayed standing. "How do you know who I am?"

Naomi rolled her eyes. "Your name is Clyde Shaw. You work for Georgia Jacobs on *Topical*, and up until a few minutes ago, you've been doing a commendable job."

"Then why—"

Naomi held up a plump hand. "My impression is that for you this is both personal and professional. But you have to respect the family's privacy. If you don't, I will have to take certain steps. Do you understand what I'm saying?"

She wanted me to back off. "I'm just following Diskin's orders."

"I will be happy to discuss the situation with him." Naomi called the shots. Until the deal with Maldone Enterprises was etched in stone, she controlled the network, she controlled Diskin, and she controlled me.

She straightened her posture, pulling at the hem of her knit jacket. "Now, please take a seat. I have some questions of my own for you."

# twenty-one

I remained standing. "What do you mean, questions for *me*?"

"What's your connection to this family?"

I told her about my childhood friendship with Olivia, and how she had helped me get my job at the network.

"Before last Monday, I'd never heard of you. Now I'm spending my time meeting with lawyers about you getting drugged at a company party, and not just any party, but a party celebrating the pending merger of FirstNews with Maldone Enterprises." She paused, studying my face. "Don't take this the wrong way, but what were you doing there?"

It was a fair question, so I gave her an honest answer. "Georgia asked me. She thought I could meet a man there. I'm single."

"Ah." She nodded in comprehension. "Did you?"

"The only man I talked to was Prentice Maldone, and he only wanted to talk about the case."

"What did you tell him?"

"Nothing we haven't already reported on air."

"Good." Her mouth curved into something approaching a smile.

"Ms. Zell, is there something I should know? Is Olivia's death related to the merger?"

"Call me Naomi." She again motioned for me to take a chair. This time I obliged. "Was Olivia opposed to the sale?"

"Olivia was adamantly *in favor* of the merger. She knew her father was ailing, and she wasn't interested in taking on a larger role herself. The economic conditions could have been more favorable if we'd waited, but she wanted out now, even if it meant everyone walked away with less."

"What about you? Is this what you wanted?" I asked.

"All good things must come to an end, Clyde. In terms of what was best for the company, the board ultimately reached the consensus that this was the right decision. This was the best scenario we could have hoped for."

The way she was talking made me think that there had been a fight to keep the company in Kravis hands. "Who was against it? Who stood to lose from it?"

"In every merger there are those in favor and those who aren't. In fact, it wouldn't have been normal if everyone had been in perfect agreement." Naomi folded her hands in her lap. "I know what you might be thinking, but until we are notified to the contrary, you should assume that Olivia's tragic murder and the network's pending merger are two separate and distinct events."

"And what about what happened to me at the party to celebrate the merger? Is that a separate and distinct event too?"

Naomi regarded me through narrow eyes. "This has all been off the record, you know?"

"I did not know that. Who opposed the merger, Naomi?"

She shook her head in disappointment. I wasn't the team player she'd pegged me for. "You know what, on second thought, I think I'd rather see Olivia's murder go unsolved than risk the life of another valued member of the FirstNews family." She plucked a business card from her jacket pocket and held it out for me. "Now that I have a better understanding of you and the situation, I'm going to advise Diskin to reassign you. This case will be handed to another producer."

"Who opposed the deal with Maldone?"

She put her card down and stood up. "I understand your motivations, Clyde. I do. But you are going to have to trust me that my primary concern is for the health and longevity of this network. Idle speculation along the lines of what you're suggesting could put FirstNews and its thousands of employees in financial jeopardy. Can you imagine what Wall Street would do if they even got a whiff of scandal coming off this deal?"

"I don't care about that."

She blinked. "And that is why as of this moment you are no longer covering Olivia's case. Is that understood?"

I pounded the table with my fist. "You can't do that."

"You may not like it, but this is the way it's going to be."


On my way back to the ballroom, I made a bad turn and ended up down a hall of small meeting rooms. I heard a voice, then a giggle, and being the nosy journalist that I am, I couldn't just forget about it and continue on my way like a normal person. Crouching low to the ground, I stuck my nose around the door frame.

The overheads were out, but there was enough light coming from the windows for me to make out Sabine's face and Alex's profile. From my vantage point, I could see that he had her up on the table, his face buried in her neck, his hands working beneath her short skirt. Sabine's dress fell off her shoulder, exposing a grapefruit-shaped breast. She whimpered with pleasure as his mouth found her nipple. The next thing I heard was his zipper.

I slipped back out, praying neither of them had seen me, wishing I hadn't seen what I did as I stumbled back down the hall and passed by the doors to the kitchen. A waiter burst through, carrying a tray of champagne glasses. I sped up and pilfered two of them. Then I went into the bathroom and downed them both, one after the other, the bubbles tickling the back of my throat, tasting like heaven, warming my belly. I wanted more.


"OK, so what happened?"

Georgia and I were downstairs, waiting in line at the coat check. Husband number four had left midway through the filet mignon, mumbling something about a conference call with Hong Kong, and Diskin and his wife had taken off immediately after the crème caramel. We were all free to go. "You look like a pig at a Memphis barbecue," she said accusingly.

I threw my hands up. "What does that even mean?"

"It means, sugar pie, that your face is redder than the blood that used to come out of my hoo-ha every goddamn month and your breath smells like the peppermints they got in the ladies'."

I'd grabbed a handful of them in the bathroom after downing the champagne. Then I'd hit the bar, sucked down a vodka tonic and a glass of red abandoned on a table in the reception area.

"What the fuck just happened?" Georgia asked.

"Naomi Zell and I had a tête-à-tête. I'm off Olivia's story, and I'm not allowed to get within ten feet of any of the Kravises. The network is hiding something. Or they're afraid I'll uncover something that will mess up the merger. Why else would she pull me off the case?"

Georgia took off her glasses. "You told her to stuff it, I hope."

"But I thought you didn't want me on this story either."

"That ain't the point."

Phil draped Georgia's chinchilla cape over her shoulders. The fur was overkill given the evening's mild weather, but Georgia flaunted her furs whenever possible. "That it?" Georgia asked, giving me a knowing look.

I handed Phil the claim ticket for my black wool topper. "Would you mind?"

We watched him file back into the coat-check line. Georgia linked her arm in mine and lowered her voice to just above a whisper. "Fess up, child."

Sometimes I loved that nothing got by her—other times, not so much. "If you must know, I caught Alex and Sabine going at it in one of the meeting rooms."

Georgia planted a hand on her hip, her eyes two thin slits. "Christ in heaven, you are so much worse off than I thought."

"She's my assistant. I'm his producer. It's normal for me to be weirded out."

She clucked admonishingly. "You drinking tonight?"

"Everything OK?" Phil asked as he helped me into my coat.

I shot Georgia a pleading look.

"This girl is a workaholic. I'm always telling her she needs to get a life outside the office."

"Point taken," I said.

"Get her home safe," Georgia said, giving Phil a meaningful look before leaving to find her Escalade.

"What was that all about?" he asked.

"I think she just really likes you," I said lightly as Phil led me to his Town Car. In the backseat, I slid a little closer to him, pressing my back against Phil's body. "Thanks for coming tonight. I owe you one."

"No problem." He gave my leg a fraternal pat in return. "Georgia's a hoot."

I reached for the inside of his thigh.

He pulled away. "I think you and I are in different places."

"What's that supposed to mean?"

He took a breath, adjusting his glasses. "You're beautiful, Clyde. And smart, and passionate about what you do, but I just don't see this working out."

I couldn't believe he was rejecting me. I pictured Alex and Sabine, remembering the sound of his zipper and her moans. God, how I missed that kind of sex. Urgent. Dirty. *Dangerous.* I looked out the window, suddenly furious. We were at a red light and about to turn down Park Avenue.

"Look, if things change—"

"Don't hold your breath." My voice was jagged and sharp. I opened the car door and jumped out. Then I slammed the door behind me and ran for the curb.

I stood there, angry and horny, an old, familiar feeling stirring deep within me, a hungry recklessness that had been lying there blessedly dormant. There was only one place I could think of going. Crossing Park Avenue, I hailed a taxi. "I'm going uptown. But first, I need to find an open liquor store."


Andrey opened the door to the Haverford. His jacket was off and shirtsleeves rolled up. I took his arm, tracing the scales of his tattoo.

He smiled. "Looks like someone's been having fun."

*Not nearly enough.* I handed him the open bottle of vodka in my hand. "Is there somewhere we can go?"

"Not here."

I took the bottle back, pouting. "Fine. I'll go then."

He pulled me back into him, his hands pressing my body to his so I could feel that he was already aroused. "It's not that I don't want you," he said.

"Quickly then."

He took a key from his pants and bolted the front door. In the elevator, I felt his lips on mine, his hands all over my body. We reached the basement floor. He pulled me into the hall, unzipping my dress to my waist, liberating my breasts from the satin cups of my bra. A second key led us to a small, pitch-black room. It smelled of WD-40, dust, and men's cologne. Andrey pushed me down on a couch and stood over me. I reached for his belt buckle and dropped his pants, taking his cock in my mouth. For the next few minutes, I was happy. This is what I'd come for, what I'd wanted. But when he bent back down, stripping off my wet panties, positioning himself to enter me, I pressed my hand firmly on his chest. "Aren't you going to use a condom?"

"What?" His brow was slick with sweat, his breath loud in my ear.

"A condom," I repeated, but the moment was already over. I couldn't do this. Not here. Not like this. Not even drunk as I was. Andrey was involved in my best friend's murder. Even for me, this was too far over the line. What the hell was I doing? I maneuvered out from under him, adjusting my dress. "I'm sorry, but I can't."

"You sure?" he panted.

I nodded. "Maybe another time."

He stood to buckle his pants. Then he walked a few paces in the murky darkness and flicked a switch, flooding the room with fluorescent light. I rubbed my eyes, which were struggling to adjust to the light, and realized that Andrey had taken me to the super's office. There was a desk and a computer, a shelving system lined with toolboxes and toilet plungers, and at the back of the tiny chamber, where I was sitting, a silk-upholstered couch that had probably once belonged to one of the co-op tenants. It had seen better days.

Andrey couldn't bring himself to look at me, and I got a flash of the man who looked so vulnerable in the coffee shop, talking about how Rachel had left him once Michael filed for divorce. "Take your time getting out of here," Andrey said, gesturing to the small fridge under the super's desk. "There's water in there if you're thirsty."

"Thanks."

"Just do me a favor and close the door to the office when you leave." He pivoted on his heel, gave me an awkward salute, and was gone.

I'd had more humiliating moments in more unlikely places. And yet sitting there, half-drunk, half-exposed, my bare ass on a ratty old couch I wouldn't want to touch with a gloved hand, I felt incredibly ashamed and disappointed in myself. I'd worked so hard for my sobriety. *Damn it, Clyde.*

Reaching under the couch for one of my shoes, I felt something hard and cool. It was a key ring. Each of the keys was clearly marked—"Super's Office," "Roof," and so on. One was simply marked "Keys." Andrey would be looking for these since he couldn't unlock the front door without them. I quickly finished dressing and had my hand on the door to go upstairs when it dawned on me that I was in the super's office—with keys.

Despite my warnings from Naomi Zell to back off the story, I couldn't let an opportunity like this pass me by. Olivia had been clobbered with a crystal vase; her pregnant girlfriend had been suffocated and stuffed into a garbage bag and suitcase, and someone thought I knew more than I did—why else would I have been drugged? Plus, I couldn't shake the feeling that I was somehow responsible for what had happened to these women. The text. If only I'd read it on Friday night. *It's time you know the truth.*

Yes, it was time. My eyes settled on an army-green lockbox mounted to the wall above the light switch. A second later I had it open. Someone had done a good job marking each of the hooks with its corresponding apartment number. I found Olivia's key, slipped it off the hook, and closed the lockbox just as the doorknob turned behind me. A split second later, Andrey stood in the door-way. "Did I leave my keys down here?" he asked.

I held them up. "Just found them." He walked over to me and grabbed them, finally bringing himself to look at me. "You OK?"

I wiped a film of perspiration from my upper lip. "Actually, I don't feel so well. Could I take another minute?"

His eyes danced around the room. He didn't feel comfortable leaving me there, but he nodded anyway.


Climbing sixteen flights of stairs left me winded, sweaty, and more sober than I'd been in the super's office. For the first time, it occurred to me that I was not only risking my career, I was also breaking the law and had no idea what I hoped to find. The police would have cleared out any important pieces of evidence days ago. And yet, there I was, key in hand.

I opened Olivia's front door and felt for the light. I stood in the foyer, the white marble cool beneath my bare feet, the light bounc-ing off the gleaming surface of an old Venetian mirror. Someone had cleaned. There was no sign of the crime-scene unit's handiwork, no fingerprint dust, no tape, no little evidence placards littered here and there. The kitchen was spotless, as were the mirrored dining room, hallways, and bathrooms. But in the living room, squares had been cut from the striped upholstery of Olivia's sofa and the sisal rug near it. The police had evidently found something in those places—bodily fluids were my guess—which they had then tested for DNA.

Doubling back on my steps, I crossed the vestibule leading to Olivia's small home office, a guest bedroom, and finally Olivia's master suite. It was large and spacious, and smelled like the powdery perfume she favored. I sat on the tufted stool of a vanity. Dozens of photographs were stuck inside the frame of the mirror, most depicting Olivia with the children she'd helped over the years, and a few dated back to her youth. At the bottom corner of the mirror I found a pair of photographs of us together. One was a snapshot she'd recently asked a tourist to take of us in the park. The other dated back to our childhood. We were in our bathing suits, towels wrapped around our thirteen-year-old bodies.

I remembered the summer that picture was taken. The Kravises had invited me to stay at their house on Nantucket, a gray-shingled giant overlooking the sparkling blue ocean. I was headed into the eighth grade, and would have been happy staying in a tent if it enjoyed a cool breeze and meant escaping the city's brutal summer cocktail of heat and humidity. We passed our days swimming in the pool and in the ocean, making friendship bracelets on the veranda, and hassling the cook for hot-fudge sundaes and macadamia-nut cookies in between mealtimes. Every once in a while our presence was requested at a breakfast or lunch helmed by Olivia's stepmother—Charles was always working and never in sight—but for the most part, we were left to our own devices and whims.

My stay happened to coincide with the Fourth of July weekend. That year the Kravises had planned a gigantic party—two hundred guests, including a handful of lawmakers, television pundits, and movie stars. There was a twenty-piece band, fancy canapés, and an impressive fireworks display after sundown. There was a big white tent, patriotic ice sculptures, and bartenders dressed up like George Washington and Ben Franklin. Olivia and I had been repeatedly instructed to stay away from the festivities, but we couldn't resist the call of miniature éclairs and sugar-glazed cream puffs in the shape of tiny swans. Dressed in our nightgowns and slippers, we made it to the kitchen only to discover the sweets had already been moved to an outdoor buffet. I wanted to go back upstairs, but Olivia insisted no one would notice us, so we forged into the crowd. I lost sight of her and spun around, knocking into Charles. I'd spilled his glass of red wine on his white shirt and khaki pants. He laughed it off, ruffling my red waves under his giant hand and asking me what my name was. "You're Tipsy Shaw's daughter?" I remember him asking as Monica escorted me back to Olivia's room on the mansion's third floor. A few minutes later, a member of the house staff arrived with Olivia in tow and then kept careful watch over us for the remainder of the evening. The following morning, I was sent home. That fall, Olivia was sent to Switzerland. It was years before we reconnected again.

I plucked the photo out of the mirror frame, dislodging a few others I hadn't meant to disturb. One of them fell behind the vanity. I felt for it, loosening a bunch of papers and envelopes that must have gotten jammed behind there in the same way. I stuffed what I could of them in my purse, along with the photo I'd wanted, before scanning the room for places Olivia might have hidden important documents or love letters. There was nothing under the bed or the mattress, nothing in the bedside table. I hit the home office next, plowing through more drawers. There I just found bills, pamphlets, and more business cards, all seemingly work-related.

I glanced at my watch. More than ten minutes had passed since Andrey left me in the super's office. I needed to get back downstairs, return Olivia's key, shut the door to the super's office, and make my excuses to Andrey. I grabbed my shoes by the front door and locked the apartment from the outside, then flew down the stairs to the basement to return her key to the lockbox, then back up to the lobby, pausing for a minute to regain my breath.

Andrey didn't look happy to see me. He opened the building's door with a clenched jaw and followed me outside. Beneath the hunter-green awning he grabbed my arm roughly. "Where were you?"

"What do you mean?" I asked lightly.

He dropped my arm and lit a cigarette. "I saw you took Olivia's key. Is that why you came here? Do you know what that makes you?"

I froze. "What?"

"Why'd you come here?"

"I was drunk. The rest should be obvious. I have a problem, Andrey."

"So you're a fucking sex addict?" He'd meant it as a joke.

I hesitated too long.

"You?" He blew smoke through his nostrils, deciding whether or not to believe me. "Why were you up in Olivia's apartment?" he finally asked.

"I didn't want to vomit all over your boss's office, so I grabbed Olivia's key. It was the only thing I could think of doing."

"There's a bathroom in the laundry room."

"I didn't know that. Do you really think I'm the kind of woman who would fuck someone to get into a victim's apartment? I may have a boatload of issues, but let me tell you something: if I'd really wanted to get into Olivia's apartment, I would have just asked you, or the building manager, or even the PD. I could have gotten in there any number of ways. And none of them would have involved taking my clothes off. But hey, if that's the kind of person you think I am, then fuck you for real."

"Is it because I'm a doorman?"

I stabbed him in the chest with my index finger. "That's your issue, buddy. Not mine."

Andrey threw his cigarette to the ground and grabbed me around the waist, pulling me into him.

I pushed my palms against him. "Let me go."

"Not until you tell me why you stopped."

"Call me crazy, but I don't like being called a whore."

"That was just now. I'm talking about before, downstairs."

"Because of Olivia. And because you lied to me about when things ended with Rachel."

He let me go, his hands dropping to his sides.

"Is the baby yours?"

"I didn't know about the baby," he said sheepishly.

"I want the truth. Right now. What's the story with you two? Were you sleeping together the whole time? Was she just screwing Olivia to get access to her money, so she could leave her husband, set up her life here, and be with you?"

"It wasn't like that."

"Then *tell* me what it was like."

He expelled a breath. "I fell for her. She was a beautiful woman. She didn't need to be with an asshole like him. I only wanted to help her. She broke up with me, just like I told you, but then it started up again after she got together with Olivia."

"Why did you lie to me?"

"Because I know how it looks."

"Did Michael ever hit Rachel, force her into sex? Rockwell has a history of taking what he wants, with or without permission."

"He told her that if she left him, he would destroy her. Her friends would turn on her, and because of the DUI he'd get full custody of the kids. Rachel needed money to fight him in court. Olivia was happy to help."

"Is that where Olivia came in? With that fat checkbook of hers?" I knew my friend. She gave freely and without strings. I'd paid her back every cent she'd lent me over the years, but only because I'd insisted. To a woman like Rachel, who'd had to claw herself out of nowhere to get to where she was, Olivia was an easy mark, a ticket to freedom from an abusive husband. I believed what Andrey had told me, but none of it justified how Rachel had used Olivia. I felt a fresh surge of anger. "Olivia got you your job. You two made a fool out of her—you two, screwing under her nose while Olivia wrote the checks. Is that why Rachel had Olivia get you hired here? So you two could fuck whenever you wanted?"

"I needed a job," he said meekly. "The sex was—"

"What? A bonus?" I wanted to spit in his face and tell him how much he disgusted me. "When was the last time you and Rachel had sex?"

"Friday, after my shift. Olivia had already left for work. That was one of our usual times."

"How could you not know about the baby?" My voice trembled with fury.

"How was I supposed to know? She didn't tell me. She wasn't showing."

"Did you kill her?"

He put his hands up in the air. "No! I loved her. And I would have loved that baby."

"So much so that you were ready to fuck me just three days after her body was found?"

He chuckled bitterly. "I'm not the one who showed up here begging for it. *You* came looking for *me*."

I started to walk away, but then I spun around, jabbing him one last time in the chest. "You're sick."

As I stormed off, I heard him light another cigarette. "You tell anyone about Rachel and me, I'll tell them about tonight and how you sucked me off for the keys to that apartment."

Tuesday

# twenty-two

I slept at the office that night. I'd forgotten my keys at work and by the time I got to the bureau, I couldn't walk another step. I made a bed out of Georgia's couch and throw pillows, and a down-filled coat she kept in her closet functioned as my duvet. Then I set the alarm on my phone for half past five.

Morning arrived with a throbbing headache, a crick in my neck, and a mouth that tasted like a garbage truck had exploded in a cotton mill. Plus, I couldn't stop sweating. I finally knew the truth about Rachel and Andrey, but if I told anyone I would lose my job. What had I been thinking? *You know better, Clyde.*

I dressed in yesterday's work clothes, washed my face, and reapplied my makeup and deodorant in the ladies' room. Back at my own desk, I went through the contents of my clutch. It was still stuffed with the papers I'd stolen from Olivia's bedroom: a handful of business cards; an invoice from a law firm; and a few empty envelopes, one of which was stamped with a return address to a company called Orchid Cellmark. I put the picture of Olivia and me in our bathing suits in one of the envelopes and stuffed it in my black bag. I left the rest of the papers in my desk drawer before leaving the office in search of coffee and breakfast. When I came back, about half an hour later, there was a note from Diskin on my chair informing me that he'd assigned another producer to Alex on the Kravis case. Today was a new day, a fresh start. I was off Olivia's story.

Officially.

I downed my vitamins, flicked on my HappyLight, and put in a call to Panda and another to Rachel's divorce lawyer. Then I looked up Orchid Cellmark. According to the company's webpage, they provided legally admissible DNA testing, paternity testing, and forensic DNA testing. The British government used them. So did the New York Medical Examiner's Office. This place was the real deal. And it was based in New Jersey, just a short ride away. I picked up the envelope again. The date stamp indicated it had been mailed a week before Olivia was killed. I picked up the phone to call the company and, after spending a good fifteen minutes in auto-attendant hell, I left a message on their press coordinator's extension.

While I waited for someone to return my call, I tried to sort through the thoughts tumbling around in my head. What I kept coming back to was this: my best friend was generous, but she wasn't dumb. What if Olivia had figured out Rachel was pregnant and demanded she take some sort of paternity test? I was pretty certain they could now do DNA tests on unborn fetuses. Or maybe Olivia hadn't known about the pregnancy but found a used condom or some other evidence that Rachel had been sleeping with someone else in her apartment and sent that evidence away to get tested? Say she busted Rachel on Friday night. They fought. But then what? Rachel hadn't killed Olivia, so how did her pregnancy fit into all of this?

"Hi, Clyde," said a voice behind me. "Are you busy?" Sabine handed me one of the two coffees in her hands. She looked tired, her hair was messy, and her eye makeup was smudged. She also had that new-love glow. "Thought you could use one," she said.

I caught her eyes flicking to my computer screen, so I quickly clicked the back button on my browser. I lifted the lid off the cup. "Thanks for the java. Can't seem to get enough this morning."

She propped herself up against my desk, and I tried not to remember what she looked like bare-breasted, in Alex's arms last night. I tried even harder not to hate her. *Oh shit,* I groaned inwardly. Was Georgia right? Was I falling for Alex?

"Did you have fun last night?" she asked, yawning, oblivious to my inner turmoil and the thirty lashes I was mentally administering to myself at that moment.

"Been to one, been to them all," I managed.

Sabine toyed with her hair. "Mike Fischer is quite the charmer."

He was undoubtedly that and a whole lot more, but I didn't have time for office gossip. Not today. Swiveling back toward my computer, itching to get back to my research, I lifted my cup. "Thanks again. If I need you for anything, I'll let you know."

"Actually, there is one thing I wanted to ask you?" Her voice was tentative.

I swung back around to face her, hoping she didn't want to commiserate with me about her night of endless passion or get my take on the politics of intra-office dating. "As long as it doesn't have anything to do with Alex," I said.

"It doesn't. At least, not really."

I raised my eyebrows.

"The thing is, I've really enjoyed working with you these last couple of weeks, and he suggested that I ask you to become my mentor. I know I can learn a lot from you."

"Wouldn't you rather ask someone like Georgia? I'm assuming you have on-camera aspirations." All pretty, young girls in television do, whether they admit to it or not. I had, for a time, until I proved myself incapable.

"I might like to try going on-air one day, but right now I need to understand what it takes to nail a story. You're the best around at nurturing sources and following leads. Everyone here says so."

I couldn't help feeling flattered, and despite the mountain of research I had to do, I invited her to sit down. "I'd love to be your mentor, Sabine. Later this week we should grab lunch, just the two of us. You can tell me more about where you see yourself in five years." I hadn't forgotten my original intention of helping her. Even though I wasn't in a position to promote her, I could ask Georgia or Wallace to give her more responsibilities. My phone rang, interrupting us. It was Panda, and his tone was all business. "What in the hell were you doing breaking into Olivia Kravis's apartment last night?"

I covered the receiver with my hand. "Sabine, do you mind if we finish up later? I need to take this call."

She slid off my desk. "Sure, of course, later."

I watched her prance happily across the bull pen to her cubicle. "Who turned me in?" I whispered.

"Who do you think?"

The only person who could have: Andrey. The bastard sold me out. "The doorman and I, we—" I began to say.

"I know."

I cringed. Panda knew I'd hooked up with the doorman on a dirty couch. "Neal, I was drinking. I made a mistake."

"You're damn right you did." He was pissed at me, and rightfully so.

"Andrey and Rachel were sleeping together," I said, changing the subject. "He admitted that to me last night. Rachel was using Olivia to pay for her legal bills. Plus, last night, the chairman of my company warned me off investigating a connection between Olivia's murder and the merger with Maldone Enterprises. She said Olivia wasn't opposed to the deal, but who knows?"

"Hold up, Clyde. I get that Olivia was your friend. You want to see that whoever did this to her gets theirs. But you aren't a cop. You don't have access to all the information we do. Let Restivo and Ehlers do their jobs. Believe me when I tell you they *will* solve these murders."

I wish I had his faith. I'd been in the business long enough to know things didn't always turn out that way. Killers went free. Some families never got justice. I took a deep breath, forcing my brain to slow down and the hysteria out of my voice. "When I was in Olivia's apartment last night, I found something," I said levelly. "An envelope from a company called Orchid Cellmark. Postmarked a week before her murder. They do DNA testing. Forensics. They're the guys that solved that cold case in London, the one involving the woman who was raped and stabbed forty-nine times in that square, right in front of her little boy."

Panda coughed. "Where are you headed with this?"

"What if she knew Rachel and Andrey were sleeping together but wanted proof?" After spending more than a decade covering crime, I'd learned two things: one, proof is everything; and two, trust your gut.

"Rachel was just ten weeks, not even showing. How could Olivia test her lover's unborn child?"

"You can test the fetus. Obviously it's more complicated than a cheek swab, but it's possible. Does Ehlers know the father is Andrey?"

"I can't tell you that."

Panda had trusted me with knowledge far more sensitive than this for years. "Why not?" I demanded.

"Because you're wanted for questioning."

"Me?"

"You broke into a murder victim's home."

I could have tried denying it—it would have been Andrey's word against mine—but my fingerprints, which the PD had on file, were all over that key box, Olivia's apartment, and the bottle of vodka I'd left behind. Long story short, ten years ago, long before I'd gotten my shit together, I'd been thrown in the slammer for disorderly conduct and public nudity. It hadn't been my finest hour, and neither was last night.

"Why didn't you guys find this envelope when you searched the apartment?" I asked.

"Despite what you see on TV, the crime-scene investigators don't have enough time to put every piece of trash under a microscope."

I lowered my voice to a whisper. "This isn't trash. How can you not see DNA testing as significant?"

Panda relented. "OK, kid, let's talk this through. You're the detective, right? You've got the body; you've got the fetus. What do you do next?"

"I'd see if the DNA from the semen found in Rachel's autopsy matches any other DNA picked up from the crime scene. Then I'd see if there was a match with the fetus. And then I'd run it through CODIS." CODIS was the national database of DNA profiles from convicted felons and missing persons.

"Good."

"What did Ehlers find?"

"I can't tell you," he said wearily. "And you're gonna have to hand that envelope to Ehlers. Don't even think about plastering it on TV."

"I couldn't, even if I wanted to. I'm off the story."

"Then what are you doing asking me questions about what my partner knows?" Panda growled. "Christ, Shaw! Give Ehlers the envelope. Don't put it on air. And I'll see what I can do to make this go away."

I'd never heard him lose his temper before, and it left me feeling off balance. "Anything else?" I asked.

"A thank-you would be nice," he grumbled, softening finally.

"Thank you."

"When Ehlers comes by, offer him something to drink this time. That fancy network of yours can spare a can of soda."

"Wait, he's coming here? No!" If Ehlers came to the offices to see me, Diskin would be notified and demand that Hiro Itzushi be present for my questioning. Then everyone would find out I'd almost slept with a source and broken into Olivia's apartment. Both were clear violations of our ethics code. Best case, I'd get written up. Worst case, I'd get fired without severance. My second line beeped. I recognized the extension: human resources. This wasn't good. "I gotta go," I told Panda.

"Listen, kid, I'll talk to Ehlers. But make sure you check in with him in the next hour, and don't run. You know enough about how this stuff works to make that mistake."

I said good-bye; Panda wished me good luck.

The way I saw it, I had two choices: give Ehlers the envelope and avoid getting arrested and further drawing the ire of the police, or give it to Diskin to put it on air, and have a shot at keeping my job. Audiences loved anything related to DNA, and this envelope was proof that Olivia was on to Rachel and Andrey's affair. Hand over the envelope, maybe keep my freedom. Give it to Diskin, maybe keep my job. Either way, I lost something.

I needed time to think, which meant I needed to disappear—just for a few hours, until I could figure out what to do. I grabbed my trench off the back of my chair, slid the envelope from Orchid Cellmark in my pocket and my computer in my handbag, and tucked my Rolodex under my arm. Then I made a run for the elevator.

# twenty-three

I didn't get very far. "Come on," I muttered, jabbing the elevator's down button again. The door finally pinged open and I lunged inside.

"Hey, where are you going?" I spun around. Alex was leaning against the elevator door so it couldn't close.

"Can you move?"

He stepped inside with me. "Aren't we supposed to be going to the Haverford?" The door closed. We were alone. He pulled my trench coat open with the crook of his index finger and saw the Rolodex. His playful expression turned serious. "What's going on?"

I watched the floor numbers descending. If I could just get out of the front doors, I'd be home free for the time being. "Oberlink is your new producer," I said.

Alex's frown deepened. "Back up. What's happening? All I heard was that I was supposed to be in the truck. Does this have anything to do with me taking Sabine to the benefit last night?"

I had to laugh. "Don't flatter yourself. Believe it or not, I have bigger problems than your proclivity for public sex."

He looked at me, confused.

I arched an eyebrow. "Next time make sure the door is shut all the way when you're screwing my assistant on a conference table."

He ran his fingers down his face. "You saw us?"

The elevator door slid open. We were in the lobby. I walked at a normal pace, my eyes focused on the door, my heart thudding in my chest. Alex followed me onto the sidewalk. "Can you just wait a second?"

"No." I flagged down a cab. It pulled up, idling.

I yanked open the door.

Alex wedged himself between the door and me.

"You getting in?" yelled the cabbie.

"Give us a second, man," Alex said.

"Move," I hissed.

"I'm coming with you."

The cabbie yelled at us again. "In or out?"

"In!" Alex and I screamed back in unison. I dove into the backseat, and Alex climbed in after me. I gave the driver my home address and put my Rolodex on the seat between us.

Alex turned to me, expectant.

"You're better off not knowing."

"Try me."

I looked out the window. It was an unseasonably warm day for early November—probably the city's last taste of temperate weather before the cold set in for good. I fished my phone out of my bag. It took a moment to gather my courage before dialing Restivo. A few seconds later, his gravelly baritone was in my ear. "What a coincidence. We were gonna come pay you a visit. I've always wanted to see what the Sixth Circle looks like." He was referencing Dante Alighieri's Circles of Hell, where heretics spent eternity in fiery graves.

"It's nice of you to make the trip, but I'm not at work," I said.

"Yeah, I bet."

"I have something to give you."

Alex elbowed me. "What?" he wrote on his pad, holding it up in my face.

I snatched the pen and pad from him and threw them on the floor of the taxi.

"You unlawfully entered a crime scene," Restivo continued in my ear. "You tampered with crucial evidence related to an ongoing criminal investigation." He was wrong about calling Olivia's apartment a crime scene. There hadn't been any police tape over the door, meaning the cops no longer considered it active. Still, I wasn't in a position to squabble over details. I was guilty of unlawful entry, crime scene or not, and they could book me on that charge alone if they wanted. "I'm no Tom Brokaw, but I'm guessing that breaking the law is a fireable offense."

"You'd be surprised." Truth was, this sort of thing was tacitly encouraged; it was getting caught that could land you in trouble. "Like I said, I have something for you. Would you like to meet this afternoon?"

"Sure, Red. That would be swell," Restivo said dryly, and we made a plan to meet at the precinct in a few hours.


The cab let Alex and me out in front of my apartment building. Alex paid the fare while I rummaged in my bag for my keys.

"This where you live?" Alex said, looking down on me. "There's no doorman."

"So?"

"It's not safe for a single woman to live alone in a building without round-the-clock security."

"Doormen are overrated," I muttered, jamming my key in the front door. We entered the small vestibule, walking past two rows of brass mailboxes. "How do you know I don't have a roommate?" I unlocked the second door and pushed it open.

"Because you would be impossible to live with."

"That's nice to hear." We climbed up three flights of creaky stairs, Alex behind me, pestering me to tell him what I had that the police wanted, why I'd left the office in such a hurry. "Here we are," I said once we arrived on my floor. Right away, I noticed my door was ajar, a wedge of sunlight spilling onto the hall's mottled red carpeting. What the hell? No one had a key to my apartment. Not even the super. I hadn't had a chance to give it to him since I'd had the locks changed.

Alex put his arm out in front of me protectively as he crept forward and pushed the door open wider. The doorjamb was splintered near the lock. "Stay there," he whispered.

I ignored him, stepping around him and putting one foot past the doorjamb, where I halted. The place was trashed. Someone had ripped down my curtains and tipped over my lamps. My bedding, including the quilt that had once belonged to my mother, was slashed to pieces; an old can of paint from my closet had been dumped all over my beloved Persian rugs. Smashed glass littered the floor. It looked like my desktop computer had escaped unscathed, but aside from it and the pearls fastened around my neck, nearly every material thing I valued in the world had been destroyed.

Alex grabbed my shoulder. "Let's get out of here. It's a crime scene now."

I shook him loose and walked into the wreckage. Everything was upended. It would take me days to clean and sort out the mess.

"They were looking for something," he remarked.

I dove for my desk drawer. I had some papers from the case, printouts and other interview notes I'd taken. Everything was still there. As I leaned against my desk, my hand accidentally hit the mouse to my computer. The screen lit up.

"JIFFY" was written in big, bold letters.

A string of images crowded my brain. I was sixteen again, a sophomore, a social outcast. Jiffy was my nickname. Maybe I'd done some bad things, but nothing as bad as what the other girls did to me. The name-calling, the prank phone calls to my home, the day they locked me in the janitor's closet in the basement. It was two hours before the art teacher heard me screaming for help. I took a breath and forced myself to focus on what was going on here and now, and what any of *that* had to do with *this*. And that's when I put it together, that the person who had killed Olivia and Rachel, and drugged me and trashed my apartment, either had known me as a teenager or knew someone who had.

I put my finger on the delete button.

# twenty-four

"What in the hell are you doing? Don't touch anything!"

I backed away from the computer, retracing my steps out of the apartment, my eyes glued to the floor. In the hall, Alex dialed 911. In the stairwell, he reached out for me. I let him hold me, his arms wrapped tightly around my shoulders. Then his phone buzzed in his pocket.

I stepped away. "Get it." We both knew it was the assignment desk trying to locate him. "Get it," I repeated. "Let's not both get fired on the same day."

"You got fired?"

"Take the call."

He answered, giving whoever was on the other end of it some false coordinates before clicking off. Then he took my hand, led me down the rest of the stairs, and regarded me in the afternoon sunshine.

"I'm not leaving you. Not until you tell me what's going on. The police want something you have, you're getting canned, and someone just broke into your apartment. If this has something to do with the Kravis case, you have to tell me."

"No, I don't."

"Jesus, Shaw. Do you have to be so stubborn all the time?"

"Yes. Now go. I'll be fine here."

Alex threw his head back, exasperated. "Where will you go afterward? You can't stay here."

I shrugged.

"Clyde, you're not just in trouble. You're in *danger*. What did you see on your computer screen?"

*Jiffy, because I spread so easily.* I'd hooked up with the wrong guy. He'd gone down on me in his parents' bed while they were skiing in Aspen, come once in my mouth and twice in the ribbed-for-her-pleasure condoms he'd had at the ready. How was I supposed to know he'd tell his girlfriend about us the next day? How was I supposed to know he was dating Missy, my old tormenter from the swim team? She forgave her Yale-bound boyfriend but spent the rest of her senior year making sure everyone knew what a whore I was.

Alex grabbed me by the shoulders. "What did you see?"

"It was something from my childhood."

"You know what this means. This person, the murderer—"

"Is connected to my past."

"They want to kill you. They're targeting *you* now."

"If that were true, I would be dead by now. The purpose of all this is to scare me."

He squinted into the sun. "Even if you're right, you can't honestly be thinking of staying here tonight. What's one night in a hotel?"

"I am about to lose my job. I don't have four hundred dollars to piss away on a hotel." A pair of uniformed patrol officers in a squad car pulled up in front of my building. "They're here. You can go," I told him.

"Juan's the doorman. I'll let him know you're coming." Alex dug into his pocket, tossed me his keys, and rattled off an address on the East Side before breaking into a sprint.

"What?" I yelled after him.

"You're staying with me tonight!" I would have argued with him, but he was already halfway down the block.

The cops killed the engine and stepped out of their car. The woman, a tough-looking brunette, asked me questions while her partner, a tall, dark-skinned cop with a shaved head, took notes. When I was done, the female cop asked me to let her into the building and her partner returned to their car to radio the information into the precinct.

Thirty minutes later, I was waiting on the front stoop when a blue Crown Vic pulled up behind the cop car. Detective Restivo got out wearing rumpled chinos, one of those knit ties I hadn't seen on anyone since my high school math teacher, and a face that looked like it hadn't seen a pillow in days. He greeted me with a curt nod.

"I thought we were meeting later," I said.

"So did I." He sounded even more pissed than before. "When were you last home?"

"Yesterday morning, around eight thirty."

He removed his sunglasses. "And you came back when?"

"Maybe an hour ago." My watch said it was a quarter past noon.

He muttered some curse words and looked up at my building. "Wait here with Officer Rivera." It wasn't a question.

I returned to the stoop and waited for Restivo to come back downstairs. When he did, the hostility I'd gotten accustomed to receiving from him had been replaced with concern. "Do you have any enemies, anyone you think might want to hurt you?"

"I've been in this business seventeen years. Yes, I've got enemies."

"Anyone stand out in your mind?"

"On this case? Michael Rockwell. Andrey Kaminski," I volunteered.

"I meant people not involved in this case."

"Jack Slane. He's a lawyer at Rockwell's firm. I dated him a few years ago, and I saw him again for the first time last week. He tried to get security to throw me out of their offices."

"That's it? Rockwell, Kaminski, and this Slane guy? No one else has been hounding you, sending you notes? No phone calls or threats?"

"Other than my drugging, no. But—"

"What is it?"

I told him about the message on the computer screen.

Restivo opened the building's front door. "I think you should come upstairs. Let's go over this all again up there."

Seeing my apartment was worse the second time. Now I noticed all the little things that had been destroyed and could never be replaced. I crouched over a pile of broken shards, remnants of my mother's collection of Herend porcelain.

"Don't touch it," the female cop barked from behind me.

I wiped away a tear and stood up. Restivo called to me from the galley kitchen. "What'd you eat yesterday for breakfast?"

I walked over to him. "Nothing, why?" He gestured at the empty packet of crackers on the kitchen counter. "I didn't do that."

"Perp was here for a while and got hungry. My guess is that they were waiting for you to come home."

"That's what I thought the killer did—wait for Olivia and Rachel to come home. Am I right?"

"We need more than a few cracker crumbs to link these cases." He looked around the room. "Did the perp target any specific kinds of items? Is anything gone?"

"No."

"Let's assume the perp picked the lock sometime last night. They trashed everything except for the computer, which they used to leave you a message connected to your past. We need to talk about why you were at the Haverford last night and not here." He

240

sighed and I heard his stomach rumble. "It's been a busy morning. Is there a place I can grab a bite to eat around here?"

"Pizza OK?"

He nodded once.

I pointed westward. "There's a place on the corner."

"That'll do."

Restivo had me pack up a few of my things in an overnight bag. We walked down the street to By the Slice, a neighborhood place that served thin-crust pizza with gourmet toppings, a few dozen wines by the glass, and five or six beers on tap. It got popular at happy hour. The rest of the day it was mostly empty.

Restivo and I got our pick of tables. He chose the rickety two-seater at the front window, and tucked one paper napkin into his collar and patted another on the top of his slice. I wanted to do the same to his forehead and nose. If he ever went on camera for us, the makeup artists would have to powder the hell out of him.

He twisted off the cap of his orange soda and took a sip. Then he said, "You have something to show me?"

"It's an envelope." I handed it to him.

Restivo peeked inside. "Nothing's in it?"

I pointed at the embossing on the front. "It's from Orchid Cellmark. They are one of the most highly esteemed labs in the world specializing in forensic DNA testing."

Restivo laughed. I could count his gold fillings while waiting for him to stop. "Sorry, Shaw, but every reporter I meet's got a boatload of theories—none of them right. Now, thanks to you, we won't be able to process this envelope for fingerprints."

A call came in from FirstNews on my cell, the third since we'd sat down. I pressed the ignore button and tapped the return address on the envelope with my finger. "But you can go to the lab and find out why Olivia was corresponding with them. They have a location in Princeton."

He carved off another triangle of his mushroom and sausage. "How about we talk about what you were doing at the Haverford last night?"

I was better off telling him the truth. The worst they could book me on was unlawful entry since I hadn't taken anything of value. If the case ever went to trial, which was unlikely, I would probably be able to plead out with community service.

After giving Restivo a minute-by-minute PG-13-rated account of what had happened the previous night, he asked me a few questions about my brief but revealing conversation with Andrey at the end of the night. I filled him in on everything as best as I could remember, and at the end Restivo closed his notebook. He removed the napkin under his chin and wiped the corners of his mouth with it. Then he drained the last of his soda before slipping on his sunglasses, stuffing his notebook and the envelope from Orchid Cellmark in his pocket, and getting up from the table. "You know if it were up to me, I would've read you your rights hours ago. You're lucky the Kravises aren't pressing charges."

I followed him outside. "Why would they not—"

"Apparently they consider you a family friend, which is kind of funny, because where I come from friends don't break into your house."

Although I should have felt relieved, I didn't. The only reason the Kravis family hadn't pressed charges was because of the firestorm of press coverage that would have been ignited if they had. Getting me fired, conversely, could be done completely under the radar. I was screwed.

Restivo and I walked back down the block to my apartment building. The female officer had joined Rivera on the stoop. The crime-scene techs were upstairs and I had to find somewhere else to stay while they swept the place for evidence. "How long will that take?" I asked.

Restivo shrugged. "A day, maybe more. It's not safe for you here anyway."

"Then give me protection."

"We're not the FBI. I can't put a team on you twenty-four/seven."

"What if I make a formal request?"

"By all means, do it. But you're gonna get the same answer I just gave you." Restivo got into his car and popped open the passenger-side door. "You want a lift to the Haverford? I'm going back there now."

I shook my head. "They already took me off the story."

He pulled the car door shut and fired up the engine. "Not for nothing, but you might want to switch on the news when you get to wherever you're going."

So there'd been a break in the case. That's why I'd gotten all those calls from FirstNews, and why the assignment desk had been relentlessly trying to reach Alex. "What happened?" I yelled, but he was already gone.


I ran the whole way to Alex's apartment building on Sutton Place, my overnight bag slowing my pace only minimally. Between deep breaths, I introduced myself to the doorman on duty. In response I got a smile that told me I wasn't the first woman Mr. Amori had handed his keys to.

"It's not what you think," I said. "Alex and I work together."

He pressed the eleventh-floor button for me, his mouth still crimped in a smirk. "None of my business, ma'am."

Inside Alex's apartment, I threw my purse on the ground and flipped on the TV in the living room. It had been on ESPN. Typical. I clicked over to FirstNews and sat through a series of commercials and the latest headlines. Finally, Jean Chan, the afternoon news anchor, tossed the broadcast to Alex. He was standing in front of the Haverford. In the background I saw a cluster of cop cars, their red lights flashing.

"I'm here in Manhattan, at the Haverford, an exclusive Upper East Side building where just this morning authorities made an arrest in the murders of Olivia Kravis, Rachel Rockwell, and Ms. Rockwell's unborn child. According to our sources, Andrey Kaminski, a building worker here at the Haverford, was taken into police custody just a few hours ago."

I felt my knees give out and sank to the floor. Andrey was the killer. My best friend's killer. Less than twenty-four hours ago, I'd been alone with him, feet away from where he'd hidden his girlfriend's body. *My God, my God, Clyde, what have you done?* I rapped my knuckles hard against my forehead. I'd never forgive myself for this.

Alex's face filled the television screen. "Olivia Kravis, the daughter of Charles Kravis, this network's founder, was found dead in her apartment early last week. The body of Rachel Rockwell—a mother of two from Greenwich, who was estranged from her husband, Michael Rockwell, an attorney at a prominent New York City law firm—was found in the basement of the building several days later. The two women are believed to have been romantically involved. It was revealed just two days ago that Rachel was pregnant at the time of her death. Sources tell us that Andrey Kaminski, the man the police have arrested, met Rachel in the Rockwells' local community of Greenwich, Connecticut, and was rumored to be having an affair with her long before he took a job as the overnight doorman at the Haverford. Police aren't releasing any more details about the arrest at this time."

I pulled myself up from the floor to the couch. The broadcast jumped back to Jean Chan. "Has anyone suggested that this is a case of a love triangle turned fatal?"

The screen split between Alex on the scene and Jean in the studio. "There's been speculation that Kaminski was the father of Rachel Rockwell's unborn child," Alex said. "But none of the investigators have given us an official word on the matter."

"Thank you so much. Keep us posted on any further developments?" Jean said from behind her desk.

"Sure thing, Jean."

I muted the television and stood up on shaky legs as another wave of fury and disgust hit me with full force. My hands balled into fists at my sides; my nails dug into the flesh of my palms. I'd been *with* a murderer. Alex's place was outfitted in typical bachelor fashion, except the kitchen was six times the size of mine and stocked with expensive-looking gadgets: a KitchenAid mixer, a Vitamix blender, a bread-making machine, and a Nespresso coffeemaker. The cabinets were filled with spices and gourmet crackers, bottles of olive oil, Swiss chocolate bars, and homemade granola. Only thing missing was what I needed most at that moment: a stocked bar. A quick search through the kitchen cabinets yielded only some cooking sherry and an opened bottle of wine that had turned to vinegar. The freezer, which held a bag of ice, a vat of cookies and cream, and a few packs of chicken, was no better. "C'mon, Alex. Nothing? You've got to have something," I muttered to myself.

In his bedroom I found a pile of dirty clothes, an unmade bed, and an open box of condoms on his bedside table. There was an en suite bathroom with a travertine tub, and a small half bath off the combined living room/dining room. There wasn't a guest bedroom. My bed, I presumed, would be the leather couch.

I sat back down on it and buried my head in my hands, forcing myself to get it together, to see that it was better like this, not getting drunk. I reached for my phone. I'd missed three calls and had one new voice mail. I tentatively hit play.

"Cornelia Shaw, this is Catherine Feinberg from the human resources department. I have been trying to reach you for the better part of the day. I'd like for you to come directly to the eighteenth floor tomorrow morning at eight a.m. The receptionist will be expecting you. Mitchell Diskin and Hiro Itzushi from our legal department will be present for the meeting. If you have any questions, I can be reached via e-mail."

Catherine Feinberg, a woman I'd never met in person but knew from the umpteen thousand memos I'd received from the HR department over the years, spoke quickly and with a strong upstate accent. If there had been any doubt in my mind as to the fate of my job at the network, her message had it sealed. I was history. Knowing the efficiency of the FirstNews legal department, I could safely assume that my termination contract had already been worked up, my key card deactivated, and computer intranet access shut down. After the meeting ended, I would be handed a booklet explaining my rights, options, and temporary benefits and turned over to a security guard, who would take me to my desk to collect my personal effects and then escort me out of the building. All this would take place before most of my colleagues arrived at the office, thereby avoiding any disruption of work and productivity. Those assholes had it down to a science.

But I could only blame myself. I'd broken the law, messed around with a source against my better judgment, and ignored everyone's advice to back off the case. Tomorrow, I'd have to take my punishment. Except, I still had one card to play, and it happened to be buried at the bottom of my bag.

Prentice Maldone's office was located in a Midtown commercial building known for its architecture and exorbitantly high rents. One of his willowy assistants—Val, a different girl than the one who had found me passed out in the gallery's bathroom—offered me a bottle of water, which I declined with what I thought was a reasonably funny joke about the safety of beverages at Maldone Enterprises. She wasn't amused. "It'll be a few minutes before he can see you," she said tersely. "But feel free to wait."

Val let me in an hour later. I didn't care; I had nowhere else to be. Prentice greeted me and led me to a long couch at the opposite end of his gigantic office. It featured a broad view over Fifth Avenue, several seating areas, and what looked like some fine Chinese antiquities. He settled into a grommet-studded armchair facing my perch on the couch. "Shouldn't you be down at the Haverford?" he asked. "I was just watching the coverage."

He motioned to the TV monitor mounted on a wood-paneled wall.

"I've been pulled off the case."

"By whom?"

"Naomi Zell." I took a deep breath. "She told me last night at the gala that I should assume Olivia's murder wasn't connected to the merger, and when I pushed a little and asked who on the board of directors had been opposed to the deal, she said she was going to have Diskin reassign me. It's obvious she's afraid of me uncovering something."

Prentice stood up. "Tell me exactly what she said." I summarized my conversation with Naomi Zell. He sat down again and ran a hand over his bald pate. "So that's everything?"

I gulped. This was the part I was dreading. "After Olivia threatened me, I went to the Haverford to see Andrey Kaminski."

"They guy they just arrested?"

"Yes. He took me to the super's office, where I stole Olivia's apartment key, which I then used to break into her apartment. The police aren't going to arrest me because the Kravises have declined to press charges, but I just got a call from HR asking me to come in tomorrow morning—early. I suspect I'm going to be fired."

"And you want me to intervene?"

"I was doing my job, and now I'm getting fired for it. If it was your friend who got murdered, you wouldn't give up so easily either."

He gave a rueful chuckle. "I don't have many friends at the network now, Cornelia. There's a limit to what I can do."

"They'll listen to you."

Maldone walked over to his desk. He buzzed his assistant. "Get me Naomi Zell."

Then he looked up at me. "Would you mind waiting outside?"

I let myself out and tried to sit down and relax but found myself on my feet again, pacing the room, checking my phone for messages and the latest news updates on the Internet about Kaminski's arrest. I was hitting the refresh button when he came back out.

This time he didn't invite me into his office but remained standing in the doorway. "This is more complicated than I thought," he began, and I knew what was coming next. FirstNews was going to fire me and none of the national networks would touch me, not if people found out why I'd been canned. And they would. These things always got out. "Call me in a couple of months. I may be of more help then," he said, but we both knew he didn't mean it.

I returned to Alex's apartment to find him at his kitchen counter, unloading a sack full of groceries. "Why are you here?" I asked. It was only five o'clock.

"Thought I'd grill us up some steaks after I get back from *Topical.* My butcher gets beef from a farm in Pennsylvania. You can't believe this meat. I also picked up some new potatoes, but the deal is you have to prep them for me."

"Shouldn't you be at the bureau?" I asked him.

"Georgia wanted me to check on you."

I slid him a sideways look. Had she told him to keep me away from alcohol? "You can tell her I'm fine," I said. "Who else besides her knows I'm here?"

He put the steaks in the fridge and set the vegetables in the sink. "Just Georgia"—he paused—"and Sabine."

I got up and went for my purse. "I should leave. They've caught the killer. There's no point to me being here."

"Just stay, OK?" He took my bag from my hands and held it tucked under his arm. "One night's not going to kill you."

I wanted to be alone with my misery. I could find a shitty hotel somewhere. Maybe I'd go out to a bar and find someone to keep me company in the aforementioned shitty hotel room. Then I would sleep through my meeting tomorrow morning. Fuck Catherine Feinberg, whoever she was. I didn't owe her anything. I grabbed for my bag.

Alex pulled it away, tossing it on top of a bookshelf. "You're not going anywhere. I promised Georgia I would look after you."

"Why do you care?" I asked hotly.

"I feel responsible for getting you into this situation. I practically forced Diskin to give you the assignment."

"*You* did? Why?"

He walked back into the kitchen and poured a glass of water. "I'd heard good things."

"It wasn't because you wanted to get in my pants?" I asked, less angry now.

He grinned. "The thought did cross my mind. But no, that wasn't the reason."

I wandered over to the sliding glass doors. His balcony overlooked the Queensboro Bridge, and I could watch the cars as they whizzed across the span.

Alex handed me the water. "The view's better from out there."

"It's good enough from in here," I said.

He looked like he was about to ask me something when he remembered the time. "I have to get back. Help yourself to anything in the fridge. You'll be all right while I'm gone?"

I nodded. "I'll be fine."

"Call me if you need me."

He was almost at the door when it occurred to me I should say something nice. "Alex," I said, feeling suddenly at a loss for words. "Thanks for taking me in."

He grinned. "If you hadn't noticed, I've been trying to get you on my couch for a long time."


While he was gone I busied myself scrubbing the potatoes, making the salad, and setting the table with plates, linen napkins, and silverware. I took a bath and changed into an old T-shirt and sweats I found in one of Alex's clothes drawers. In my haste, I'd packed only a skirt suit, a few extra pairs of underwear, and toiletries in my overnight bag.

Alex walked in at half past ten. He took one look at the place and me and loosened his tie. "How are you doing?"

"Reasonably well, considering the circumstances."

"You watch the broadcast?" he asked, turning on the stereo. I nodded as I dimmed the overhead lights and lit a trio of candles in hurricane lamps. "You think we did OK?"

"You did great," I said, straightening a napkin on the table.

Alex moved to the kitchen, rolling up his shirtsleeves to get to work. He seasoned the steaks with salt and cracked peppercorns and whipped together what he promised would be the best béarnaise I'd ever tasted. "You like tarragon, right?"

"Sure." It was an herb—I knew that much. "Since when have you been such a cook?"

"Since I realized that chicks dig it."

I rolled my eyes.

He laughed. "Actually, my mom taught me. You haven't lived until you've tasted her beef Wellington."

"Where does she live?"

"DC, which is why I want to get back there. My dad's cancer came back."

"I'm sorry, Alex."

He turned back to the stove, where two filet mignons were sizzling on a pan. He flipped them over, picked up a whisk, and started emulsifying the eggs and butter together for the sauce.

"Can I ask you something personal?"

He started chopping the herbs on his cutting board. "Shoot."

I migrated to the couch. "Why Sabine? Aside from the obvious reasons."

He didn't answer straightaway. Finally he asked with his head cocked to one side, "Why do you want to know?"

"I'm a journalist. I'm curious by nature."

He pointed his big knife at me. "And nosy."

"That too."

"You really want to know?"

I nodded. "That's why I asked."

"She's easy. And I don't mean it the way you think I do."

*Easy.* That was a good word to describe what most men wanted: pretty and uncomplicated. On a good day, I could pass for pretty, but I'd never be uncomplicated.

Alex wiped his hands on a striped tea towel and sat down next to me on the couch. "I got a call from Olivia's assistant."

"Emma?"

"She was trying to reach you at the bureau, but they already shut down your voice mail. The desk sent her to me."

"What did she want?"

"She said Olivia didn't take a taxi the Wednesday before she was killed. She took a hired car. The bill came in yesterday."

I sat up straighter. "We didn't know where she went. She was gone all afternoon on personal business, but we didn't know what she was doing."

"Emma gave me the number for the car service Olivia took."

"And?"

"I called over there. The dispatcher said she was taken to an address in New Jersey. I looked it up, and—"

I beat him to the punch. "Orchid Cellmark. The DNA lab."

Alex's eyes widened. "How did you know?"

I told him about the envelope, the call from Catherine Feinberg, and my visit to Maldone's office. When I was finished, he asked if I'd gotten any updates from the police about my apartment.

"I spoke briefly with Restivo before you came home. They're still processing the scene. Right now they're treating it as part of Olivia's case, and since he's lead detective, he's my go-to. But when I asked him about Kaminski's arrest, he refused to give me any other info. He said I had to go through the IO for anything like that. It's bullshit, since I'm not even covering the case anymore."

He shook his head. "What's bullshit is that you're getting fired."

I shrugged. "What can I do at this point?"

"Don't sign anything in Feinberg's office. They have to at least give you twenty-four hours. I'll take a look at the documents they give you."

"I don't want a fight." If I made trouble, it would get around to other networks. Not that it mattered at this point. I was already going to have to move to Topeka to find work.

252

The steaks were done. Alex brought them to the table with the rest of the food. We ate our meals quickly. Neither of us had much appetite, although the food was delicious and I told Alex so. "You should let me cook for you more often," he said. "Under better circumstances."

"I'd like that." I stood to clear the dishes. I knew I couldn't trust myself around him much longer.

Alex followed me to the sink. "I was there when Diskin told you to go after the story. They can't fire you for following his orders. And if they do, when it comes time to negotiate my new contract, I'm going to fight to bring you back. This situation is only temporary. I won't let you take the brunt of this, Clyde."

I was touched by his desire to help, surprised by it too, but I knew he was making a promise he couldn't keep. I finished the dishes and took to the couch. Outside the sliding glass doors, the sky was inky black behind the illuminated bridge. There were no stars visible, just a sliver of moon hovering over the East River. I thought of my mother and of the darkness that sometimes clouded her face when she'd come into my bedroom long after I was supposed to have fallen asleep. She'd sit on the edge of my bed and just stare out my bedroom window for what felt like hours. Even before she killed herself, I'd known there was something wrong, something that eventually forced her onto our fire escape and down to a horrific death.

Alex brought out a pile of fresh sheets and blankets and began making a bed for me on his couch. I spied a box of chocolates on the coffee table that hadn't been there before. "Are those for me?" I asked, pouncing on the gold *ballotin*.

He fluffed an afghan over the length of the couch. "Those are actually for—"

"Sabine."

"I was planning on going over to her place."

"So late?" It was close to midnight.

"She didn't exactly love the idea of you sleeping over." He grabbed his keys, cell, and blazer and hovered by the door. "You keep the chocolates."

"No way. They're for her." I threw them in his direction, harder than intended.

The corner caught his chest. "Ow!"

"I'm sorry," I said.

"Jeez, Shaw." He gave me a small smile. "You hit hard for a girl."

I remembered my previous reply: "I'll take that as a compliment."

"You should." He let himself out, and I fell into my makeshift bed. Sleep couldn't come fast enough.

Wednesday

# twenty-five

That night I dreamed that I was back in that super's office, on that ratty couch with Andrey, my back arching and fingers digging into the muscles of his back as I climaxed. Afterward, he lit a cigarette with a match, and in the light of the flame I glimpsed Olivia's and Rachel's bodies. They were lined up one next to the other, naked, their eyes glassy and lips blue and cracked. And there was a strong, almost overwhelming smell—a putrid mix of decomposition and human feces—I hadn't noticed until that moment. How had I missed it? I opened my mouth to scream but no sound came out. I tried to move to no avail. And there was Andrey, standing now before me, acting as though nothing were wrong, telling me I could take my time getting dressed.

When I woke I was covered in sweat, freezing cold, and I couldn't shake the feelings of guilt and fear that had paralyzed me in my dream. I stared at the ceiling for an hour, maybe more, trying to will myself back to sleep before I gave up and reached for my phone. It was 5:00 a.m. I thought I might as well get the day started.

On the way to the bathroom I passed by Alex's room. I'd expected to find it empty, but Alex must have come home in the middle of the night because he was asleep in his bed, chest down, his body uncovered to just above his rear end. I allowed myself one longing glance at the two dimples at his lower back.

In the kitchen I found flour, butter, milk, and eggs and began whipping them together. Pancakes were one of the only things I knew how to make, and I wanted to reciprocate for dinner the night before. I'd ladled my first two circles of batter and was looking for maple syrup in the fridge when the fire alarm went off. Alex appeared suddenly at his bedroom door and raced to the stove. Grabbing a tea towel, he pulled the pan off the burner and tossed it into the sink.

"I can't believe it. I left it for one second," I said.

He ran the tap over the pan. Smoke rose between us. He was wearing nothing but a bedsheet, his bare torso once again putting all sorts of thoughts into my head, thoughts I'd already taken a cold shower to try to forget. "What were you cooking?" he asked.

"Pancakes, unless the smoke has totally put you off. Maybe we should just get bagels."

"You'll have to work a lot harder than that to put me off." He took my coffee cup off the kitchen counter and took a sip. I turned around and got to work on a new batch with a fresh pan. Alex stood behind me, close enough that I could feel the warmth rising from his body. "I see what your problem is now," he said, reaching around me to turn down the stove's burner. His hand grazed my hip.

"It's the flame," he said. His body pressed into mine.

"What's wrong with it?" I asked, not daring to move an inch.

"It's on too high," he said into my neck.

I finally turned around. There was hunger in his eyes. I'm sure it was in mine too. He inched closer, his hand on my hip. "Alex, I—"

The doorbell rang. We both jumped. "I'll go see who it is. Don't move," he said.

Alex looked into the peephole before opening the door. It took Sabine all of one second to notice Alex's bare chest, his T-shirt on my body, and the heady tension still suspended in the air. "Good morning," she said in her too-bright voice, her long hair gliding over her shoulders as she lifted the paper bag in her hand. "I brought bagels."

I turned back to the pancakes, not trusting my face. Alex went back to his room to shower and dress, closing his bedroom door behind him—something he hadn't bothered to do since I'd gotten there. Sabine hovered by the table, emitting nervous energy.

I was really too old for this. I took a sip of coffee and turned around. "I'm going back to my place today, Sabine. The police must be done with it by now. There's nothing going on here, if that's what you're worried about."

"I'm not worried." She did her best not to sound hostile. "I just wanted to say you could come stay with me. I've got a couch."

I poured another circle of batter. "All I want is to be back in my own place, surrounded by my own things." Not that there was that much to salvage in my apartment.

We were both quiet. I finished making my pancakes; she set out her bagels. I heard the squeak of the shower being turned off. Soon Alex reappeared in his bedroom doorway fully dressed. "Who's hungry?"

Sabine put a bagel on her plate and one on Alex's. "I got you sesame and cream cheese, lightly toasted." Alex took a seat at the table. Sabine slid into his lap. Behind her, Alex gave me an apologetic look.

It was my cue to leave. I looked at my watch. "It's later than I thought."

My pancakes were left to cool on the countertop as I scuttled off to the bathroom to change my clothes; then I was out the door to face my future.

Catherine Feinberg was waiting for me at the appointed time in an eighteenth-floor conference room. It was decorated in a beige grass wall covering, abstract oil paintings, and a heavy walnut table big enough to accommodate twenty people, although there were only four of us that day: Catherine, Mitchell Diskin, Hiro Itzushi, and me.

"Please take a seat, Cornelia." Catherine had the look of a life-long paper-pusher—pallid skin, frown lines, a brown tweed skirt suit that proclaimed a distinct lack of imagination. Before her lay a file folder marked with my name.

I nodded hello at Diskin and Itzushi as I chose a chair.

Feinberg spoke first. "Do you know why you're here?"

"I have an idea," I acknowledged.

Itzushi cleared his throat. "It has come to the network's attention that you illegally entered Olivia Kravis's home Monday evening. Is this correct?"

I conceded the point only partially. "It's true I was in her apartment on Monday night."

Itzushi scribbled something on the yellow legal pad in front of him. "Did you have permission from the owner of the apartment to enter it?"

I shook my head.

"Is it also correct that you procured a key to the Kravis apartment from the superintendent's office at the Haverford, and that you gained access to the aforementioned office through Andrey Kaminski, a source you interviewed for air and with whom you have developed a relationship that could be categorized as inappropriate?"

"Define *inappropriate* for Miss Shaw," Feinberg clucked.

Itzushi referred to another stack of papers to his right. "All FirstNews employees are discouraged from engaging in sexual or romantic relations with sources, and are, moreover, required to make such relationships known to the appropriate parties so that correct actions or steps may be taken to eliminate the existence or appearance of a conflict of interest.'" He looked up at me. "Your relationship with Andrey Kaminski suggests a breach in the code of conduct, which you, and every FirstNews employee, have signed as a condition of employment at this network. Is this true or untrue?"

I blinked. "I'm sorry, what exactly are you asking me?"

Feinberg snorted. "Did you or did you not have sexual relations with Olivia Kravis's murderer?"

"Alleged murderer," Itzushi interjected.

"Is she really asking me that?" I asked Diskin.

Itzushi put his hand on Catherine's sleeve. "I think what's important here is to establish exactly what happened, while at the same time respecting Cornelia's privacy."

I shifted in my chair. "I'd like to point out that technically, at the time, Kaminski wasn't my source. Naomi Zell had already informed me that I was going to be reassigned to another story. It is my understanding that Barton Oberlink was already the lead producer on the story. I hadn't known Barton was going to take over for me at the time, but I had known I was going to be taken off the case—and I couldn't help but throw the idiotic move back in their faces."

Catherine Feinberg and Hiro Itzushi glanced at each other. For a moment, I thought I had them, but then Diskin rapped his Montblanc on the table. "Your relationship with this source isn't why you're here, Shaw," he boomed. "The reason why you are here is because you broke into an apartment. You broke the law."

My neck itched beneath my jacket collar. I couldn't believe he was leading the charge against me; I thought he'd be the one person I could trust at this meeting. "Every day at this network, producers make unethical calls to get access to the information they need or book guests they want. We say we don't pay for interviews, but we do pay for first-class airline tickets, hotel suites, fancy dinners, and Broadway shows. And what about the time Greg Lanier hacked into that sports agent's voice mail? As I recall, he got a promotion for landing that baseball doping story. You and I both know the only time anyone ever seems to get in trouble around here is when they get caught. Not one week ago we were sitting in your office—Itzushi was there; he knows this—and you told me in no uncertain terms to pursue this story through any means necessary."

Diskin set his pen down on the table, his lips thinned with indignation. "I didn't think someone of your experience needed clarification that *by any means necessary* meant any means necessary *within the scope of the law.*"

I squared my shoulders. "I haven't been charged with anything by the police, so whether or not I have broken the law is debatable."

Feinberg spoke next. "We're terminating your contract, Miss Shaw."

"On what grounds?"

"Multiple ethics violations including, but not limited to, not informing your superiors at the network of a conflict of interest related to your inappropriate relationship with Andrey Kaminski and using unlawful means to gain entry and access information related to the Olivia Kravis case."

I glared at Diskin. "Way to have my back, boss." How many times had he stood before us in that dreadful conference room, swearing his allegiance to us, the staff, proclaiming to be our greatest champion here among the number crunchers on the executive floor? I'd always known his bluster was just that. Diskin was a company man through and through.

Itzushi slid a manila envelope across the table to me. "We believe this is an exceedingly fair offer considering the circumstances."

I opened the package and skimmed through the documents inside. FirstNews was offering me fifteen months of severance, health insurance for two years, glowing recommendations. My departure would be publicly owed to my desire to pursue personal interests. In return, I'd walk away quietly. I'd expected zilch. This was a hell of a lot more. This was a buyout. A payoff. "Feeling generous, Mitch?"

Diskin fiddled with his expensive pen again, eyeing me evenly behind his gold-rimmed spectacles. "You've been with the network a long time, Clyde. We have appreciated your loyalty."

"Beth Stern worked for FirstNews for almost twice as long as I did, and all she got was three months and a coffee mug when you canned her." I shot the folder back across the table.

Itzushi intercepted it. "You may consult an attorney if you wish. The offer is good until Friday, barring any further unlawful actions."

"What gives?" I pressed.

Diskin checked his watch. "I guess we're done here."

I jumped to my feet, my body pitched forward over the table, bridging the distance across. "Are you kidding me? After everything I've done for this network? You're the one who put me in this position. You're the one who told me to go after this story. Now I get myself in a little hot water and you decide to throw out ten years of good, solid work? Do you have any idea what kind of sacrifices I've made for this network? I have no life. FirstNews is my life. You know that."

"Clyde, you broke the law and you violated our code of ethics. You did it to yourself. And this time, Olivia's not here to save your behind," Diskin said without any trace of empathy.

"How dare you talk to me about Olivia. You never gave a shit she was dead. Get the story, get the story. That's all we're ever told. But this time even *you* knew the victim. How many dinners did you sit next to Olivia at? How many luncheons? She was a real, living human being, not just to me but to you too, and still her murder— her brutal fucking murder—was just another story to you. Another fucking ratings grab." I grabbed a shaky breath. "What I want to know is what wouldn't you do for ratings, Mitchell? What wouldn't *you* do to keep *your* job?"

He stood up. "What in the hell is that supposed to mean?"

Feinberg, the old battle-ax, had heard enough. "You sign the agreement or you don't. Either way, as of this moment you are no longer an employee of this network. Your personal effects will be sent to you via courier later today."

I turned to Itzushi. "This is wrong and you know it."

He refused to look at me.

"Cowards." I stood to my full height and regarded Diskin one last time, my voice cool and words deliberate. "You threw me under the bus, you spineless hypocrite. I hope Maldone fires you as soon as the merger is complete." I backed away from the table, feeling better than I thought I would. I was out of a job and none of the networks were hiring, but hell, I'd said my piece—or almost all of it. At the door, I turned around and looked Diskin in the eye. "Isn't it curious how none of you seem to care what it was I found when I was in Olivia's apartment?"

"It's over, Clyde," he said, possibly referring to the case, possibly to me.

# twenty-six

Under the watchful eye of Eugene, one of my favorite security guards, I descended to the lobby. I was handing in my key card when Barton Oberlink showed up, chomping on his breakfast. "Tough break, Clyde. We're really going to miss you." Barton took a bite of his onion bagel. He stood there chewing, staring straight at my breasts. Then he adjusted his crotch.

I snapped my fingers next to my face. "Up here, perv."

His ears turned pink. "What? I wasn't—"

"Yes you were."

He swallowed and readjusted his spectacles, leaving a trace of cream cheese on the rims. "Sorry, jeez."

"Go. Away."

He took a backward step, his hands in the air. "Nice attitude. No wonder you're out on your ass."

"You're next!" I shouted after him.

It was time to go, but I wanted to see one more person before I left. I turned to Eugene. "Any chance you could turn your head for five minutes?"

He barely hesitated. "I'll be by the elevators."

Georgia was in her office, staring at her computer screen. "Get the fuck in here," she hooted, getting out of her chair to shut the door behind me. Then she gave me a hug. "I'm so sorry, girl. I tried to intervene, but you know how these things go. I'm gonna fight for you to get back here. As soon as the merger's final. Diskin knows you're a valuable part of my team."

"I wouldn't bet on that."

Georgia's gold bangles clinked together as she crossed her arms over her chest. "What did you do?"

"I called him a spineless hypocrite. There may have been more."

"Oh, Clyde." She shook her head.

I leaned against her bookshelf. At least once a week she asked me when I was going to finally get my act together and write a true-crime book. My answer had always been the same: when I'm not working from nine in the morning to nine at night, Monday through Friday and sometimes on weekends, I'll *think* about it. Maybe now was the time.

"Will you do me a favor and let me know if you see anyone from the Kravis family around the office today?" I asked.

She scrunched her face. "Why?"

"The network's buying me off. HR offered me fifteen months of severance in exchange for my silence. Olivia's murder may not have had anything to do with the merger, but they're covering up something. I can feel it."

She lifted her eyebrows as her phone rang. Georgia craned her neck to check the caller identification. "Diskin," she muttered. I hovered by the door. Georgia glanced up at me and mouthed the word *sorry*. "Taped not live, I got it. Exclusive to us?" There was a long pause. "OK." She replaced the phone. "Delphine and Monica Kravis apparently just agreed to go on *Topical*."

I couldn't believe it; I'd been hounding Delphine for days to tape another interview with us, and Monica had been totally off the table since the get-go.

"Charles Kravis was admitted to Lennox Hill last night," she added. "They think he may be on his last days. They want to talk about that and refocus the media attention on their family to what Charles did, his accomplishment in building this network and changing the cable industry and how Americans get their news. With the merger pending, it's smart strategy."

"You don't think Diskin made a deal? An interview for my head?"

Georgia rubbed her temples. "I don't know, honey. You think you know someone, but truth is anything's possible. Not too many people you can trust in this world."

I found Eugene near the elevator bank. Alex was there waiting with him.

"I just heard." Alex put his hands on my shoulders. "You OK?"

"I'm fine," I said, but inside I felt uneasy, and not just because my future was entirely up in the air. There were still too many unanswered questions churning in my head about the merger, about the message on my computer screen, and about Olivia's last text to me. *It's time you know the truth.* It dawned on me then that had she been referring to Andrey and Rachel, she would have worded it differently. Whatever she had to tell me was *personal*, like the message the perp had left on my computer. The *truth*. My *past*. But what did one thing have to do with the other? *Did* they have anything to do with each other?

Eugene and I stepped inside the elevator.

Alex put his hand up against the door. "Any word from the cops about your apartment?"

"They said I could go back and pick up some clothes with an escort if I wanted."

"So I'll see you at home tonight?"

"I promised Sabine I was leaving."

"You don't have to," he said.

"Oh yes I do."

"She understands."

He was wrong about that. "I wouldn't."

Alex let the elevator go. A few minutes later I was in a cab heading uptown. Panda was about to go on his lunch break. I was planning on hitting him up for a ride to New Jersey.


I secured the corner table at Pastrami Queen and ordered us a couple of sodas and a knish for Panda. He hobbled inside, his knee acting up again. Before he could say anything, I told him about getting canned.

"These people never hear of probation?" he asked in reply.

I slid him a root beer. "Probation's for cops, criminals, and teenagers. I'm none of those."

"Well, they made a mistake. They're gonna beg you to come back, kid."

"When pigs fly." I nodded at his choice of cravat. "Like your—"

"Nah, try again."

I shook my head.

*"Swine flu."*

I hung my head. "Second one I've gotten wrong. I'm losing my touch." Panda's knish arrived at the table in a red plastic basket. I pushed it to his side.

He picked up a fork. "You not eating?"

"I had a late breakfast." Truth was, my stomach was in knots. I was nursing a ginger ale, but it hadn't done much good. "How'd you pin Andrey?"

Panda dusted some crumbs from his mouth. "DNA."

"The baby?"

He nodded. "Our break was finding Rockwell's body, and linking up the DNA. It took some time to get Kaminski's sample, though. And then another twenty-four hours to get it tested."

"That can't be all you got. All that proves is he was the baby's father."

"You're right. But he also left plenty of his DNA around the apartment. Hair and clothing fibers, bodily fluids." I thought back to the two squares removed from the carpet in the living room. "There were also fingerprints on the suitcase and all over Rachel Rockwell's clothing."

"Couldn't that all be circumstantial? He could have helped Olivia with her suitcase the last time she came home from a trip, and he was having an affair with Rachel."

"It's a lot of evidence, Red."

"Is he talking?"

"Kaminski claims he didn't know about the baby. And we think Rachel was not planning on keeping it."

I sloshed the ice around in my glass. "Had she made an appointment at an abortion clinic?"

"No, but she'd had a conversation with her gynecologist, who had referred her to a clinic in Stamford."

"Olivia would have wanted Rachel to keep the baby. She wasn't a staunch conservative like her dad, obviously, but she did share some of his values."

"We don't even know for sure Olivia knew about the pregnancy."

"But they were fighting, remember? The neighbors overheard them."

Panda sighed. "They could have been fighting about anything."

"I'll buy that Rachel didn't want the baby. I'll even give you the possibility that Olivia didn't know about it, but I think Andrey was telling the truth when he said he didn't know about it either. So if he didn't know about the pregnancy, he couldn't have known Rachel was planning on getting an abortion. And if he didn't know that, what's his motive? Why kill two women?"

"We know Rachel liked the lifestyle. So it fits that the pregnancy could have been her wake-up call. She realizes how reckless her affair with Kaminski is. She tells him again that it's over between them. Maybe she's mean about it, and maybe this time he decides he's not going away quietly."

"Sounds like you've got it all figured out."

"It's the only way it could have happened. But to tell you the truth, we hardly need motive with all the physical evidence we've got. I'm talking phone records, fingerprints, DNA, and if that ain't enough, a personal history of anger-management issues. One of Kaminski's ex-girlfriends called 911 on him a few times. No restraining order, but cops showed up on their doorstep, and there's a record of him threatening her—and that crap is admissible in court. It'll go a long way with a jury."

Michael Rockwell also had a history of roughing up his women. Rachel had a type, just like I did; and so did Olivia. There was never a romantic spark between my best friend and me, but Rachel and I were one in the same—broken little birds attracted to trouble and prone to self-destruction via men and booze.

"I'm a fool," I whispered. Why had I believed Andrey? Of course he killed Olivia and Rachel.

Panda patted my hand. "You're not the only one. Rachel trusted Kaminski too, and there were probably plenty more before her."

It was because he was good-looking. Like Scott Peterson and Joran van der Sloot, Natalee Holloway's presumed killer. Or Ted Bundy, who murdered, raped, and battered over thirty women before they caught him, or Charles Manson, whose body count is still unknown. By the time their victims saw the monster behind the good-looking face, it was too late.

We got up to leave. Once we were outside, I asked Panda where he was heading. "New Jersey with Ehlers," he said. "To that lab, actually."

I raised my eyebrows. "Orchid Cellmark?"

He nodded.

"Can I go?"

Panda rocked on his heels. "No way, kid. I can't take a reporter on a fact-finding mission. This isn't even technically my case."

I clenched my molars. "I'm not a reporter anymore."

He flashed me a look. "You're close enough."

We walked together to his squad car in silence. At the curb he promised to let me know what they found out at the lab, but I had to make him a promise. "Anything," I said.

"We can't be sure Kaminski was the one who drugged you and broke into your place. Whoever was in there was real careful not to leave behind any prints. It's gonna take some time to sift through everything they bagged and figure out if they've got anything useful. In the meantime, there may still be someone out there who wants to hurt you. For the time being, you can't stay in your apartment. I know they're gonna tell you that you can go back there tomorrow. But you gotta promise me you won't."

I offered my hand for a shake. "You have a deal."

That night, I had Alex's place to myself. He arranged to stay with Sabine again. I imagined she'd put her foot down with him after what she'd witnessed that morning. I showered and ate a dinner of takeout Chinese while watching Georgia's taped interview with Monica and Delphine. There were no surprises. Mostly the women talked about Charles's career, Olivia's philanthropic endeavors, and how the family was coping in the aftermath of such a terrible loss and with Charles's failing health. At the end of the interview, I changed the channel, disheartened.

My phone buzzed on the coffee table with a text from Sutton Danziger. She wanted to know if we could have lunch after Olivia's memorial service the following morning. I picked up my phone. There was one more favor I had to ask of her.

# Thursday

# twenty-seven

I woke up at 8:00 a.m., groggy from a restless night of sleep. I showered and dressed in the black skirt suit and pumps I'd been allowed to pick up from my apartment along with a few other necessities. By the time I left the apartment, Alex hadn't made an appearance. After what had almost happened between us yesterday morning, I couldn't blame her for keeping him on a short leash. I locked the door behind me, made a stop for coffee and a bagel, and took the subway uptown to Lexington and Seventy-Seventh, walking the rest of the way to the Frank E. Campbell Funeral Chapel on Eighty-First and Madison.

I was two blocks away, on a quiet street between Lexington and Park, when I saw Michael Rockwell striding from the opposite direction. At the corner, I crossed Park. He followed. I kept walking uptown, quickening my pace, but he stayed in step. "I want to apologize," he said, catching up to me.

I stopped abruptly. We were on a stretch of open sidewalk. It was broad daylight, plenty of eyewitnesses around, and there was a cop car not more than fifty feet away. Rockwell wasn't stupid enough to try anything on me right there.

He ran a furry hand down the length of his blue silk tie. He was dressed in a dark suit and starched white shirt, his hair slicked back with an overabundance of gel. I surmised he was headed the same place I was. "I said some things the other day in the woods behind my house that were uncalled for." That was an understatement, but I let him finish muddling through his mea culpa. "Rachel and I didn't have the perfect marriage, but I loved her. I never wanted anything like this to happen to her."

I crossed my arms. "Why are you telling me this?"

"Her parents are fighting me for custody."

In other words, Rockwell was afraid I was going to testify against him in court, that I'd tell the judge what a brute and bully he was. Rachel's parents had been on Georgia's show almost every day since I'd wrangled them for our show, and Rockwell, not knowing that I wasn't working for the network anymore, had assumed that I'd been getting close to the Harts, possibly commiserating with them about the upcoming custody battle.

I decided to make use of his fear and vulnerability. "Why didn't you tell me Rachel and Olivia met through you? Why hide that?" I asked.

"The Kravises were clients of my firm. They find out I'm blabbing to the press about how their murdered daughter stole my wife from me, how do you think that's going to blow over with my partners? Lawyers are paid for their discretion."

"That's cliché." I felt a slight wind at my back. The forecast predicted heavy rains, but not until the afternoon. "So is being the husband who threatens to take away the kids when his wife decides she's had enough. You roughed her up, didn't you, Michael? Did you fool around too? Good for Rachel for having the courage to leave you."

"I wasn't sleeping with anyone and I never once hurt her. Not once. That's what she told people to make her affair with that trainer of hers seem less awful," he protested, his voice rising. "I found her with him. Did you know that? And he was such a sleazebag. I couldn't let a guy like that near my kids. I was hoping she'd tire of him and come back to us. But the next thing I knew, she'd hired a lawyer and was spending nights with Charles Kravis's daughter."

"You filed first."

He nodded soberly. "On advice of counsel."

"Did you know Rachel liked women?"

Rockwell looked at his feet. "I knew it wasn't the first time."

"But it was for the money, right? She was attracted to Olivia because she liked her lifestyle?"

He looked back up at me, squinting in the morning sun. "Rachel grew up on an American Indian reservation. She was the third girl in a family of five. She wore hand-me-down clothes, played with hand-me-down toys, and she had an uncle who couldn't keep his hands off her when he had too much to drink, which was every week, like clockwork, right after he got his paycheck."

"The Harts, they never said anything." And Olivia had obviously never mentioned it to me. I wondered if she'd even known.

"Why would they? Rachel got out, but not without her demons. She liked to drink; she liked to shop. It made her feel like she was a million miles away from being that little girl on the reservation, clutching her one-armed Barbie, hoping her uncle would pass out before he got to her bedroom door." He stood there, his massive size somehow diminished, like a balloon that had come back down to earth after spending a long time lost in the clouds.

"Then why Kaminski?" I pressed. "He has no money."

He shrugged. "I guess there's only so much you can truly understand about a person."

Sutton was waiting for me out in front of the funeral chapel, her face pinched and pink from being made to wait for me outside. She knew nothing about what I'd been through the last week, and met my somewhat haggard appearance—the dark circles under my eyes and patchy skin—with a disapproving stare. "You have got to take better care of yourself," she hissed in my ear, linking her arm in mine as we filed in line to make our way inside the home.

Sutton craned her neck to look around, and I did the same. By the looks of it, there were over 150 people crowded into the receiving room. We spotted Delphine and Monica, who were seated next to Delphine's husband, Naomi Zell, Mitchell Diskin and his wife, and a few members of the FirstNews board. Noticeably absent was Charles Kravis.

Sitting down on an empty bench near the back of the room, we put our phones on mute as a string quartet began to play a somber piece by Mendelssohn. Then Monica read a poem and Delphine recalled memories of their childhood. Naomi Zell spoke of Olivia's tireless efforts at the foundation and all the lives she'd touched. I would have liked to say a few words, and kicked myself for not insisting on it when I spoke to Delphine.

At the end of the service, the Kravis clan began to make their way down the aisle and out of the chapel. Monica, Delphine, Naomi, and Diskin filed past us, ignoring me deliberately. Sutton nudged me in the ribs. "You should say hello."

"Another time," I whispered back.

I hadn't told Sutton about losing my job. I'd have to explain the circumstances, and Sutton, despite her best intentions, wouldn't be able to keep from passing along the news to our former classmates. By sundown, everyone would know I'd almost had sex with an alleged murderer. And not just any murderer, but the one who'd killed our friend.

Outside, the block was littered with reporters and news vans, including one belonging to FirstNews. Alex spotted us coming out of the funeral home and beat a path through the crush of onlookers and mourners. "Are you ready?" he asked Sutton. I'd convinced her, in lieu of having lunch with me, to agree to give FirstNews a quick on-camera after the service. It was my parting gift as Alex's producer. Not that the network deserved my help.

She fluffed her hair. "How do I look?"

"Perfect." I stepped aside and asked Alex if we could meet up after he wrapped up filming. He glanced behind him to Sabine. She had her eyes trained on us. I waved and smiled. She did the same. "Say no more," I told Alex.

He caught the tightness in my voice. "Hey, I've been thinking about you."

"That and a buck fifty," I said lightly, waving good-bye to Sutton and my old crew and walking away.

Good-bye, indeed. Good-bye, producers screaming in my ear. Good-bye, blowhard newscasters and prima donna correspondents. Good-bye, crime-scene gore. Now what? At times like these you're supposed to think about the big picture, but I found it a hell of a lot easier to focus minute to minute. It was easier to think about going to Alex's apartment and then mine, briefly, to pack my bags. It was easier to think about going to see my dad upstate and the really decadent slice of chocolate cake I'd buy on the way to the train station. It was easier to think about anything but Olivia. Or my job. Or Alex.

I passed by a boutique with silver picture frames in the window and thought of the photograph of Olivia and me I'd taken from her apartment. Overhead the sky had turned slate gray. A few drops of rain fell on my shoulders and hair. I took refuge inside the store, digging for the picture in the depths of my bag. A sales lady glanced over my shoulder. She plucked a simple beveled-edge silver frame from a display table and handed it to me. I didn't bother to ask the price.

"Do you want me to throw that away for you?" She gestured at the envelope I was holding in my hand, one of the ones that had fallen from behind Olivia's vanity. I'd stuffed the photo in it for safekeeping.

I turned it over in my hands. The envelope was old and yellowed, and addressed to Charles Kravis. There was something familiar about it. "Wait," I said, flipping the envelope over and back to the front again. There was no return address. But that didn't matter. Looking closer, I realized I recognized the handwriting.

It was my mother's.

And it was postmarked the year before I was born.

# twenty-eight

In the drizzling rain, I walked back toward Alex's apartment, losing myself in my thoughts, attempting fruitlessly not to jump to any conclusions. Maybe Charles Kravis and my mother were just friends. Maybe this meant nothing. But why then had no one ever told me they knew each other? And why would Olivia have had the envelope? Eventually I arrived at Alex's apartment. I was in the living room, unbuttoning my suit jacket, when my phone rang. I scrambled to answer it.

"I've got something to tell you," Panda said.

"Is it about the case?"

"We're on our way back from the lab now. It took longer than expected. They wouldn't hand over the information without a subpoena," he said stiffly. "It turns out that Olivia wasn't doing a paternity test. It was a sibling test."

A sibling test. It wasn't difficult to take the next mental leap: my mother and Charles Kravis; an affair a year before my birth; a sibling test; a secret. *It's time you know the truth.* This was why Olivia had a copy of my birth certificate in her desk drawer at work. I felt my stomach bottom out, my breath turn shallow. Was it possible? Could Olivia and I be half sisters? I swallowed hard, my mouth suddenly dry. "What were the results?" I asked, but I already knew the answer.

"Positive. Do you have any idea who she might have been testing? There are no names attached. They're faxing over the results. Forensics will see if either makes a match with what we picked up at the scene." There was a short pause. "Crap. Now?" Panda huffed into the phone.

Police business. "Go. I'll catch up with you later," I said, hanging up the phone. I sank to the floor. A gray cloud moved overhead, submerging Alex's living room in dull light. In the distance, a first bolt cracked against the sky. I heard the low growl of thunder, then the rain beating down on the cement floor of his balcony.

I fumbled for my bag, ripping into the box holding the silver-framed photograph of Olivia and me. There we were: same smile, same red-tinted hair, same smattering of freckles across our noses. Our eyes were different, and face shape, and bodies. As we'd aged all those things became more pronounced. But when we were young, they used to mistake us for sisters. Old people especially. We'd laugh and look at each other and wish it were so. I gazed down at the framed picture as anger, grief, and guilt took over my mind, forcing out every thought except for one: Who didn't want me to know I was a Kravis?

My mother, for starters. She must have known about my true father and never told me, never even given me a clue. But she had to have been haunted by her guilt. To have had a child with one man and live a lie with another. Was this the reason she'd killed herself?

"Life will teach you this in time," she'd told me once, a lone moment of unvarnished candor. I was five years old, too young to understand, but not too young to remember. "Men make promises they can't keep. Friends become enemies. It's the people you trust the most who hurt you the worst." She'd smoothed the copper curls off my face, pulled the covers of my bed up to my neck and called me by my pet name. "And do you know why that is, Princess Bumblebee?"

I can't recall what I'd said. Probably nothing.

Her answer came in a whisper laced with regret. "Because we let them."

Charles Kravis was my biological father. My parents had always avoided discussing the fact that I was born less than nine months after their wedding, and I'd assumed it was because my dad had knocked up my mother. But there had been more to the story than that. The question was, had my father known? Suspected, at least? I looked down at my cell phone and started to dial his number and then stopped. This wasn't a subject you broached any way other than face to face. Olivia must have thought the same thing: I'll wait to see her in person. Then I'd canceled on her. And then someone had killed her. The police thought Andrey had killed her, and had a pretty good theory on why he'd done it, but what if it hadn't been him? What if Olivia hadn't been murdered because of Rachel, but because of me, and because of this secret that she'd uncovered about us being related? Again I asked myself who didn't want me to find out I was Charles Kravis's daughter. Who would have been willing to brutally kill not just one but *two* people to keep this secret?

I heard Naomi Zell's voice ringing in my ear: *What's your connection to this family?* And then my mind reached deeper, to the shadowy figure towering over me in the bathroom at Prentice Maldone's party, to the strong hands pinching my cheeks, and the swish of hair against my face. Long hair. A woman's hair. I flashed to another moment, to Delphine standing with Prentice Maldone in the lobby of the FirstNews building, her hand so tightly clenched around the strap of her handbag her knuckles had turned white.

I dialed Panda on my phone. It went to voice mail. "Call me as soon as you get this. The party Prentice Maldone threw at that gallery in SoHo—you guys still have the surveillance footage, right?

283

I need to know when Delphine and her husband left the party. I think she drugged me, and I think . . . I think she killed Olivia."

I hung up. Delphine must have found out about my past. She'd written "JIFFY" on my computer and destroyed all my belongings. I thought of those cracker crumbs Restivo noticed on my countertop. She'd waited in my apartment for me to come home from the benefit, just like she'd waited for Olivia to come home from dinner with Rachel. She waited.

Inside my head, I heard an alarm bell ringing. *Leave now.*

Another bolt of lightning lit up the sky, illuminating the room. On the wall, I caught a split-second of shadow.

It was too late.

The first thing I saw was the gun. Next the blue latex gloves. And finally the person wearing them. Delphine Lamont stepped out of Alex's bedroom.

I looked to the front door. It was dead-bolted by my own hands. I looked behind me to the balcony. I could try climbing down, but Alex's apartment was on the eleventh floor. If I fell, I'd die.

"How did you get in here?" I asked, struggling to keep the tremor out of my voice.

"Look at me," she said, a sneering smile on her face. "Do I look like a burglar? A murderer? There's no building in the city I couldn't get into if I wanted to." She took a step closer. "Now drop the phone."

I stared at the phone in my hand.

"Drop it," she repeated, taking another step. She was wearing the same clothes she'd worn to Olivia's funeral: low-heeled designer pumps, a heavy gold necklace, and a beautiful black suit. Her thick brown hair was up in a blue hairnet. She was going to finish me off now. My only hope was to stall her and call for help without her noticing. "Don't come any closer. Don't or I'll scream," I warned.

She shook her head pityingly. Then she lunged for me, 140 pounds of muscle and rage railing on my body, wrenching the phone from my grasp. I grabbed for her hair, lost my balance, and felt her elbow connecting with my spine. A moment later I was on my hands and knees, blood dripping from my temple onto the rug. My head had slammed against the corner of Alex's coffee table. I managed one ragged breath before Delphine nailed me at full force with the pointed toe of her shoe. She aimed the gun at my face. "Get up."

"Please don't do this," I begged, gasping for air. "I don't want any money. I won't ask for any. I promise."

She snorted. "Charles is worth hundreds of millions of dollars. If he knew he had another living daughter, he'd want you to have your share of it. But you don't deserve it. You never spent a day with him in your life." Her cold eyes were lit with fury. "He was planning on leaving Olivia *everything*. My mother was getting a pittance. Me, fucking five million dollars. And I'm supposed to just *accept* it? I was *entitled* to more. And now I'm going to get it, everything except for what he's giving that charity of hers. Do you realize how much money is at stake here?"

Outside the rain was coming down in sheets. Thunder growled from overhead. "Were you the one who opposed the merger?"

"That was Naomi Zell. The rest of us realized the sooner we cashed out the better."

"How did you know to find me here?" I asked, still hoping to stall her.

"There was a girl in the news van. Pretty. I don't know her name. She was more than happy to give me the address."

Sabine. I knew she felt threatened by me, but she wouldn't have done this on purpose. She, like everyone else, thought Olivia's killer was behind bars. She'd assumed I was no longer in danger, and that Delphine, in her jewels and kitten heels, wasn't a threat.

Delphine kicked me again in the side, knocking the breath from my lungs. "Get up now and start undressing, or I'll shoot you right here. Do it slowly. And don't try anything."

I reached for my first button with dread. Delphine wasn't going to just shoot me. She had something else planned, something worse. My eyes searched the room for a weapon, anything I could use to get the upper hand. Nothing was in my grasp, but my keys lay just beyond, about a foot away from the coffee table. In self-defense, we'd learned to aim for the side of the neck: jugular vein, carotid artery, and no bone protection. I had to distract Delphine, throw her off balance, get her to lower her gun for a second if I was going to have a chance at nailing her in the right spot.

I worked another few buttons on my blouse. "How did you know to pin it on the doorman?"

Her face lit up with self-satisfaction. "Olivia suspected Rachel and Andrey might be messing around in her apartment. Turns out, she was right. I told her if she wanted, I could find out for sure, sneak into her apartment and catch them in the act. She wasn't sure she wanted me to do that. But I didn't need her permission. I have a key, and I knew how to get into the building unnoticed. From there, it was a fucking cakewalk. All I had to do was bide my time until Rachel and Olivia came back from dinner; then I tied the whore up in the closet and took care of Olivia in the hall." The whole time she was talking I was slowly undressing. I'd so far removed my blouse, strategically tossing it so that it concealed my keys. They were my only hope.

"Hurry up." Delphine seemed to suddenly remember the task at hand. I removed my skirt and stockings and placed them on top of my blouse. She gestured at my clothes. "Now pick it all up and go to the bathroom," she said.

I did as I was told, scooping up my clothes and the keys. As soon as I had a firm grip on the largest key, I hurled myself on top of Delphine, bringing it down on her neck. She cried out in shock, staggering backward. We struggled. I felt the butt of her gun connecting with the side of my head, her knee with my ribs. I gasped for breath, my diaphragm protesting against the force of inhalation as I hit the floor.

"Look at me," she panted, the gun at my temple again. "This isn't a fucking dress rehearsal." She pulled me up by my hair and dug the barrel of the gun between my shoulders. "Walk."

"What are you going to do to me?" I whimpered, fear blunting the edge of my pain. I felt nothing, just a quiet panic eroding my sense of reality. For a moment I wondered if I might be dreaming, but then I heard the click of the gun's safety being taken off.

"Bathtub. Razors. You know the rest," she said in a singsong. "No one will question it. You've lost your job. You're all alone. You fucked the man who killed my stepsister. This wouldn't exactly be the first time you tried to put an end to your pitiful existence, would it?" She pointed at my arms. "I saw the scars."

I turned to face her. "It won't work. The medical examiner will see my wounds. The police will see the blood on the carpet. They'll know there was a struggle."

"You stumbled and fell, picked up a few bruises on the way. Not unusual for someone on as many drugs as you are." She shook a trio of pill bottles. Even at a distance, I knew what they were.

"Those aren't mine." Georgia had thrown out all my painkillers when I was in rehab. She'd gone back to my apartment soon after she'd taken me to Hilltop and dumped all my drugs in the trash and all my alcohol down the toilet.

"So what?" She threw them at me one by one. "Now start swallowing. You're still good at that, aren't you? Swallowing."

I squared my shoulders. "I'm not taking these."

"If I have to force you, I will."

I opened the first bottle and placed two pills on my tongue. "Faster!" Delphine shouted, pointing the gun at my face. I looked down at the handful of pills in my hand and wondered who would find my body first—Alex or Panda or Restivo? After I'd swallowed the last of the pills, Delphine prodded me toward Alex's bathroom. The bath was full to the top, still steaming. On the sink, one of Alex's razor blades had been dismantled. Three thin pieces of metal glinted against the green marble.

"No one will believe I did this to myself," I said.

Delphine's mouth twisted into a sadistic smile. "Why not? They say suicide runs in the family. And apparently so do other things."

Her words hit like a blast of cold water. "What does that mean?"

"You remember what the other girls used to call you in high school?" She waited for my response.

"How did you know about that?" By the time I was in high school, Delphine and Olivia were in a Swiss boarding school.

"You don't fuck half the Collegiate basketball team without word getting around."

"It was two. Just two of them."

"At the same time," she snarled. And then, like a slow twist of the knife: "You are a slut and so was your mother."

*How dare you.* Delphine hadn't known my mother, her sweetness, her patience, the way she used to grip my hand when we crossed the streets, how gently she used to comb the knots from my hair, how she read to me every night until my eyes grew heavy and my breathing slowed. And then she'd kiss me on the forehead, pull the covers to my chin, and whisper in my ear how much she loved me—*today, tomorrow, forever.* I launched myself into Delphine, my fingernails tearing at her face, but it was like trying to tackle a seven-foot lineman. She threw me to the floor with ease.

"People are going to see that," I hissed, pointing at the long scratch I'd managed to inflict above her right eyebrow. "I've got friends on the force. They won't give up until they bring you to justice."

"Shut up. No one cares about you." Her lips thinned. "Your mother was supposed to get rid of you. She told Charles she would."

So Charles didn't know he had a daughter, had never known. And then I remembered the look on his face at that Fourth of July party. *You're Tipsy Shaw's daughter.* He must have put two and two together. Is that why Monica had sent me back home to my father the next day? I grabbed the towel bar and pulled myself up to standing with effort. The pain and pills were starting to take their toll.

Delphine cackled. "Olivia found the letters from your mother. After Charles's second stroke, we had to help with the memoir. We were looking for documents, pictures, and memorabilia. Instead, we found a stash of old letters. I thought they were nothing. Some stupid old letters? Who the fuck cares. I had them in the trash. But Olivia dug them out and read them, and then she had you tested. She got your hair from your hairbrush. She was going to make Charles do right by you. I had to stop her. Charles is about to die. The fuck if I was going to lose my inheritance to his redheaded slut of a stepchild."

"Except I'm not the stepchild. You are." I looked her dead in the eyes.

"Enough!" Delphine shrieked.

I felt the blood trickling down the side of my face, my brain swimming in a sea of medication. *Stay awake,* I commanded myself. But my belly had turned warm, my vision cloudy. My fingers tingled. I thought I heard my mother's voice reading to me from a favorite book. *It's bedtime now, Bumblebee.*

"Get in." Delphine's eyes flicked to the water.

I stepped one foot in the bath. "Too hot," I protested. My ribs sang out in pain as Delphine pushed me down toward the water. It felt certain now, my impending death. A tear escaped my eye, and then another and another. I thought of my father, the one who had raised me; my mother, the one who had sacrificed everything for me; and Olivia, the one who had died for me.

Delphine regarded my sobbing and my almost-naked body. She rolled her eyes. "Get over it."

"I promise I won't tell anyone," I bleated, sinking farther down into the tub. "Please. Please, *please*. Let me live."

She placed the gun on the sink and pulled my right arm out of the water, holding the razor steady for a moment before plunging it deep into my flesh. I felt a sharp sting and watched as a red stream poured into the bath.

"One more," she said in a soothing voice, the razor poised to slice into me again.

The mist rose from the bath in the shape of my mother's face. She was frowning as she shook her head slowly. *No, Cornelia. Not like this. Fight back.*

I grabbed the first thing I saw, a glass bottle of bath oil perched on the side of the tub. Delphine never saw the blow coming. It caught her just above the ear, one blow, hard enough to make her lose her balance and fall to the side. I jumped out of the bathtub, slipping and careening forward as I dashed through Alex's living room and slid open the door to his balcony with a bang. Outside the rain beat cold against my hot skin. I lunged for the railing and swung a leg over.

Delphine appeared on the balcony a moment later. "You'll die either way!" she roared through the storm.

*If you're watching, Mom, help me.*

I swung my other leg around. Delphine shoved me in the chest with all her might. I lost my footing and was dangling, clothed only in my underwear, the rain pummeling me as I clung for life eleven stories up. I had no voice to yell for help.

Delphine looked down at me. "This is even more perfect," she whispered.

My hands burned as I closed my eyes again and pictured my mother's face. She bared her small white teeth in the smile I'd remember always.

*It's OK, Bumblebee.*

*You can let go now.*

# twenty-nine

The gunshots startled me so much I almost did let go.

But then I heard voices, shouts, and footsteps. Delphine fell to the ground, her hazel eyes blinking blankly at me through the railing. Blood seeped onto the balcony floor. My muscles ached. I felt my grip slipping.

Two hands reached down and grabbed my wrists. "I've got you. Don't let go. I've got you." I looked up. It was Alex. Restivo appeared behind him on the balcony, assessing the situation. He called out to the people behind him. "One floor below. She's hanging."

Alex struggled to hold his grip. My arms were wet. I was slipping. "It's OK," I may have said only to myself, while below I heard the glass door to the tenth-floor balcony crash open. Arms—I don't know how many—encircled my torso, pulling me over the railing to safety, to a cold stone floor. I made a cocoon of my own body, hugging my legs, shivering in the freezing rain. Someone wrapped a towel around me and carried me inside. Hands tied a tourniquet around my bleeding arm. A pair of paramedics arrived and began ministering, checking my body temperature, my heart rate, my pupils. A flashlight shined in my eye. Their voices buzzed in my ear.

*Did you take any medication? Do you know what you took?* I tried to speak but no words came out.

Two EMTs lifted my body onto the gurney. "We need to pump her stomach now," one said to the other.

"Clyde, thank God." Alex was at my side. He gripped my good hand and kissed my forehead and then my lips. His were soft and warm.

Alex looked up at the EMTs. The paramedics hoisted up the sides of my gurney.

I tried again to thank him.

He shushed me, and kissed me again. "Later."

I laid my head back on the pillow as the paramedics rolled me away.

Friday

# thirty

I woke up in the hospital.

This time I got my own room equipped with a gigantic television and a nice view over the East River. For the first twenty-four hours, I had round-the-clock visitors. First Alex, then Georgia and Panda. Then my father, who had gotten in his pickup truck the second Georgia tracked him down and then broken just about every traffic law along the Taconic State Parkway. Ehlers and Restivo came next. Naomi Zell sent balloons. Frank Uffizo offered his services "at a substantially reduced rate," while Prentice Maldone sent flowers and a note that read "Please don't make a habit of this," and Orchid Cellmark, the lab in New Jersey, sent a DNA kit, accompanied by a very nice letter asking if I would care to submit my DNA to confirm that Charles Kravis was indeed my father. I swabbed my cheek and repackaged the kit according to the enclosed directions. After all that had happened, I wanted incontrovertible proof.

I wanted it, but I didn't need it. I knew in my heart I was Charles Kravis's daughter and Olivia's half sister. It made sense of so much—not only Olivia's text, but also the feeling I've had my whole life that something wasn't quite right. This was why my mother insisted I carry her last name and not my father's, why no one had ever wanted to talk about my conception and the date of my parents' wedding. Panda had been wrong. Sometimes all the pieces of a puzzle did fit together.

But the puzzle wasn't complete yet. After two days in the hospital, I changed out of my gown and back into my clothes, signed myself out against doctor's orders, and left a note for my dad, who was staying in a nearby hotel and was out buying papers and coffee. Then I caught a cab crosstown to Lennox Hill.

I found the hospice-care wing. The nurse at the reception desk took one look at me and handed me a pen. She was a big lady with chocolate skin, an island accent, and a name tag that said her name was Judith. "We were wondering if you'd come," she said smoothly, pointing to the visitors' log where I was supposed to sign my name.

Judith had apparently seen the news: the *Post*, the *Daily News*, the lead story on just about every cable network in the country, including FirstNews. Three dead, a rich female murderer, and a shoot-out on an apartment balcony. Like we say in the business, *You can't make this shit up.*

I signed my name. Judith escorted me down the hall to the corner room. "You came at a good time," she said, pushing the door open. Buttery morning sun slid through the slats of the blinds onto a small hospital bed where my biological father lay staring up at the ceiling tiles. The nurse pulled a chair close to his bed. "He just got up." And then, louder, to Charles, "Didn't you, Mr. Kravis?"

He nodded, propping himself up on the pillows.

"You have a visitor. Would you like to eat now or after she leaves?"

His finger crooked toward a tray of food on a countertop. "I'll eat now, Judith." The left side of his mouth slanted downward, paralyzed from the strokes, slurring his speech. He was weak of body, but his mind seemed lucid.

"Take a seat, child," Judith said to me, motioning to a chair by the bed as she began to feed Charles his breakfast. First eggs, then a few bites of oatmeal. A piece of toast stayed on the plate. As I watched him eat, I tried not to think of how frail he looked for seventy-eight years old—the gray pallor of his skin, the sound of the machines monitoring his heart—and how I really just wanted to get the hell out of there. What was I doing? Why did I think he'd want to answer any of my questions? I was the reason his daughter, the only daughter he'd ever known, was dead. He probably hated me for it.

Judith rolled away the cart, shutting the door behind her. Charles tilted his head toward me.

"My name is Clyde Shaw," I said simply. "I worked for FirstNews as a producer. And I was very close friends with Olivia."

His eyes slanted in my direction once again. "I know who you are." He spoke slowly, trying to enunciate each word as clearly as his condition allowed. "You are my daughter."

I bit my lip. "You know?"

"I do watch the news." The right corner of his mouth lifted.

It was a joke. I laughed belatedly.

"Do you want to know?" he said hoarsely. "About your mother and me?"

I blinked through a few tears, my emotions getting the better of me. "Yes. Do you remember her?"

"Of course I remember her. She looked like you."

"Skinnier."

He pointed at me with his right hand. "That's from my side."

"And the hair."

His rheumy eyes lifted to mine. "Ah, yes."

"What happened?"

"She was single. I was not. And I couldn't leave my wife, you see. She was pregnant."

"With Olivia." Two women, my mother and Olivia's mother, had been pregnant at the same time. He chose his wife. I couldn't blame him, and yet it was difficult not to feel some resentment.

Charles seemed to know what I was thinking. "I didn't know about you," he wheezed. "Not until I saw you at that Fourth of July party. Then I suspected it, but your mother was gone by then, and I couldn't have taken you away from your father." He paused again for breath. "You were all he had left of her."

I lowered my eyes. "My mother told you she had an abortion?"

"She did. That is what she said," he affirmed, grabbing on to his absolution. "I wasn't much of a family man then, but if I'd known about you, I would have taken care of you." There was another short pause and within this I understood that much more had happened, things Charles felt I should not know. I hungered for details; he wanted to spare me of them. A pair of nurses called to each other in the hall. A cart rumbled past the room.

I leaned closer to the side of his bed. "Monica made me go to my room the night of that big party, and I was told to leave the next day. Did she know I was your daughter?"

"I met Monica long after my first wife died, and long after your mother and I stopped seeing each other. She couldn't have known."

He'd married Monica in 1982, the year I'd met Olivia. I was eight, and in the second grade. My mother had died in 1980, on my first day of kindergarten. I was six years old.

"Does she know now?"

Charles coughed, slumping into his pillow. "She is upset. This has all been quite upsetting." Delphine had died on the way to the hospital. One of the bullets had pierced her liver, another her lungs.

I couldn't imagine being in Charles's position right now. His own daughter was dead by the hands of his wife's daughter, and his wife's daughter was dead at, if not my hands, then the hands of the policemen who were trying to save me. "What about the letters?" I asked. "The ones my mother sent to you. Olivia found them. Do you know where they are now?"

He shook his head. "I'm afraid I don't."

"I would like to have them."

Silence fell again as I gathered the resolve to ask the question I'd come to ask, the only one that really mattered. "Did you love my mother?"

He considered his response. "It was a very passionate affair," he said gently. "She was a beautiful woman."

I looked away, embarrassed. There it was: I was the product of something other than love—of lust and subterfuge, of my own jaded axiom: *People lie and people cheat.* My mother had an affair with a married man who loved his wife better. I knew how terrible she must have felt.

"I'm sorry," he said, his hand inching toward mine.

I wiped away my tears with the heel of my hand. "All those years that you did know about me, or suspected I was yours, why didn't you try to get to know me?"

"I did know you in a way. Olivia kept me informed."

"She did?"

He nodded. "She didn't know why. I said it was because I found the stories about you entertaining."

"Did I get my job here because of you?"

"I may have put in a word at the very beginning." The right corner of his mouth rose once again. "Everything else you accomplished on your own." Charles sat up a little straighter on his pillows. "I tried to help more. My offer of financial assistance was declined."

So my father had known.

"I had planned to leave you a good sum, Cornelia."

A pit opened in my stomach. Delphine had killed Olivia to keep her from telling Charles about me, or so she'd said. I no longer believed that. She'd wanted *all* of Charles's money, not just whatever portion of the pie that would have been set aside for me. Still, finding out about me seemed to have sparked in Delphine's mind the idea that she was entitled to more than she was getting.

Charles looked out the window. "I was so sorry to hear about your mother's passing. I sent flowers."

I didn't remember much about my mother's funeral. I remembered what I wore—a navy dress and matching tights, the black patent Mary Janes that pinched my toes. I remembered my father's bloodshot eyes and his hand gripping my shoulder as they lowered her casket into the grave, as well as the leftovers from the catering company that crowded our refrigerator until finally, when there was mold growing on everything, I threw them out. I remembered my father opening the refrigerator and seeing it was clean, and starting to cry. Right there, on the floor of our kitchen, with the refrigerator door open. He cried until there was nothing left.

I stood to leave.

"Going so soon?" he asked gently.

I nodded. Suddenly all I wanted was my dad, the one who raised me. I'd thought learning the truth from Charles would comfort me. But it hadn't. It couldn't. He'd given me answers, and it turned out they weren't what I needed.

I paused with my hand on the door.

Charles regarded me sadly. "I am sorry, my dear."

# thirty-one

I drove back with my father upstate. He picked me up outside Lennox Hill Hospital in his silver truck. He was dressed in his usual uniform—plaid flannel shirt, Levi's, and scuffed brown boots—and greeted me with worried brown eyes. "I thought the doctors said they wanted to keep you under observation for another day," he said, popping my door open.

"They're just being overly cautious," I said, trying not to wince as I climbed into the cab of the truck. "I'm fine."

He gave me a dubious look before putting the truck in gear. "You don't look it."

I gestured at the bandages around my head, ribs, wrist, and hands. "These are just for show."

"Should we swing by your place? Pick up some things? You'll need a heavy coat. Forecast says snow tomorrow."

"I'd rather not, if that's OK." I didn't have enough energy to face my apartment. Alex had brought over what I'd left at his home, which amounted to a few changes of clothes, some toiletries, and my handbag. A trip to Walmart in Greenport would have to fill in what I couldn't borrow from Dad. "You'll loan me your Patagonia?"

"Sure, kiddo."

It took us two hours to make it to Hudson, New York, a little town that had started as a whaling community way back when. After falling on hard times, it was rediscovered by antiques dealers, foodies, and other New York City transplants, who helped revive local commerce and cultural landmarks. Dad's place was a little more than five miles outside of town but he said he wanted to swing by Olde Hudson, our favorite little grocery store on Warren, the town's main drag, to pick up some bread and cheese for dinner. I stayed in the truck while he went into the market. Ten minutes later, he came back out with two huge bags filled with goodies for us. "Hope you're hungry," he said, placing the bags by my feet.

We drove along half a dozen tree-lined country roads before pulling into Dad's little two-story. In one direction it overlooked an apple orchard, in the other, a cornfield. The field wasn't his, but the neighbors let him hunt on the land—wild turkey in the spring, deer in the fall. He never shot the does. He never said it, but I was sure it was because he didn't have the heart to take a mother from its fawn.

I shrugged off my bag in the living room. Stone fireplace, old wood floors, some couches and chairs that were as beat up as Dad's truck. Milton, a Norwich terrier, lifted his head from the fleece-lined dog bed by the fireplace. His fat little body jumped into my arms. I let him lick my chin and scratched his round belly. I called out to my dad, who was unpacking the groceries. "Who looked after him while you were gone?"

"The neighbor," he said.

Not a girlfriend, then. "You're overfeeding him again."

"Am not," he protested.

I put Milton back down and joined my father in the kitchen. Dad had bought the house about ten years earlier and made few adjustments in that time. The kitchen, for example, was still papered in a yellow floral print the previous owners had selected. There were etched-glass light fixtures, green-painted cabinetry, and an old stove that looked like it was on its last legs but still worked just fine. I gazed out the bay window at the desolate field below and took a seat at the round oak table after setting it for dinner. We were having a light dinner, just cheese, cured meats, some crusty bread, and a cucumber salad. Tomorrow, Dad planned to make his beef Wellington and roasted new potatoes.

He sat down in the chair opposite me. "You ready to talk about it?" he asked.

In the hospital I'd told him that I wasn't ready. I needed some time to get over the shock and process some of the emotions I was feeling. But it had been three days since I'd learned the truth about who my real father was, and I still wasn't sure how I felt. Or what I was supposed to feel.

Dad flipped his blue-checkered napkin onto his lap. Later, we'd rent a movie off the cable service. Milton would fall asleep at my feet. I wanted to fast-forward to that and get over with *this*, but it was time to put the elephant out of its misery. "You knew," I stated.

My father's chin dipped to his chest. "Of course I did."

I could have been mad. I probably *should've* been mad. But I wasn't. I loved my dad. He'd taken good care of me, stood by me when a lot of other parents might not have, and considering I wasn't even his flesh and blood, that meant double to me now. "Did Mom tell you?"

"I can do math, Cornelia. It wasn't a matter of weeks."

"She didn't try to make you believe I was yours?"

He half smiled. "I can tell why you're good at your job."

I rolled my eyes. "Please, Dad."

He clasped his hands together under the table, straightening his posture against the hard back of his chair. "Yes, in the beginning. I think she hoped I wouldn't put two and two together."

"Why didn't you leave her? She tried to trap you."

The corners of my father's mouth sagged. "It was no trap. I was in love. Your mother told me she had no contact with the man who had gotten her pregnant. It was a short-lived affair."

I balked, angry at him for not being more upset with my mother. But this is how it had always been between us—him defending her, her "choice" to take her life, while I'd condemn her as a selfish coward. "Fair enough," I finally said. "But my understanding was that it wasn't a passing fancy. Mom wanted him to leave his wife."

He shrugged. He didn't care.

"She never told you it was Charles Kravis who had gotten her pregnant?"

"I'm sure she would have if I asked. I didn't want to know."

"But you did find out."

"Several years later. After your mother had died and you'd gone to stay with Olivia on Nantucket. Charles figured it out, and I was terrified he was going to take you away from me."

"Charles told me he offered to give you money."

"Through his lawyers, yes. I said no thank you, through mine, and that was the last we heard from him." He rapped the grained surface of the table with his knuckles. "Listen, kiddo, are you mad at me for not accepting his help?"

"No. That's not it. I just wish you'd been honest with me."

"Long ago your mother and I decided to leave the past where it was. You were—and are—as much mine as any child could be. So what if you didn't share my DNA? That didn't matter to me. And in the eyes of the law, I was your father. My name was on your birth certificate."

I reflexively touched the bandage on my head. It still hurt, as did my hands and ribs. "I'm sorry, Dad, but I still think I had the right to know."

"Yes, of course," he replied calmly. "Of course you did. But at first you were too young, and then, once your mother passed, there were other considerations. You'd already lost one parent; I didn't want you to feel like you'd lost another." He got up to arrange the cheese platter. "You were all that I had left in the world once your mother left us. What if knowing the truth made you want to leave? What if you wanted to go live with your grandparents?"

"I barely knew them. The last time I saw them was at Mom's funeral. Why would I have wanted to go live with them?"

He shook his head. "It was my biggest fear, losing you. I didn't want to take any chances."

I sighed. "I forgive you. But it's harder to forgive Mom. She lied to Charles and told him I was going to be aborted, and then she lied to you and to me, and then she killed herself, leaving all of us to clean up her mess. If she'd been honest from the start, Olivia wouldn't have died trying to make right her wrong."

My dad was quiet for a long time. I'd gone through an angry period in my teens and after college and whenever we fought— about grades, boys, curfews, and later my drinking and spending habits—we'd always end up here: me, furious with my mother, blaming her for everything; and my father, furious with me for invoking her name with such hostility and disrespect. After a while, we just stopped talking about her and everything wrong I was doing with my life.

"I'm sure Charlotte had her reasons," my father finally said. "We all do."

I'd hoped to find peace in the truth, but all I felt at that moment was the heaviness of my father's sorrow and the same low-grade anxiety that had followed me my entire life. I beat my fist against the table in frustration, startling Milton. "Let's just talk about it once and for all, Dad. Will you just put all the cards on the table? Why did Mom kill herself? Was it because of me? Did she regret having me? The life she had to choose for my benefit?"

"No, of course not."

"Then was it you? Was she unhappy in your marriage? Did she hate *you*?"

He jolted back, wounded.

I should have apologized, but I didn't want to.

"What your mother wanted was a way out of her life," Dad said. "Not the one she built with me, but the one she wanted me to save her from. If she were here today, I believe she would tell you that."

I regarded him with skepticism. "What did she need saving from? Boring cocktail parties, bossy housekeepers?"

"Her family," he said, his chin jutting out an inch. "They were not kind people."

I snorted, still skeptical. I don't remember much about my grandparents other than what my father had told me about them over the years, which was never positive, and the few photos of them in one of our family albums. I didn't even know if they were dead or alive. "That's an awfully vague statement, Dad."

"Your grandfather wanted a divorce, but your grandmother wouldn't give him one. *They* had a terrible marriage. Your grandmother became a very angry woman. She was abusive to your mother. Mostly verbal but there were a few physical incidents as well."

All this time I'd thought my mother was unhappy with her life with us, the smallness of it. I thought she'd killed herself because she couldn't take it anymore.

"Before your mother died, she was in therapy," Dad continued. "Working through the past, coming to terms with what she had seen and survived. I thought she was making progress. So did the psychologist. We were going to try and have another child, a sibling for you. The doctor decided to adjust her medication, actually, to decrease it. But your mother did not respond well. The way she died, Clyde, that wasn't Charlotte. She was a very private woman.

She wouldn't have done it like that, for everyone to see. That's how I knew she wasn't thinking straight." His shoulders slumped. "She wanted to get better. And she loved you more than anything. She believed you saved her. Once you arrived, she had a reason to live."

"Why didn't you ever tell me this about her?"

"She made me promise not to. She didn't want this to be your legacy."

"But she gave me her name. Why would she make me a Shaw if she didn't want any part of her family?"

"There was a gift."

"Financial?" I asked.

He nodded. "They agreed to create a trust for your education. We didn't want to deny you that opportunity. And, personally, I didn't care what your last name was."

"If I'd been truly yours, would you have felt differently?"

"You *are* mine." He reached his hand across the table. "You have the right to be upset and confused by all of this. But if I had to do it all over again, I would."

# thirty-two

I ended up needing that winter coat.

I stayed with Dad for almost three months. I watched late fall turn to deep winter, filling my time reading novels, cuddling with Milton, and watching football with Dad. I shoveled snow, drank hot chocolate, and spent a lot of time doing the things I thought would make me feel better—journaling, meditating, and taking yoga classes. None of it really worked, but I got a hell of a lot stronger. My head healed. My hands, wrist, and ribs were as good as new. But I was never going to be normal again. For one, I was rich.

Charles Kravis died in December, a month after I met with him, leaving me an obscene amount of money, about $50 million after taxes. The rest of his fortune was divided between his foundation, other charities, his wife, and Delphine's two children. My money was in probate, and would be for a while, so I didn't actually get to go crazy spending it on new stuff, but Dad and I talked a bit about how I was going to use it, and what I was going to do with my life now that I didn't have to work.

"Don't let this define you," Dad had said one night to me as we were sitting by the fire, reading the papers. It wasn't clear what he'd

meant by this—the money, my mother's suicide, or the murders—
but he was right.

"I just don't know what to do," I said.

"That's the beauty of it. You can do anything."

I said nothing. I should have felt liberated, but the money made
me uncomfortable. I hadn't earned it; I'd barely known the man
who'd given it to me. And I believed the real reason Charles had
left it to me was because he felt guilty—not just about what had
happened with Delphine, but for abandoning my mother in her
time of need.

My father got up to add a log to the fire. "It's an incredible
luxury to be able to think about what would make you most happy.
If the money does anything for you, let it do that."

"That's just it, Dad." I tossed the magazine I'd been reading
back on the coffee table. "I don't know what makes me happy.
Besides work." I missed the camaraderie, the adrenaline, the race to
find sources, the hunt for the truth.

"Then go back to work."

He was right. Lying around was doing me no good. I couldn't
sleep at night, I was avoiding talking to my old friends and colleagues, and despite my hours on the yoga mat, I still felt unsettled.
I may have finally found out the truth, but that didn't mean I'd
made my peace with it. "Do you think I should give the money
away?"

Dad considered my question. He'd already refused my offers
to buy him a new house or a new truck. He wouldn't even let me
take him on an around-the-world vacation once I got my money. "I
think you shouldn't do anything until you're sure about it," he said.

The next morning I opened my laptop and started dealing with
everything I'd put on hold since I'd left Manhattan—namely, my
job situation. The incident had turned me into a minor celebrity
and done more for my career than any of the awards or scoops I'd

landed in my tenure at FirstNews. I'd fielded dozens of job offers, plus a couple of offers from major publishing houses to write a memoir about my ordeal. I'd turned the book deals down flat, but I hadn't said no to some of the jobs—the most surprising of which came from GSBC News. Of all people, they wanted to team me up with Penny Harlich.

The network president, a woman by the name of Janine Saltz, claimed it was all Penny's idea, before admitting that within the network there were concerns Penny wasn't being taken seriously enough by her audience. "We think you can help," she said before offering me a 30 percent bump in salary, a sizable signing bonus, matching 401(k) plan, and all sorts of other benefits I'd only dreamed of in the past. I'd told Janine I needed a few weeks to think it over. Considering the circumstances, she said she was happy to give me time to mull over my response.

Soon after that, Alex called. He was a star now—FirstNews's biggest draw, second only to Georgia Jacobs, who had been pulling in record ratings every night since the Kravis scandal. Alex had offered to come visit me in Hudson, but I had some things to do in the city anyway and agreed to meet him for lunch at Michael's.

The restaurant was Alex's choice, a favorite Midtown cantina of media-industry heavyweights. The fare was good, but the people-watching was unparalleled, particularly on that sunny day in late winter. Sarah Palin with her literary agent, Keith Richards with his. Michael, the restaurant's namesake proprietor, greeted Alex by name at the door and personally escorted us to our table within spitting distance of George Stephanopoulos and the executive producer of *Good Morning America*. They nodded their hellos as we took our seats.

Our waiter arrived tableside, unfurling one of the restaurant's heavy, oversize white napkins in my lap. I ordered an iced tea and a burger, while Alex opted for the day-boat scallops and a Perrier.

"So how have you been?" I asked after the waiter left.

"Good." He planted his elbows on the table. "The network green-lighted my show."

I'd heard and I was genuinely happy for him. "Congratulations. You deserve it."

I raised my glass of iced tea and clinked it against his over the small floral centerpiece. "To your success."

He took a sip of his water and placed it back on the table. "When I signed the deal, I told Diskin I had two conditions. One, I wanted to move back to DC, and two, I wanted you as my executive producer. I can't do this show without you, Clyde."

I was speechless. I hadn't been expecting this. Finally I said, "Washington, huh?"

He rubbed his hands together. "You're gonna love it there. Wait till you see what kind of apartment you can rent."

"How does Diskin feel about me coming back on board?"

"He said you would have been his first choice."

I cocked my head. "C'mon. Tell me what he really said."

He nodded enthusiastically. "I'm telling you, he's all for it. The network is prepared to offer you a big package."

I smiled to myself. Little did Alex know that Georgia was also hounding me to come back to work for her. Not a day went by that I didn't receive an e-mail or voice message from her. I missed her, but I couldn't fathom going back to doing what I'd done before Olivia died.

"It's a tempting offer," I acknowledged.

Alex could read my ambivalence. "But?"

"I'm still sorting some things out."

"Where are your things?"

He'd misread my meaning, but I humored him anyway. "In a storage unit upstate." My dad and I had driven down in a U-Haul one morning in early December, a few weeks after I realized it was going to take me more than a few days to be ready to face city life again. We salvaged what we could and put the rest in trash bags, then left my key with the super.

"I won't need you to start for another few weeks," Alex said. "That'll give you plenty of time to move."

I sat back in my chair, took another sip of the iced tea. "I've got other offers on the table."

"I don't doubt it." He leaned forward, lowering his voice before adding, "Whatever they're offering, we'll give you more."

A server deposited our entrées. Alex picked up his knife and fork and sliced into one of his scallops. "Anything new from the Kravis case?"

I shook my head. As grateful as I was to Alex for saving my life, the case was personal to me. I could no longer discuss it like it was just another news story. Besides, I didn't want anyone finding out about my inheritance. Talking openly about the millions Charles had left for me would have invited more intrusive questions about my private life and past. I wanted to get back into the news business, but I was done being the day's lead story.

"Your turn," I said, picking up my burger. "What's new at the network?"

He set down his utensils. "Well, Charles Kravis died, as you know. And the sale went through, as I'm sure you also know. FirstNews is now officially part of Maldone Enterprises. The stock is on the rise. Ratings are good. But they could be better, which is where I come in . . . and you. What's holding you back, Shaw? I thought this is what you wanted." His brown eyes regarded me intently.

I balked. "You're actually surprised I might be a bit hesitant to go back to work for the network that unceremoniously canned my ass not four months ago?"

Alex picked up his silverware again. "Back to prickly so soon? You must be feeling better."

I crossed my arms in front of my chest. "I am."

We glared at each other across the table.

Finally Alex sighed. "Look, I invited you here to offer you a job. Say the word, you're on the team. No, more than that. You're the head of the team."

There was no question I'd be smart to take the executive-producer job. The network was fully invested in the success of his show, and Alex had the natural charisma and smarts it took to make it for the long haul. The money would be good too, not that I needed to worry about my finances, but it was a measure of my value to the network, and I still wanted that, as well as the respect of my peers. With this job, I could finally get to call some shots, make great TV, and maybe get nominated for an Emmy. Truth be told, even moving to another city appealed to me. I could use a fresh start, a real honest-to-goodness chance to start over.

But then there was the fact that I was attracted to Alex, an attraction I was slowly and unhappily realizing had only intensified in the months we'd spent apart. He'd visited me in the hospital, sent flowers to me upstate. He'd said he wanted to see me again, as soon as possible, but before that week I hadn't been ready. Every time I thought of him, my stomach felt like it was pulling taffy.

I could close my eyes and imagine him standing next to me at his stove, the heat radiating from his body, his breath on my neck. I could picture his eyes, those warm brown eyes, as he promised not to let me go, my body dangling eleven stories above the sidewalk. And I could feel his lips against mine, soft and warm, the kiss that promised everything I yearned for—companionship, passion, love. Working with Alex in such close proximity would be torture. I had a million good reasons to want to be his executive producer and only one not to be. But that one was enough. I'd fallen for him, hard, which meant that taking a job with him wasn't just a business decision. Not when my heart was involved.

"How's Sabine?" I asked, my posture stiffening.

"She still feels terrible. She really had no idea Delphine was the killer."

He'd said it without saying it: they were still together. I'd had a feeling they were, but until that moment I'd allowed a part of myself to fantasize that Alex had realized how he felt about me and broken things off with her. But that hadn't happened. In my confused and medicated state, had I read something in his kiss that wasn't there?

"I know she didn't mean to put me in danger," I said quietly. As envious as I was of Sabine, what happened wasn't her fault, and I didn't hold her accountable.

Alex finished his scallops. "She'd love to apologize to you in person. And it would mean a lot to me, personally, if you would let her do that."

"I'll call her," I said, meaning it. I took the last sip of my iced tea. Beyond our table, a quartet of bone-thin socialites was being seated, all of them trying to catch Alex's eye, all of them wearing door-knocker-size diamond rings. I crooked my thumb in their direction. "Your new fan club."

Alex reached for my hand across the table. "Look at me, Clyde." My eyes met his.

"This isn't about her. It's about us. I can't think of anyone else I'd rather have as my partner in all this."

My eyebrows arched. Did he mean the job or *us*? "Why me?"

"You're smart, Clyde. You're ethical. And tough. Nothing gets to you. Nothing scares you. And to top it all off, you're pretty damn fine to look at. You're the one I want by my side. Since the very beginning I pictured us together."

I felt the rest of the room slip away. We were alone once again, back at his dining-room table with the tea lights flickering and music on the stereo. Almost dying had brought a few things in my life into sharp focus, including the fact I'd never been in love. Sure there had been men. Too many, actually. And too much meaningless sex. But love? Even when I'd gotten my act together, I'd dated men like Phil Drucker precisely because I knew I wasn't in any danger of falling for them. With love came vulnerability, abandonment, *pain*. Still, I couldn't live the rest of my life like that. It was a misery of its own kind, and one I'd known for far too long.

I wasn't a teenager anymore, and I didn't want to act like one. "Alex, be honest with me. What's the deal with you and Sabine?"

He let go of my hand and sank backward in his seat. "She's pregnant," he said flatly. "She's coming to DC and we're moving in together."

And just like that, the waiters, the media titans, the rock stars, and the social gadflies reappeared, buzzing around us, stealing center stage. Alex and I sat in silence, his announcement hanging between us like a toxic cloud. "I suppose I should say congratulations." I would have lifted my glass again but it was empty.

"You don't—"

"No," I said firmly. "I do. She's a lucky girl. And I wish you both the best of everything."

"It wasn't planned," he said, as if that made a difference. "If this hadn't happened, Clyde, I would have wanted—" He stopped himself. "I'm trying to do the right thing."

"So am I."

He nodded. "No doubt." A beat later: "What about the job?"

I stood up, let my napkin tumble to the floor. "Can I get back to you?" I asked, though my mind was made up. For once, everything—what to do and what I actually *wanted* to do—was not only crystal clear, but in agreement.

Outside, I dug into my purse for a business card and my phone. Janine Saltz's assistant put me right through. "If that job offer is still on the table, I'd love to accept." I wasn't going to be an executive producer, but at least with Penny Harlich I wouldn't be in any danger of having my heart broken. Janine and I spoke for twenty minutes, arranging a start date and negotiating some of the finer points of my contract.

Then I hung up and put the phone in my bag. I walked eastward, crossing Park and Lexington, and then north, on Third Avenue. It was cold outside, with a brutal wind coming off the East River, the weak winter sun barely visible behind a swath of gray clouds. But it felt good to walk. I felt light and free, excited about starting over with a new network and new colleagues. Hell, maybe Penny and I would be friends.

At the corner of Eightieth Street, I looked up. I was at my old building, the one I'd lived in as a kid, where my mother had killed herself. The redbrick façade looked like it had been cleaned, and there was a new green awning overhead. At the building's entrance stood a man in uniform. He opened the door for a young mother. She was pretty and well dressed and pushed a little girl in a stroller. The tot waved at me with a small, chubby hand as she went by.

And then I remembered something, something small. In the hospital during my recovery, my palms had been bandaged. I'd hurt them holding on to the railing of Alex's balcony.

*My mother.*

Her hands.

They'd been chafed too.

She hadn't jumped.

# Acknowledgments

Some books come into the world easily and without complication. This book did not, which makes me all the more indebted to everyone who provided support, encouragement, and wise counsel while I labored over this love. I am grateful to my fellow writers' group members—Lauren Lipton, Sandra Waugh, and Melanie Murray—for their sound commentary and good company, and to Brooklyn Assistant District Attorney Joshua Charlton for answering my questions about criminal law. Thank you as well to television producers Howard Rosenberg and Michael Heard for sharing their insider knowledge about the business of broadcast news. There aren't enough words to express my gratitude to Cindy Eagan for her editorial notes. You are a master literary surgeon and a true friend. I am beholden to Alison Dasho for falling in love with Clyde and bringing me into the Thomas & Mercer fold. Thank you. My children give meaning and bring joy to everything I do, as does my husband, the love of my life, my dearest Max. Thank you for your unwavering belief in me.

# About the Author

Born in South Dakota, New York–based author and magazine editor Tatiana Boncompagni was raised in Tennessee and Minnesota. After graduating magna cum laude from the School of Foreign Service at Georgetown University, Boncompagni worked for the *American Lawyer* magazine in New York, the *Legal Times* in Washington, DC, and the *Wall Street Journal Europe* in Brussels. Her writing has appeared in dozens of publications, including the *New York Times, Wall Street Journal, Financial Times, Self, Marie Claire, InStyle,* and *Vogue.* Her novels include *Gilding Lily, Hedge Fund Wives,* and her latest book, *Social Death,* the first in the Clyde Shaw Mysteries series.

Married with three young children, Boncompagni splits her time between Manhattan and a farm in the Hudson Valley.